I0695032

RIVERWALKING

Mark Paleologopoulos

ISBN
Edited by
Cover design by

Printed in the United States of America

Otherwords Press
www.otherwordspress.net

DEDICATED TO NIECES EVERYWHERE

CHAPTER ONE

At the bend before Route 5 rises into the hills, a well-maintained farm stand is flanked by a grove of trees brimming with red and green apples and a seemingly boundless corn field. Hidden from the view of passers-by, amidst the checkerboard of fields, stands a stately, well-maintained red farmhouse at the end of a long gravel driveway.

Several generations have made this house their home since the walls were first raised more than two hundred years ago. The Stantons have been stuffing every room with their laughter and their tears for so long that the house is now part of the family. The warm, well-ordered home remembers every triumph, every mundane happenstance, and every catastrophe. No matter what state of mind you may be in when you step through the door, if you settle into any seat or cushion and close your eyes, you will sense a warm, welcoming affection settle like a blanket on your soul.

Still, one person is unhappy here. One person feels as if the crushing weight of the world is resting on her shoulders and no one understands her. One person feels she is being treated unfairly by cruel parents whose only purpose in life is to prevent her from doing anything fun. It may shock you to learn that this person is a twelve-year-old girl.

The unhappy girl's parents are actually quite delightful people, a very far cry from being the wicked fun-blockers their daughter would have you believe. Thomas Stanton, III lives with his wife, Cecelia, and their daughter Charley in that wonderful old farmhouse. Thanks to the quality of workmanship during its construction, the house itself has weathered many a storm over the years. However, it has never had to deal with the recent weeks of alternating high and low pressure systems and the sustained battering of gale force energy that is Storm Charley.

On this particular afternoon, the entire county was experiencing a sun-kissed autumn day, but the Stanton house was not enjoying the weather. Microbursts had been reported touching down in the kitchen and a back bedroom on the second floor. A tornado warning was in effect for the greater Stanton homestead area. The walls groaned as the house held its breath. The air inside tasted like lightning and a deafening silence waited for the violence and destruction soon to follow.

The wooden screen door flew open with a loud, violent *clack*, causing the house to exhale as if in pain. Four feet, nine and a half inches of barefoot, pony-tailed fury strode out onto the back porch with fire in her eyes. Charley Stanton stomped on the planks with as much destructive force as her light frame could muster. She stood shaking, fists crossed tightly against her chest. With her back to the door she lifted her face to the skies and screamed at the top of her lungs, "You are the worst parents ever!"

Sweeping up a pair of sneakers from the mat, she tramped down the steps to the yard, throwing shoes ahead of her, one at a time. She set out in a huff for solitude and freedom, punctuating each step by chanting 'It's not fair' over and over like a volley of verbal darts aimed at her parents' hearts. Farm workers, the chickens, and Whiskey, the family dog, scrambled to get out of her way.

She slowed her march of rebellion only long enough to snatch her sneakers from the ground. She strode down the hard-packed dirt lane between the corn fields, not stopping until her rage had subsided to a simmer, and Whiskey had stopped barking. Turning, she caught the house staring at her. The windows seemed ready to cry, and the screen door yawned wide open in dismay, but her parents were nowhere to be found. Her anger towards them increased exponentially for not calling her back to the house. With her nose in the air, she turned and resumed her march around a bend, out of sight, and alone.

The dirt lane gradually became more rutted and rocky as she walked. Her bare left foot landed on a cruel and uncaring stone, forcing her to execute some athletic right-footed hopping as she rubbed her injured sole. She only had time for a brief shriek of pain before a regrettable stubbing of her right big toe on an entirely different, yet equally indifferent, half-buried stone drew her undivided attention.

In her desperate need to make her exit as dramatic as possible, she had delayed the donning of her sneakers. It was too late now. If she had planned it out to the last detail it would have taken away from one of her most spectacular histrionic performances. Creativity and originality are crucial when crafting a truly compelling scene. As it was, Charley might never know if her mother had even witnessed her skillful and authentic performance. So, she suffered for her art, and rubbed both her feet to massage the pain away. She muttered curses at rocks for being hard, sneakers for not putting themselves on, and parents for being heartless.

When the pain subsided, Charley collected her sneakers and pulled them onto her dirty feet. She stood and resumed walking, taking the opportunity to look at her surroundings. To her right, a tall, tightly-packed hedge lined the crest of a small rise for as far as her eyes could see. To her left, the familiar, seemingly endless corn-field stood at resolute attention like thousands of green soldiers. The road ahead stretched on forever, without a jog, bend, or dip. Turning back so soon was out of the question. Not enough time had passed. How could her mother learn her lesson if she didn't believe Charley's performance was genuine? If she stayed on the road and continued to take left turns whenever the opportunity arose, she would eventually return to the house.

She chose to continue on , looking down and picking her way with care around ruts and rocks. The usual assortment of beasts, bugs, and birds bounded and buzzed around and above her on their own vitally important business. The rows of tall corn now blocked the sun. The shade, combined with a breeze that set the stalks rustling, led directly to her second regret. Out here on her own, with no mother to say '*I told you so*', she could wish without embarrassment that she had been smart enough to bring a sweater or jacket with her.

Charley marched on and a third regret poked her belly. She rubbed her stomach to soothe a pang of hunger; skipping lunch had been a mistake. The probability that dinner would not be delivered to her caused a twinge of worry to cloud her face. She lengthened her tiny strides until a brief moment of light-headedness stopped her progress. A familiar flutter in her lungs reminded her she had also skipped her medicine today; a fact her mother would undoubtedly factor into a future lecture.

She stopped and looked to the sky, noticing the afternoon getting ready to leave and call it a day. Summer was also saying good-bye, reminding her of the familiar dread she associated with autumn and another year of academic torture. Another moment of dizziness led to her stepping into a small puddle of mud that seemed ecstatic to meet her right foot and claim her sneaker. She lost her balance and fell to her hands and knees. She pulled her sneaker free from the sucking muck, collapsed, and rolled over to face the sky. Lying fl at on her back, with her small store of determination depleted, she inhaled deeply, admitting defeat. Her father would, no doubt, be rumbling by in his rusty red pickup truck soon to pick her up.

Charley remained on her back on that dirt road wondering what else could go wrong. What had started out as a protest against parental tyranny had rapidly turned into a cold, painful, and dirty mistake. She could admit as much to the birds and the bugs and the beasts. They wouldn't care. They wouldn't look at her with that mixture of smugness and annoyance that was plastered on her parents' faces day in and day out.

Her body was running on empty.

"It's exhausting being me."

Fatigue washed over her, and she allowed her eyes to close. "Only for a second," she told herself.

Charley's eyes fluttered open. The color of the sky was an odd electric blue, as if she had been transported inside a video game. As she blinked to gain focus, a rush of wind came whipping through the corn rows, setting the stalks crackling, blowing sand and grit into her face. The squall passed quickly, ending with a vacuum-like pop, leaving behind a swirling fog to fill the spaces between the rows.

Rising to rest on her elbows, she looked down to find a grasshopper had landed on her chest. It remained motionless, facing her down with cold and disrespectful insolence. They stared at each other. The grasshopper flinched first, cocking its head insolently. Charley's eyes widened, shocked at the grasshopper's attitude. Who was he to judge her? She swiped him away and rolled over to rise unsteadily to her feet.

She brushed herself off and took stock of her situation. Looking left and right repeatedly offered no guidance. Tendrils of fog crept onto the road in both directions, obscuring her sight. Charley reached up to spin the hair above her right temple around her index finger.

Before she could make a decision, a flash of color zipped past her face. She startled and turned to see a large bird swoop up to alight above her on a tree branch poking through the hedge. She stared at its exotic regal plumage— a dark purple hooded cape over a gold vest. It settled on its perch and seemed to take an interest in her as well. It chirped several notes in a short burst, ending in a questioning tone. The bird repeated the question several times, each time giving Charley a chance to respond. She was forced to answer just to be polite.

"I'm fine. How are you?"

The bird responded with a shake of the head.

She tried again. "My name's Charley Stanton. What's yours?"

The bird threw up its wings in a shrug and turned its back. After a sufficiently cheeky amount of time, it dropped off the branch and cruised down to land next to Charley.

She knelt to look into its perceptive eyes. "I'm sorry. I don't understand you."

The bird repeated the question one more time, slower and louder.

"I don't speak bird," said Charley in frustration. "Now, who's being rude?"

The bird's casual chirping turned into a squawking tantrum, complete with mad hopping and flapping of wings. Charley countered by crossing her arms, pursing her lips, and setting her feet in a perpendicular stance; a ballet form learned from her mother. It always annoyed Charley to the point of madness, so she applied it herself in this situation.

The bird continued to rant, providing Charley more than a little pleasure. As the pair faced off, a shadow cast by something large flying overhead passed between them. The bird stopped squawking and flew back up to the tree branch. Charley looked up to see a hawk circling in the sky. Her eyes darted up to the strange colorful bird. It chirped a terse, dismissive statement this time, not a question.

"Don't go," pleaded Charley, surprising herself.

The bird chirped once more. Charley surprised herself by responding.

"Don't be stupid. I can't come with you. Why don't you stay here?"

The bird ignored her plea and took off, flapping three times and disappearing over the hedge. Charley shouted after him in the rarely effective, not-so-commanding voice of a twelve-year-old and waited expectantly for the bird to return. When it didn't submit to her authority, she shook her fist at the hawk, now long gone. Gathering clouds were there watching, unimpressed by one angry girl wearing a single shoe. Charley hung her head, surrendering to the disappointment. She asked the corn, "Where is Dad? He should have picked me up by now."

Charley retrieved her muddy sneaker and looked down the road in both directions. With a sour, reluctant expression, she pulled the soggy shoe onto her filthy foot. Neither seeing nor hearing a pick-up truck approaching, she heaved a sigh.

She climbed the rise and looked in the direction of her house. The weathervane poking the sky from the tip of her house was the only thing visible above the corn. Farther south, out of sight, lurked the educational gulag she would be forced to endure for the next nine months.

"Maybe without me around, you guys would have one less thing to argue about," she said softly. "Maybe it would be better for everyone if I took a little vacation."

She took one last look toward home and reached a conclusion. She left her troubles behind and followed a stranger to parts unknown.

CHAPTER TWO

Charley approached the hedgerow, searching for a break to breach the wall. Finding none, she turned sideways in order to sidle through and carve out her own gap. After five minutes of scratches, struggles, and sweat, she found herself trapped in a cocoon of green fir. She spun and rocked and shook branches in a fit of rising frustration.

In the dim light, it was impossible to tell which direction was which, much less the direction toward freedom. Panic set in. She rocked back and forth to find movement in one direction painfully impossible. Movement in the opposite direction met slightly less resistance. She allowed the hedge to choose her heading. Anything was better than being trapped inside a cramped forest of sharp needles and unyielding branches insistent on poking her repeatedly in inconvenient places. She pressed on and found the going progressively easier. She forced her way through the obstinate green pin cushion with a sheer force of will, until suddenly she was through– and falling.

The price of freedom was a headlong pitch forward down a steep slope. Luckily, her four sessions of gymnastics training last year served her well as she instinctively tucked her shoulder to avoid a painful face-plant. She rolled like a boulder, eventually coming to a painful stop, flat on her back.

She lay still for a moment, calmly watching clouds floating serenely across a blue, blue sky. Their voyage was decidedly more graceful and calm than the bumpy journey she had just experienced. She flexed her fingers, testing them. She wiggled her toes. When she was satisfied everything was in working order, she beat the ground with slamming fists and kicking heels.

"I am having an awful day!" she shouted to the clouds.

A voice startled her. "That looked painful. Are you hurt?"

Charley rolled over, scrambled to her feet, and assumed a defensive stance similar to one drilled into her head during the three weeks of tae-kwon-do training from last winter.

On the opposite slope, facing her with a totally relaxed and non-combative attitude, sat a girl, older by perhaps four or five years. She was barefoot and dressed in dirty, ripped jeans and a severely stained tie-dye tee shirt. Bits of leaves and twigs poked out of the girl's wild, bushy red hair and a wide gap-toothed smile cracked her grimy, smudged, or possibly freckled face. She rose and approached Charley with her hand extended. Charley accepted the handshake with a wary eye.

"I'm Rachel."

"My name's Charlotte."

"That was quite a tumble. Are you always so graceful?"

Charley bristled. "That's rude. Are you always so filthy?"

"I was kidding. It's what friends do."

"We're not friends. I don't even know you."

For a wild-looking, feral girl, Rachel was remarkably calm and well-mannered in the face of Charley's frosty attitude.

"Well, I want to be your friend. Everyone could use more friends. We should get to know each other. What do you want to know about me?"

Charley looked down at her feet, admitting, "I could use a friend."

She lifted her face and thrust out her chin. "Alright, where do you come from?"

Rachel waved in the general direction of the hedge behind her and returned to her seat on the rock. "Not far," was all she said on the subject.

"What else do you want to know?"

Another identical hedge ran along the crest of the slope on Rachel's side of the riverbed. A wide stripe of bone-dry rocky ground stretched down the center of the grassy valley bending out of sight in both directions. Small trees dotted each of the grassy banks. A dark gray strip formed by chains of faraway mountains divided the forest green hedges from the deep blue sky.

"We're practically neighbors, but I don't remember seeing you before," said Charley, her eyes narrowing in suspicion.

Rachel mimicked her expression. "I don't remember seeing you either."

After an uncomfortable pause, Charley pointed back toward the slope she had rolled down moments before. "I live on a farm on the other side of that hedge. Stanton Farm, you must have heard of it," she said with a trace of pride in her voice.

Rachel sat still on the rock with her hands clasped in her lap and a half-smile on her face. "It sounds familiar."

Charley looked around at her surroundings again, stalling for a topic of conversation. Rachel waited patiently with an expression that could possibly be interpreted as enjoying Charley's discomfort.

When this uncomfortably long pause had dragged on long enough for Charley, she said, "I thought I'd explored everywhere around the farm, but I don't remember being here before."

Rachel shrugged in disbelief. "Really? It's quite nice. I live here."

Charley laughed at her. "Shut your face hole. You can't live here. Where's your house? Where are your mom and dad?"

"I couldn't live with my parents anymore," said Rachel as she looked down at her feet.

Charley stopped laughing. She gulped, nearly choking on her embarrassment. The pauses were getting painfully awkward for her.

"Me neither," she said, hoping it would make Rachel feel better. "Why did you run away?"

Rachel looked like she was reliving an anguished memory. Her voice cracked as she spoke, "I was miserable. I was suffocating. Every day was a struggle just to breathe. I couldn't take another day like that."

She fell silent and poked at the pebbles at her feet with a twig.

Charley bent down to pick up a rock, not knowing how to respond. Somewhere nearby, a woodpecker's search for food mimicked the ticking of a clock, making an already uncomfortable situation painfully worse. She made an attempt to throw the rock over the hedge, but her effort fell far short. Those few innings last summer spent picking dandelions while a softball game went on around her proved useless. The rock bounced and rolled down the slope all the way to her feet.

Rachel looked up at her. "What about you? Why did you run away?"

"The same. You know. My Mom and Dad are always telling me either what I'm doing wrong or what I'm not doing right. I live in an old house with old furniture and old everything. I never get to go anywhere or get anything new. The other kids at school always have new clothes, brand new phones, new everything. And everyone treats me like I have the plague or something. Which I don't!"

"Do all the girls at your school wear two different shoes?" Rachel teased.

Charley bristled again, "They aren't different shoes. I stepped in a mud puddle." She pointed a finger a Rachel and snarled, "You're making fun of me again. We'll never be friends if you keep being cruel to me."

"I'm sorry, Charlotte. What else would you like to know?" She motioned for Charley to sit with her.

"What is this place? It looks like a river without the water."

"Bingo," replied Rachel.

"So how long is this river and where's the water?"

"I don't really know how long it is, but there hasn't been any water flowing through as long as I've been here."

Charley glowered at the girl and her insulting questions and non-answers. Still, this girl smiled and paid attention, which was something her classmates never did. Charley couldn't remember the last time someone close to her age had been so interested in what she had to say. She chose to ignore her new friend's irritating habit of mocking her and instead take advantage of her seemingly sincere interest.

"What is with this hedge? I can't get through to go back home."

"It is stubborn," Rachel admitted.

Charley climbed back up the bank to repeatedly pull and poke at the hedge, trying to find a gap. Eventually, she gave up with a growl. She turned to look across the way at Rachel, still calmly sitting on the ground, twirling a lock of her hair.

"What's next, Charlotte? Are you going to dig a tunnel?"

"I want to go home!" Charley shouted. "Now!"

Rachel maintained her calm and looked at Charley with a quizzical expression. "Why are you yelling at me? I'm not stopping you."

"This overgrown weed is stopping me!"

"Insulting the hedge isn't going to help. Why don't you try asking nicely?"

"Would that work?"

"Maybe," offered Rachel.

Two years ago, after receiving rave reviews for her starring role in her father's local television commercial for the farm stand, Charley had begged her parents to send her to acting classes. Although she only attended three before losing interest, she did remember how to bow. She faced the hedge and bent stiffly from the waist.

"Mr. Hedge, would you be so kind as to let me pass through you so I can go home for dinner?" she asked in a poor semblance of a British accent.

Nothing happened. Charley turned to Rachel, shrugging her shoulders in silent question. Rachel shrugged back at her. She looked again at the green wall. Realizing her request had been ignored, she grabbed hold of fistfuls of the ferny obstacle and shook them as violently as she could.

What followed next was what her mother called her 'angry dance'. Charley stomped, twirled, and jumped up and down to a beat of unintelligible shrieks, wild accusations, and unladylike words she had learned from eavesdropping on the field hands. When the tirade finally stopped, she was dizzy and out of breath. Rachel gave her a round of applause.

"That was amazing. You're so cute," she said, laughing.

Charley could only glare at her as she stooped over with her hands on her knees. Rachel rose and approached her.

"Face it, Charlotte, we can't leave here."

A tremor crept into Charley's voice. "Ever? That's not fair."

"I don't know about ever, but I've been here a long time. And what do you mean, not fair? You ran away from home, right?"

Charley composed herself to answer, "I didn't run away forever. I have to go home sometime. Soon," she muttered.

"You said your Mom and Dad were mean to you and they wouldn't let you do anything. You said they didn't want you. Why would you want to go back to that? Are you a child?"

She straightened at Rachel's challenge. She wiped her runny nose with the back of her hand and said in the most mature voice she could muster, "I never said they didn't want me. I just don't get what I want."

Charley scowled and winced, hearing herself.

"I'm not a child."

Rachel consoled Charley by putting her arm around her, while at the same time rolling her eyes dramatically in derision. "Of course not, Charlotte. Anyone can see that."

Charley waited for Rachel to expound on the subject or perhaps give her a compliment, but Rachel changed the subject too quickly.

"Do you want me to show you where I sleep?"

"Is it a pile of leaves?" asked Charley with a nasty grin.

Rachel led Charley away. "Good one, Charlotte. It's okay for you to make jokes, but not for me?"

Charley almost apologized. "I'm tired."

Rachel put her hand on Charley's shoulder. "You should be tired. That fit must have taken a lot out of you."

Charley ignored the fact that Rachel was teasing her again. It had taken a lot out of her. -- She he was glad her new friend was unaware of the three earlier tantrums she had thrown at home. She ignored the sarcastic comment since she didn't have the energy to think of a nasty remark anyway.

"I'm so sleepy," Charley said as she shook her head. "I could doze off right here."

"That would be a truly dangerous idea," said Rachel. "Come on. It's not far."

Charley felt Rachel's hand take hers and allowed herself to be led downstream, or upstream. She couldn't tell.

CHAPTER THREE

Charley kept an eye on both banks of the stream, looking for a break in the tall hedges. From time to time, she caught strange circular images in the periphery of her vision, formed by contrasting shades of green glossy needles on the walls. The branches of the hedge swayed continuously in the breeze resulting in constantly changing patterns. Guessing the light must be playing tricks on her, she kept her suspicions to herself. There was no sense giving Rachel any ammunition to make fun of her again. As they walked, four more probably-not faces came and went, the last one winking at her. That was enough for her. She stopped Rachel and pointed where the face had been.

"Did you see that? There was a face in the hedge. It was looking at us and... it winked at me!"

Rachel was unfazed. "No, I didn't see it. Whose face was it?"

A new layer of surprise appeared on Charley's face. Instead of taking the opportunity to mock her for imagining things, the news of plants with the ability and the impudence to wink hadn't shocked Rachel at all.

"I...I don't know. I think..."

Rachel continued her line of casual questions. "Was it a man or a woman? Or was it an animal?"

Charley continued to stare at the spot where the face had been. "I couldn't tell," she said, her voice trailing off.

She whipped around to face Rachel.

"Wait, you've seen them too?"

Rachel nodded.

"And you don't think that's nuts?" asked Charley, in disbelief.

Rachel casually shook her head. "They're happy to stay in the hedge, and they don't bother me. I just wave and go about my business."

"What are they?" asked a bewildered Charley.

Rachel shrugged her shoulders in dismissal. "No clue. Come

on. We have to pick up the pace."

Charley continued to look for more faces and, hopefully, a way out. At one point, the hedge to their right did end. More accurately, it was blocked by a dense thicket of sumac and bramble bushes growing next to the path. Unfortunately, any hope of exit was blocked by the number and the size of long thorns bristling throughout. Charley's disappointment was slightly diminished by the delicious wild black-berries they were able to gather.

Further along, they came upon taller mature trees here and there on both sides of the riverbed, both before and beyond the hedge. Vegetation would sometimes hide the hedge for a distance, but it always reappeared to Charley's growing frustration. She checked out each tree for any branches that might reach over the hedge, only to be continually disappointed. Although most branches were out of her reach, she was able to pull herself up into the crook of one stunted pear tree. Her efforts to escape turned out as fruitless as the tree. She took off her shoes, one at a time, and rubbed her feet as she sat in her perch.

"Rachel, when are we going to get there? I can't walk any far-ther.

"We're close. Come on down."

Charley dropped to the grass. She collected her sneakers and limped down the slope.

"Ooh! What's that?" she exclaimed, pointing to something glowing in the grass at their feet.

Rachel backed away, and Charley bent down to pick up a per-fectly oval stone. It fit neatly into the palm of her hand, felt slippery smooth, and glowed with a faint, warm red light. Charley looked it over from every angle.

"It's so beautiful. I've never seen anything like it before. Have you?"

Rachel seemed disinterested. "I've seen rocks before, sure."

Charley didn't let Rachel's casual reaction temper her ex-citement. "Don't be stupid. You know what I mean. It's glowing like there's a fire inside." She passed it back and forth between her hands. "But it's cool." She couldn't take her eyes off it. "It must be worth a fortune. I'm going to keep it," she declared with more than a hint of greed contorting her expression.

"As you wish."

Charley's gaze snapped to focus on Rachel. "You don't mind?" asked Charley in surprise.

Rachel shook her head. "Why would I mind? Finders, keepers."

Charley clapped her free hand over the stone in her right fist and held it close to her chest. She tried to sound as magnanimous as Rachel had been.

"Still, I wish I had another one like it so we could both have one."

Charley emitted an exclamation of surprise and spread her hands to find a second stone in her left, identical in all aspects to the one in her right hand, apart from the inner glow. The original stone faded as she watched, turning to a soft blue. Her jaw dropped. She held one stone in each palm to show Rachel.

Rachel enjoyed the look on Charley's face. "That's a neat trick, Charlotte."

"I didn't do anything. At least, I don't think I did anything," said Charley, staring with wide eyes at the stones.

Rachel laughed.

"What's so funny? What did you do?"

"I'm laughing at the look on your face. Don't you see? Your wish came true," said Rachel, as if a wish coming true was as common as the sun coming up in the morning.

Charley was still confused. "What do you mean?"

"You wished for another stone, and you got one."

Charley's eyes lit up with a mixture of wonder and greed.

"Wait. Are you saying I can make a wish on a stone, and it will come true?"

"It happened, didn't it? Don't you believe your eyes?"

Charley stared at the stones again.

"Can I have my stone now, Charlotte?" Rachel asked, holding out her hand.

Charley reluctantly handed her the brighter red stone. The glow from the bluish stone was almost gone now. Rachel dropped Charley's generous gift into a pocket, turned her back, and walked away briskly.

She called over her shoulder. "Come on, Charlotte. It's getting late. And dark."

Charley hurried after Rachel to stop her by tugging on her sleeve.

"Wait, I want to wish again," she insisted.

She held the now-ordinary stone to her mouth and spoke directly into it as if it were a microphone, "I wish I had some socks."

Although she had a sinking feeling the stone was going to disappoint her, she was still crushed when nothing happened.

"What did I do wrong?"

"Nothing, luckily."

"I don't understand."

Rachel dismissed her with a wave of her hand and an urgent and ominous tone in her voice. "I'll explain later. We have to go. Now. It's not safe to be caught outside after dark."

She trotted away. Charley dropped her cold stone to the ground and raced to catch up.

"Wait!" she cried. "Caught by what?"

She overtook Rachel, blocking her path. She reached out to hold the older girl's hands.

"Rachel, we're friends, right?"

"We're going to be best friends," Rachel replied with a nod and a smile.

Charley stared into Rachel's eyes and nodded vigorously in a vain attempt at mind control.

"Well, best friends do favors for each other, right?"

Rachel agreed without hesitation.

"Then, could I use your wishing stone? My feet hurt so bad. I'm getting blisters on my blisters."

Rachel gave her a disapproving look and a shake of her head. "I don't know. I might need a wish soon."

Charley began pleading with a quality of earnestness and desperation that could only have been attained from many hours of practice. She employed an onslaught of desperate and shrill vocal exercises with accompanying facial expressions that can amount to sheer torture for any victim.

"Please. We're best friends. I could wish for socks for you too. Please!"

Charley clasped her hands in front of her face to form a megaphone thereby concentrating a rapid-fire chant aimed directly at the Irritation Center of Rachel's cerebral cortex.

"Please, please, please, please, please, please, please, please."

Rachel fell victim to the assault. "Alright!" She fished the rock from her pocket. "Here. Take it. Just stop!"

Charley was thrilled that her skills were still as sharp as ever. "Thank you. Thank you. Thank you," she gushed.

"Now, be careful," warned Rachel, heading off another barrage of verbal assault.

"What do you mean?"

"If you're not specific, you won't get exactly what you wish for. Come to think of it, something close to what you wish for isn't guaranteed either. Once, I was cold and I wished for a coat. I blinked, and the next thing I knew I was covered with fur, like a collie."

Charley looked at her doubtfully.

"I used another wish to fix it," explained Rachel.

Charley stared intently at the stone in her hand, barely registering surprise at Rachel's story.

"That sounds awful. Thanks for warning me. Now, let me think."

She chewed her lower lip for a minute while Rachel looked up at the sky and gestured with her hand for Charley to hurry. Her face grew serious.

"Charlotte, come on. I mean it. It's not safe to be out after dark. The night belongs to creatures that'll eat little humans like us for dinner."

Charley was not intimidated. "Wait a second, okay?" She held the stone to her lips and said, "I wish we had socks. Oooh, wait! Heavy, warm, soft socks!" She pointed to a flat stone nearby. "Over there!" She added, "White!" for good measure.

Four socks of various colors and sizes appeared at Charley's feet. She dropped the stone like a rapidly cooling potato. She chose the two socks that were most closely matched and looked at Rachel for her reaction.

Rachel sighed. "Not bad for a first try, Charlotte. Now, hurry up and put them on." She reached down and snatched up the two remaining socks and stuffed them into the back pocket of her jeans.

"Happy now? Can we go?" she asked with her last shred of patience.

Charley clapped and smiled for the first time since crossing the hedge. She sat on a rock and pulled the socks onto her filthy feet. The white sock on her left foot stretching up to her knee was printed with comically drawn penguins. The other was calf-length and black with a silver spider web pattern. Charley bit her lower lip for a moment as she lifted her feet straight out in front of her to inspect the socks. She shrugged her shoulders and proceeded to put on her sneakers. Rachel hurried away, and Charley ambled after her, laughing.

Rachel looked at the sky, and Charley followed her gaze. The sun disappeared, as it was needed elsewhere , leaving them on their own. Rachel turned to Charley, her voice sharp and severe.

"We're going to have to run. Can you keep up?"

Charley ignored the urgency in Rachel's voice. "I can try. I'm super-fast but only for short distances. I'm faster than most of the boys in my grade. One time we had a race in gym class..."

Rachel sprinted off downstream, and Charley found herself alone in the deepening darkness. Finally, after adding up all the clues and multiple direct appeals, she sensed Rachel was in a hurry and tore after her. Rachel led her along the grass at the start of the slope, avoiding the treacherous footing of the rocky riverbed. As they ran, a slab of darkness settled down on the hedges like someone placing the lid on a shoebox. Night was upon them. Behind them upstream, a wolf bayed. The mournful howl was answered by other voices from ahead and around them.

Rachel called out to Charley over her shoulder. "Almost there! Run faster!"

Charley squinted to her right to see a large shaggy bear emerging from the hedge. It stretched and yawned as they sprinted by. More figures emerged. Shaggy and filthy young men and women shambled aimlessly, mumbling to themselves and apparently unable to get the hang of the traditional left-right-left-right rhythm of human bipedal ambulatory locomotion. Their faces were slack-jawed, eyes unfocused. Charley yelped, "Rachel?"

"We're here!"

Charley could barely make out the outlines of a shack ahead. Rachel crashed into a wall and rebounded, pulling open a door. Charley barreled into her soon after and they both hurried inside. Rachel slammed the door behind them, shutting out the predators and shutting themselves into a void of pitch blackness.

CHAPTER FOUR

"**L**ock the door! Lock the door!" hissed Charley in a panicky whispered shout.

Rachel's voice from the inky nowhere reassured her. "Relax. They won't come inside. We're safe now."

Charley shivered as her imagination listened to the sounds of hundreds of creatures, great and small, prowling and growling and roaring outside the cabin in the wild night, some natural species and some the creatures of her darkest nightmares. Something scratched at the door. Some thing-- or perhaps multiple things- scuttled on the roof. She jumped in fright when Rachel shuffled nearby.

Charley's voice trembled. "Rachel, are you sure we're safe in here?"

The sound of a match being struck caused her to swing her head around in time to see Rachel lighting a candle. The candle gave off barely enough radiance to allow Charley to see they were standing in a small, one-room cabin. Rachel lit two more candles as she moved about the room, seemingly without a care in the world.

"I've never been bothered when I'm at home, but then again, I don't go outside after dark."

She walked casually to a window and closed it. Charley looked around to find two cots and a table. A small metal sink with a hand-operated pump jutted from a wall below a second window. Rachel smiled at Charley as she closed the shutters, not noticing a hairy baseball bat-sized insect leg poking inside and searching for prey. It quickly pulled back out as Rachel closed the last shutter, barely avoiding being pinched. Charley's eyes were as wide and round as her mother's pancakes. She backed away to crash into and fall onto a cot, letting out a frightened squawk as she landed.

"What's wrong?" asked Rachel, oblivious to how close she had come to death.

Charley pointed at the window. "I saw..."

Rachel hurried over to help her up. "Saw what?"

"It looked like a spider leg. Only huge. It was trying to get in!"

Rachel nodded, unconcerned. "They do grow big here. There aren't many around this part of the river, though. There are some parts where it looks like Spider City."

The sounds outside had decreased, but something was still scrabbling on the roof. Charley held her breath, but Rachel casually went about her business. After a few more seconds of what could only be the sound of a thousand blood-sucking spiders parading above them, silence jarred Charley, forcing her to inhale.

"I can't sleep here, Rachel."

Rachel pumped some water into the sink. She bent over and splashed some onto her face, with little discernible effect.

"Don't be silly. You can't go outside until sunrise. Relax and get some rest. We'll have fun tomorrow."

"What about dinner?"

Rachel reached into her pocket and pulled out a blackberry and popped it in her mouth.

"You're hungry? Don't you have more berries?"

"I ate them all."

Rachel shook her head in motherly judgment. "You need to learn to control yourself."

"Excuse me. I'm new here, you know."

"Calm down, Charlotte. You can't be sheltered forever. There's no supermarket down the street, and your Mommy isn't here to tuck you in at night. No more excuses."

"I thought we were friends. Friends teach each other. Don't they? They don't try to make their new friends feel stupid."

Rachel sighed. "I'll teach you what you need to know, but it would help if you didn't act like you were Queen of the River."

"Is there a Queen of the River?" asked Charley with a hopeful tone.

"Not as far as I know. If there is, she doesn't have many sub-jects."

Charley pumped some more water into the sink and washed herself as Rachel had. She cupped her hand under the pump to get a sip and wiped her mouth on her sleeve. Rachel walked to the table and lifted a cloth revealing a bowl with three glowing stones.

"If you're hungry, help yourself."

Charley hesitated. "There's no food around here? Do I have to use a stone? We could wish for something a lot more valuable."

"What's more valuable than food?"

"Money, a really nice car, new clothes and shoes for every season..."

"Charlotte, none of that is valuable here. You're going to have to get used to it. If you're not going to eat, let's get some sleep."

Charley picked up a stone. She looked at Rachel, who nodded to go ahead.

"I wish I had a hot fudge sundae with mint chocolate chip ice cream."

The edible ingredients of an ice cream sundae appeared on the table in front of Charley. Charley clapped her hands and gave Rachel a smug, but short-lived smile. The sundae had appeared with a plop on the dirty table, hot fudge streaming off the rapidly melting ice cream to make a sticky mess. She also had no spoon to eat it, even if she was brave enough to try. She stuck her finger into a possibly uncontaminated glob and placed it in her mouth. Unsatisfied and embarrassed, she bit her lower lip and looked at Rachel.

Rachel picked another stone out of the bowl and tossed it to Charley.

"Try again."

"Maybe, I should try something simple."

"Yep. Good idea."

"I wish I had a banana. Wait, no, a bunch of bananas!"

A single banana appeared on the table.

Rachel yawned. "Well, at least it's edible. Now, can we turn in?"

Charley peeled the banana and took a bite. Although she still hadn't mastered the art of the wish, she was happy to find it was the best banana she had ever tasted. She heaved a sigh of relief and ate her dinner. She even dipped the banana carefully into the ice cream puddle on the table.

While Charley smacked noisily, Rachel gathered the dimmed stones and opened the window a crack. She tossed them outside and closed the window again. She walked to her cot, picked up a blanket to wrap around her shoulders, and lay on the cot with a sigh. Charley finished her banana and pumped another mouthful of water, slurping it down.

Rachel blew out her candle and lay on her back with eyes closed and one arm behind her head. Charley blew out one more candle and carried the last lit one to her own cot. She placed it on a wooden log functioning as a night stand. After removing her sneakers and her new socks, she looked at her dirty feet with disgust. She shrugged, deciding there was nothing to be done about them at this point. She left the candle lit and lay on the cot, covering herself in her own blanket.

The girls lay without speaking for a time. Charley was not ready to settle down yet, so she broke the silence.

"Rachel, my friends call me Charley."

Rachel murmured an inaudible question to Charley at her mention of having friends.

"Well, actually my Mom and Dad call me Charley."

"It fits you. Are you going to blow out the candle?"

"It's going to be dark. I don't like the dark," Charley admitted in a quiet voice.

"It's going to be exactly as dark as it gets every time you close your eyes."

"Hmm... That's true. I never thought of it that way."

"That's what friends are for, Charley. To help you look at life in different ways."

"I wouldn't know. I don't know many kids my age. I didn't even go to school until a couple years ago."

Rachel waited for her to go on.

"Nobody wanted a new friend – especially someone like me. I'm little and…"

"And what, Charley?"

"I just don't fit in. Everyone whispers behind my back and laughs at me. They used to call me Pygmy. I wish they still did. Now they have worse names. I tried to explain why I'm… so small, but it only made it worse."

The noticeable sound of nothing at all greeted them as she fell silent once again. Charley strained her sense of hearing to the breaking point, but it seemed the monsters outside had moved on in their search for a late dinner. She propped herself up on one elbow and looked at Rachel drifting off into carefree slumber.

"I have to go home tomorrow," said Charley in a loud voice.

Rachel managed to summon enough energy to feebly blink her eyelids and allow a quiet breath of incomprehensible mumbling to escape from her lips. Charley kept up her monologue, taking Rachel's inarticulate moan as an invitation to go right on chattering.

"Don't get me wrong. I'm glad I ran away. No one's going to tell me what to do here."

"So, why do you want to go home?"

"It's just… I remembered something I had to do. Never mind," said Charley.

Rachel answered warily, "What's that?"

"I didn't brush my teeth before bed."

Rachel snickered, and Charley joined her, their giggles blooming into full-blown laughter.

"Good one. Good night, Charley."

"We could stay up a little longer and talk," said Charley, hoping to put off the loneliness of night.

Rachel ignored her. Charley was exhausted, but the possibility of the return of giant spiders to the roof or hungry wolves outside the door scared her. She looked over at Rachel to find her with her eyes closed, already snoring.

Charley blew out the candle and lay back. Alone in the dark, the constant worries about her illness always returned to torment her.

"I'll be fine. What's one day?" she said to her sleeping friend.

Her health had been improving for months. Although she had missed her medication, the day's exertion didn't produce the same feeling as those scary times in years past. She was sleepy; just normal, every night sleepy – the kind of sleepy that young children feel after a long day of living every moment. She pulled the blanket up to her nose.

"If she can sleep with wild animals and monsters running around, I can too. I hope."

CHAPTER FIVE

Despite her fears, Charley quickly fell into a fitful sleep. She jerked and twitched in her cot, trapped in a nightmare. She staggered around a primeval jungle, chased by a Tyrannosaurus Rex. For the entire night, she screamed as she ran about, dodging and weaving, with the dinosaur roaring in playful response to her terror. Time and time again she fell into and crawled out of gigantic claw prints, as the terrible lizard stomped all around her. At one point, the huge dinosaur was distracted by a large purple and gold dragonfly. It turned its attention away from the shrieking girl to the buzzing insect, giving her a chance to escape at last. Charley scrambled forward over muddy ground only to fall with a squeak into yet another deep claw print. Rolling over, she looked up to see the massive head of the monster closing in on her. Its teeth were razor sharp and its breath was horrible. She held out her hands in an ineffective attempt at pushing its massive head away and inexplicably called out, "No, Grace, no!"

The dinosaur paused, possibly to sneeze, or possibly, though far less likely, because her name actually was Grace. In any case, Charley had an opening. She tried to get up and run away but was swatted back down to the ground by a sweep of the dinosaur's massive head. With one more deafening roar, Grace lifted her foot and prepared to flatten her. Charley closed her eyes so as not to see the claw descend, but the end never came. Unable to tell if she had been squashed, she opened her eyes to see wooden beams and cobwebs above her head.

She was still alive, a dirty little girl in a dirty little shack and Rachel was nowhere to be found. Her cot was empty, the blanket neatly folded next to her pillow. The cabin was still dim despite the light of the early morning peeking through gaps in the walls and windows.

Charley rose and discovered a breakfast consisting of a stack of pancakes and a small pitcher of milk sitting on the counter. Knives and forks were set out beside the pancakes along with another smaller pitcher containing syrup, and a note. Charley dipped a pinky into the syrup and tasted. She gave an exaggerated yummy sound for no one's benefit.

Charley made a mental note to thank Rachel for breakfast later. She stood at the counter and cut up her pancakes. She poured the entire pitcher of syrup over them and began spearing chunks into her mouth. As she chewed, she looked around at her shelter.

Cobwebs could be found in every nook, cranny, and corner, made by what must have been hundreds of ordinary everyday spiders. A stone chimney rose from an empty, sooty fireplace and a moose head with one antler stared at her from the opposite wall. Other than their cots, everything was covered with a heavy carpet of dust. As she chewed a large mouthful of pancake, she asked no one in partic-ular, "How does Rachel live like this? You thought my room was bad, Mom? You should see this place."

She looked around for a glass for her milk. Not seeing anything handy, she drank directly from the pitcher, gulping it down. When she was finished, she wiped her sticky hands on her shorts and walked to the window over the sink. She lifted the latch and pulled the window open a crack. Seeing no giant arachnids, she opened the window a little wider for a look at the yard outside.

Rachel was dancing with and amidst a swarm of butterflies. She waved her arms as she leapt about and the butterflies flitted and followed her hands making it seem like she was holding sparklers on the Fourth of July. Charley watched her for a while, noticing the huge smile and serenely happy look on her friend's face.

Rachel stopped dancing when she saw Charley in the window and waved enthusiastically to her. Charley returned the wave and beamed a smile back at her. Rachel dismissed the butterflies and sprinted toward the cabin. When Charley opened the door, Rachel was waiting. She took Charley's hands and pulled her outside. They giggled hysterically as they swung each other around and around until they fell down in a heap, as dizzy as tail-chasing dogs. Rachel recovered first. She rose unsteadily and reached down to Charley to help her up.

"Come on. Let's eat. I'm starving."

Charley thought about the tall stack of now-eaten pancakes and could only say, "Umm."

Rachel mistook the 'Umm' for 'Mmm' and smiled in anticipation. She pulled Charley inside with a playful tug. When she saw the empty plates and pitcher, she looked back at Charley with lightning in her eyes.

"You ate them? You ate all of them?" Her once gleeful innocent expression was now menacing.

Charley shook her head and began to recite from her well-worn excuse list. "I didn't know. It was dark. I thought you had eaten already."

"Didn't you read my note?" asked Rachel.

Charley only shook her head. Rachel stormed to the counter and grabbed the note. She crumpled it and threw it at Charley, hitting her in the chest. "You're such a selfish brat, Charley!"

She stomped out and slammed the door. Charley picked up the note and straightened it out to read.

Charley,

I'm outside. Come get me when you wake up so we can have breakfast. We are going to have so much fun. I'm so happy you rolled into my life. I hope you like pancakes.

Love, Your Best Friend, Rachel

Charley stood silently, considering how best to handle this. She could apologize. She probably should apologize. She dropped the note on the table and reluctantly walked outside. Rachel was trying to gather the butterflies again, but they would have none of it. The butterflies were apparently sensitive to angry, hurt feelings.

"Well, what do you have to say?"

Charley intended to say, 'I'm sorry'. Instead, what came out was, "It's your fault."

Rachel exploded, "My fault! How is it my fault?"

The two friends then launched into a spirited argument, unburdened by conventional logic or the slightest inclination to listen to what the other person had to say.

"You should have told me last night you were going to make breakfast for us. And I was sooo hungry I wanted to eat right away, and I was going to read your note later. I didn't want them to get cold, even though they were cold anyway and, and I thought you probably already ate. Besides, it was too dark to read. They weren't very good anyway."

"You are so inconsiderate. I used my last stones to make those pancakes, and you stuffed your face with all of them and drank all the milk too. I didn't have to make them, you know. I could have let you starve. You would have been eaten by a bear, or a spider, or who-knows-what if it wasn't for me, but you couldn't spare one thought about me, and then you think it's my fault you're a greedy, selfish, little baby?"

Rachel was shocked silent. "Not good? You think you could do better?"

"I know I could," said Charley, determined to cling to her delusional gambit.

"I doubt you can even butter toast."

"Oh, like it's so hard to wish for a stack of pancakes," Charley sneered.

"It is hard to get it right! It's the thought that counts, anyway. All you think about is yourself!"

Charley charged on. "Oh, yeah? Well, all you think about is... bossing me around."

Rachel's fists clenched. "What did you say?" she said, barely controlling her rage.

Charley clenched her own fists and repeated, "I said you're bossy." She raised her hands like a boxer. Just as her father had taught her the evening after the first time she was bullied at school.

Instead of witnessing a fistfight, the butterflies and other nearby riverbed denizens were subjected to another screeching duet. Charley and Rachel circled each other, eyes flashing, and fists clenched, until their noses were an inch apart.

"You're bossy, and you're dirty, and you're mean. The next stone I find, I'm going to wish for a big plate of spaghetti, and I'm not going to share it with you. You smell like a skunk, and you're ugly, and it's no wonder you don't have any friends, and you snore, and I bet no one even misses you."

"You are an immature child, and you're just as dirty as me. The next stone I find, I'm going to wish for a hundred pimples on your stupid face. You smell like a sweaty hippopotamus wearing skunk pajamas. I'd rather get my ears cut off than listen to your voice again and you have ugly crooked teeth, and I bet no one even misses you."

For a few seconds, there was no sound. The air was still. A knock-down, drag-out wrestling match was about to ensue. Instead, both girls were distracted by a raucous ruckus approaching from downstream. A sing-song voice accompanied by an out-of-time clacking sound reached them. They both turned their head slightly, sparing one eye to get a look at the singer while still maintaining a watchful glare on the other.

A tall, sturdy woman strode purposefully upstream, one third-humming, one third-mumbling, and one-third singing a bouncy tune. She wore a threadbare, ankle-length, green or greenish print dress. She wore what appeared to be a large window drape wrapped around her upper half with assorted bits, bobs, and odds and ends poking out of the folds. A collection of table legs had been trussed onto her back, producing the clacking sound as she walked. Her ensemble was topped by a straw hat the size of a monster truck tire.

The two combatants did not move an inch. Together, they appeared to be one statue; one tiny, furious warrior mirrored by a taller and equally furious warrior. As the woman approached, the warriors' snarling jaws dropped in disbelief at her appearance. She kept walking until their statue fell under the shade from her hat. She had a deeply tanned, wrinkly face creased by a broad, but serious smile. She crossed her arms and planted her feet in a wide stance, instantly rooting herself to the ground.

She said flatly, "I don't like the song you're singing. It's too angry for my taste. It's a morning for songs about peace and love and happy times. Would you like to hear mine? I've been working on it all morning."

Charley asked in a nasty tone, "Are there any Tra-la-las or Hey-diddle-diddles?"

The woman squinched her face in confusion and looked up to search her eyebrows for an answer. "There's a Hey-Nonnie-Nonnie."

Charley was still combative. "Then, no."

Rachel dropped her warrior stance and hissed at her, "Charley!"

The woman's face showed only the slightest bit of hurt. "Suit yourself, Sunshine. I won't waste your precious time. I have a long way to go myself."

She adjusted her load and walked away upstream.

Rachel glared at Charley.

"What?" Charley asked.

Rachel nodded her head toward the woman. Charley spread her hands, palms skyward as if she had no idea as to what Rachel was hinting.

She rolled her eyes and muttered something under her breath before calling out to the old woman, "Hey!"

Rachel sputtered in shock and gave Charley's right ear a flick with her index finger.

Charley sneered at her, but amended her request to inject some courtesy and manners. "Excuse me, ma'am. Please come back."

The woman did stop, but did not turn around immediately. Her huge hat tipped to the side as she considered Charley's request. She spun slowly and returned to them.

"Did you want to hear the song?" she asked.

"Maybe later," said Charley. "Can you answer some questions first?"

"Of course, I can," said the woman. "A better question would be, 'Would you answer some questions?' with a please thrown in. I will, but only for a short time. If I'm not where I need to be before I need to be there, I'll be too late."

She sat cross-legged at their feet and tilted her hat back until the brim rested on the ground. Charley and Rachel sat as well, as they pondered her last statement.

Charley cleared her throat. "Well, we're going this way," pointing downstream. "What is that way? I need to find where I need to be to get out of this place because I need to be home before I'm too late."

The woman frowned at her with justified disapproval. "Child, mockery is for the simple-minded. I don't abide mockery."

Charley rudely ignored her. "Where are you going?"

The woman looked questioningly at Rachel, who shrugged her shoulders and shook her head in unspoken commiseration. She said to Charley, "I am traveling to my special spot. I'm in the middle of a painting, you see."

The woman reached back into her drape/shawl and fished out a rectangular canvas. It was a landscape of a sunset over the river valley. There were no colors yet, making it more of a drawing than a painting.

"I started this years ago when I was a youngster like yourselves. I was exploring on a gorgeous afternoon around this time of year. I turned around at precisely the right moment to see the sunlight kissing the treetops. The colors were perfect. I stood there in blessed awe, taking in the supreme beauty of it all. I was frozen, in a flawless, witnessing-a-miracle kind of way. Do you know what I mean?"

The girls looked at each other and shook their heads, saying in unison, "No."

"Sad. Anyway, I decided to paint it the next day. I spent the whole night and the next day there waiting for the sun to start setting, but it was cloudy. The day after that, it rained. A whole week passed and the sun never shined the same way again. Every year, I go back to the same place around this time, but I've never seen those colors again."

"Why didn't you take a picture?" asked Charley.

The woman blinked and looked to Rachel for an explanation. Rachel was not only unable to furnish one for her, but she also looked profoundly embarrassed to be associated with Charley.

"I'm going to set up my easel and paint, thank you very much." Charley tried once again, "Don't you have a camera in that bag somewhere?"

The woman stared Charley down for more than a few moments. "Do you have any intelligent questions?" she asked at last.

Charley's mouth twitched. Rachel nudged her. "Ask her if there's a gate in the hedge somewhere."

Charley looked at Rachel, annoyed. "Why don't you ask her if there's a gate in the hedge?"

The woman answered to avoid further squabbling. "The hedge doesn't have a gate. There are no gaps. It doesn't open or close."

"But, I got in," countered Charley.

The woman nodded. "You are here. There's no denying that."

"If I got in, I should be able to get out, right?" said Charley.

The woman explained, "The river is meant to be traveled, child. There are no short cuts or off-ramps."

Charley turned up her indignation. "So, we have to keep walking, until what? We reach the ocean? Then what?"

"I suppose you could stay here in your cabin, but what's wrong with strolling along and seeing the world?" asked the woman.

Charley couldn't sit still. She began to pace. "I can't just stay here."

Rachel reached up and tried to take her hand, "Charley, sit."

Charley's pacing became more frenetic as frustration grew. "The faces in the hedge, who are they?"

The woman nodded with the look of a learned sage. "They are the hedge. The hedge are they."

Charley rolled her eyes. "That doesn't answer my question."

Despite the whiny pitch in Charley's voice, the woman maintained a calm and patient demeanor. "The hedge is here to keep you on the path.

"And I can't crawl under it or climb over it or push through it?" asked Charley.

"You know the answer to that question. Anything else?" she asked with finality.

Charley gave up on her line of questioning. Instead, she asked the woman to foretell her future, as if this strange woman had arrived from a fairy tale and therefore logically had magical powers.

"Can you tell us what we'll find downstream?"

The woman had begun the process of collecting herself to rise. She reluctantly settled back down.

"Oh, you'll find allies and enemies, friends and fiends, angels and monsters, marvels and wonders, twists and turns, pain and suffering. Nothing unusual."

"Is it safe?" asked Charley.

With lethal seriousness, the woman answered, "No, child. It isn't."

Charley scowled. "You're not being helpful at all, you know."

"You want me to hold your hand along the way? I can't coddle you. I have my own journey."

Charley was getting frustrated. "Just tell me. If I wanted to go home, how would I get there?"

"You're a headstrong young lady, Charley. If I were to tell you what to do, you'd do the opposite. Of that, I have no doubt. I'm no seer, but I sense you have a long journey ahead of you."

"No, please. I'll listen," pleaded Charley with a small measure of forced sincerity.

The woman did not appear to be convinced. "Very well, for what it's worth, I'll tell you two things about the river ahead."

Charley and Rachel both leaned forward, hoping for valuable advice.

"First, when the river forks, always take the right path. Second, use your stones wisely. Use them for practical purposes and not for fanciful notions or selfish whims. There's less chance of something going horribly wrong.

Charley shook her head. "That still doesn't help me get through the hedge."

The woman was now officially aggravated with Charley. "I told you. The river is meant to be traveled," she said crossly. "Everyone has to travel the river at some point in their life."

Charley could tell the woman wasn't going to give her the answers she wanted. She turned her back so the woman couldn't see her gnashing her teeth so hard that her head vibrated. This would also prevent the woman from seeing her scream silently at yet another inhumane injustice perpetrated against her. She waited, making sure her silent protest lasted for an impolite length of time. When the fit passed, she turned around again and abruptly bumped into the brim of the enormous straw hat. The woman had already risen and was waiting patiently for Charley, an arm wrapped around Rachel's shoulders.

"Okay, thank you," Charley managed to squeak out.

"You're welcome. I wish you well," said the woman. "I predict you won't become the person you will be until you are no longer the person that you are."

Charley pondered that while the woman knelt to give her a hug. She peered over her shoulder at Rachel through the legs of the easel. Rachel only shrugged her own shoulders, looking as perplexed as Charley felt. The woman straightened up and held Charley's face in her hands.

"Be careful. If you run into folks giving you trouble, you tell them I won't be pleased," she said with all seriousness.

She lightly squeezed Charley's cheeks to get that to sink in. She let Charley go and rooted around in her robes, eventually pulling out a small scabbard with the handle of an equally small knife sticking out. The thin handle was wrapped in a plain leather strap. She pulled the knife out to show Charley the blade. It was plain and ordinary without adornment, its thin handle wrapped in a plain leather strap. Charley looked questioningly at the old woman.

She said, "It's not made for swordplay or bear-fighting, child. It's got its uses, though."

Charley was unimpressed. "Thank you, I guess. Is it magical?"

The woman roared with laughter. "Definitely, you'll be able to magically gut a fish and magically pop balloons."

Charley turned red from embarrassment. "Okay, well. Thanks for the butter knife."

The woman slid the knife into its scabbard and into the bib pocket of Charley's overalls.

"Keep your new butter knife close at hand. You may find it has more uses than your ungrateful little mind could ever imagine."

The woman then turned to leave. Charley was blinded when her face left the shadow of the woman's hat. She threw a hand up to block the sun. She could barely make out the figure of the woman striding away.

"Wait! Tell them who won't be pleased?" she called.

The woman shouted, "Nonnie. My name is Nonnie."

Charley twirled a lock of her hair and gently bit her lower lip, embarrassed. She looked up to see Rachel looking back at her. They stared at each other and then down to stare at their own feet, the anger of a few short minutes ago almost forgotten.

Rachel spoke first. "You want to leave the river already?"

Charley waved her hand in dismissal. "No, no, I just want to be able to go home whenever I want to."

"Good," said Rachel as a small smile lit up her dirty face.

"What do you want to do today? We could try to make up a song like Nonnie was doing."

"I want to start walking. Downstream," said Charley in a resolute, putting-her-foot-down kind of voice.

Rachel considered her suggestion/demand. "I suppose we could, but she said it would be dangerous, Charley. We'll have to find a different place to stay every night. I think we should stay here."

"It's kind of boring here, Rachel."

"It's not boring. It's peaceful."

"Peaceful is another word for…" Charley closed her eyes and pretended to snore. "Let's have an adventure!"

Rachel frowned, but Charley would not be denied. "Well, I'm going, and I want you to come with me. We'll find stones along the way and wish for food." She patted her chest. "If we get in any trouble, I have Butter to protect us."

Rachel mocked her. "What could go wrong? That's a stupid name for a knife, by the way."

"I need something to protect me from the bunnies and the butterflies," said Charley flippantly.

Rachel closed in on Charley. Her face was deadly serious. "You heard Nonnie. There are dangers on the river. Threats you can't imagine. I will go with you because foolish children get in big trouble if they aren't careful."

Charley looked down at her shoes, stung by Rachel's forcefulness. Rachel relaxed, and her tone softened. "You have to listen to me, Charley, and do exactly what I say, though. You're new here, and things are sometimes not what they seem. Okay?"

"I'll listen to you, Rachel," her tone flat and non-confrontational. "But I'm not a child, and I'm not foolish."

"Of course not. I'm going to search the cabin for anything we can use. Wait here, okay?" She left Charley and headed inside.

Charley nodded and muttered at Rachel's back, "I'll listen, but I can't guarantee I'm going to do what you say."

CHAPTER SIX

Charley waited outside while Rachel gathered supplies from the cabin. She began searching the immediate area, hoping to find a glowing stone nearby. Finding none in the first fifteen seconds, she tired of the effort. She looked expectantly at the cabin, leaning precariously in a state of near collapse. It looked even more decrepit outside than in. The walls were sparsely covered by wooden shingles riddled with holes made by what must have been legions of industrious woodpeckers. A thick layer of leaves, sticks, and pinecones covered the thatch roof. The upper half of the chimney had surrendered to gravity, its stones in a tumbled pile next to the house.

She whistled impatiently and walked toward the house.

"Rachel, are you almost ready?"

The door opened, and Rachel appeared. She held the strap of a canvas backpack in her left hand and the strap of a leather satchel in her right.

"Keep your pants on. Here."

She pushed the satchel into Charley's hands. Charley accepted it gleefully as if it was a Christmas gift. She looked inside to find it empty.

"I thought you were gathering things we might need."

"I'm carrying some things from the cabin that might be useful. Your bag is for what we find on the way."

"Is it heavy? I can carry something."

"Not so much. Two full canteens of water, some twine, a candle and some wooden matches, two sandwiches, two apples, and a blanket. "I'll handle it. I don't want to overburden you."

Charley shouldered the empty satchel and gave Rachel a sweet smile. "So, we're ready. Let's start our adventure."

Rachel nodded and smiled back at her with equal artificiality.

"You know, on second thought, I think I will share some of the load."

She placed her backpack on the ground and bent down to pull out one of the canteens. She handed it to Charley and then pulled out Charley's share of the food.

"I'm going to trust you with these. Try to make them last. Now we can go."

She turned and marched confidently downstream. Charley looked skeptically on a plain ham sandwich and some walnut shards wrapped in a cloth napkin before placing it carefully in the satchel. She opened the canteen and took a long swig. She stopped it up and took a last look at the cabin before dropping it into the satchel and turning to follow her friend.

The hedges reappeared, rising out of the ground on either side. She paused and scratched her head, wondering if they had been there seconds ago. The riverbed stretched out before her in a straight line to the horizon.

Rachel was far ahead already. She trotted to catch up, with the satchel bumping at her side. As she approached Rachel, it slipped off her shoulder and her leg became tangled. She tumbled to a stop at Rachel's side.

Rachel helped her to her feet, suppressing a smile. Having grown used to Charley's outbursts, she was prepared for an eruption. The missed interpretation of a word or the subtlest of gestures taken the wrong way could lead to hours of sulking. She knew she should tread lightly here, but she couldn't help herself.

"Very graceful, Princess Charlotte. Did you enjoy your trip?"

Charley shocked her by breaking into a fit of giggles. She rolled side to side, with tears of laughter streamed from her eyes. Rachel waited, with amusement filling her heart until the fit passed, and Charley groaned, holding her belly from the pain of too much hilarity. She disentangled the satchel from around her friend's ankle.

Charley stood and sheepishly asked Rachel, "Could you fix it please?"

Rachel smirked and adjusted the strap for Charley's height. Charley lifted the strap above her head and settled it on her shoulder.

Rachel opened her mouth to speak, but Charley's palm rose to cut her off.

"Don't say anything. I can't laugh anymore," she warned.

Rachel bit her tongue, and Charley walked away with arms outstretched as if balancing on a tightrope. Rachel repositioned the backpack and followed in her footsteps and in the same deliberate manner, catching up to maintain a position two paces behind her friend.

Eventually, they settled into a pleasant amble. Charley scanned the ground for stones while Rachel took in the scenery. The hedge wound between maples, spruces, and birches. Birds swooped between the trees, their conversations filling the riverbed with song. Rachel tried her own calls to get their attention. With the exception of one wren responding with a suspiciously sarcastic trilling, they ignored her as they went about their own business.

Charley's search paid off. She squeaked and jumped to her right, stabbing her hand into the dirt, and triumphantly raised a stone to the sky. She ran to Rachel and shoved it in her face.

"Look. I found one. You haven't found a stone."

"I haven't been looking."

"Well, we can't eat twine so you could at least say thank you."

"Thank you, Charley. We don't need to worry about food yet. It's still early. Why don't you put it in the satchel? We can talk while we walk."

"I'm hungry," said Charley.

"Charley, the next shelter is a long way away. We can't stop and eat every hour, or we won't make it."

"We can talk and walk and chew at the same time," suggested Charley.

Rachel bit her tongue and refrained from commenting dubiously on Charley's suspect ambulatory skills and the possible dangers associated with combining those three basic activities.

"Let's walk until we find another stone. Then we can eat and still have a stone for emergencies."

Charley chewed her lower lip for a moment and nodded.

"Okay, it's a good plan."

"You can take the time to think of a good wish for tonight's meal."

"Wait a minute. I have an idea!"

She knelt and placed the stone in the grass. Her eyes glittered as she prepared a brilliant wish. She passed a hand over the stone in exactly the same way as the instructor in her Magic class from last summer had taught her.

"I wish I had two more wishing stones."

A sound like the crack of a whip accompanied by a flash of light startled the two girls. Charley blinked and stared at her target with laser focus. Two identical stones sat on a pile of black sand. The light within them sputtered for a few seconds before disappearing with a soft pop-pop.

"I don't suppose it would do much good to wish for a dozen then," said Charley with a frown.

"Hmm," said Rachel. "It was worth a try. I guess the stones are just smarter than we are."

Charley kicked the stones. "Nothing's easy, is it?"

"You got that right, sister," said Rachel as she began to walk.

Charley reached out to hold her arm.

"You mean you never thought to try that?"

"Nope," replied Rachel.

"I guess I'm just smarter than you," said Charley.

"Let's just say our minds work in different ways. It never occurred to me."

Charley smiled falsely and nodded. "Sure, let's just say that."

She allowed Rachel to lead on, buoyed by an unearned sense of superiority.

They resumed their march, passing the time talking about their lives. Charley waxed on and on about her family and her school and all the injustices that seemed to befall only her. Rachel contributed by nodding often and adding a sympathetic *I know what you mean*, or a sincere *'Really?'* here and there. Eventually, Charley stopped venting and changed the subject to more positive themes. She grew more animated and cheerful, relating her hopes and dreams for the future and telling stories about more recent and happier and healthier days. She stopped talking only twice to pick up stones and put them in her bag without a comment. Rachel was glad for her distraction. When she wasn't complaining or angry at the world, Charley was quite likeable.

Charley looked up and spied a group of people far downstream. She whacked Rachel on the arm and called to them, but they were too far away to hear. When the river bent, they disappeared from view. Charley ran on to meet them, and Rachel jogged to keep up until they approached the bend in the river. Turning themselves, they found no sign of the travelers.

Charley turned around to face Rachel with a confused expression on her face.

"Where did they go?"

"Beats me. Lots of people on the river like to keep to themselves. I don't know if they're in a hurry or stuck up."

"But they should be here. They weren't that far ahead."

"This is a strange place. I don't think the river is a straight line that goes from beginning to end. Nonnie said there were forks, remember?"

Charley cast a judgmental glare at Rachel. "You're starting to sound like her. Nutty, I mean."

They started out again, falling into a contented silence, taking in the sights, sounds, and scents of the tranquil, picturesque countryside. Rachel paused to smell wildflowers and sometimes wandered off to chase butterflies while Charley watched faces appear and disappear in the hedge. At one point, Rachel raced up to the top of the slope and traced her hand along the branches. The smiling faces shimmered and dispersed, only to reappear when her fingers passed by.

Her friend carried on as if there was nothing to do but sing and dance and play and experience nature with all of her senses. Charley had more important things to think about and do, including eating lunch. While Rachel climbed a tree, Charley ate most of her sandwich, all the walnuts, and a few bites of her apple before tossing the scraps to the birds. She gave the faces a distrustful look as she took the lead, assuming Rachel would catch up.

Rachel trailed behind until Charley stopped. She had come upon a building on the right bank. It was an intensely gray, three-story, clapboard shamble of a house, only one strong wind away from collapsing. As if this weren't dangerous enough, the words 'Stay away' were painted sloppily in huge white letters on the front of the house. Broken windows gave the appearance of missing teeth from a grotesque smile. It seemed as though the house was built somewhere else and subsequently carried downstream in a flood long ago to be swept up onto the bank where it rested uneasily today.

Charley looked at Rachel. "Do you know who lives here?"

Rachel shrugged her shoulders and shook her head. "If I had to guess, I would say rats, spiders, and birds. I've run by it as fast I can a few times. It gives me the creeps."

Charley's curiosity about the house coupled with her inability to mind her own business led her to give it a closer look. "Well, someone painted on the house, and look; there are clothes on the line."

There were other signs of habitation as well. Dozens of coffee mugs held red checkered tablecloths down on half a dozen picnic tables. Smoke escaped from a pipe on the roof. Charley started to march toward the house despite Rachel's cautioning advice.

"Charley, come back. It isn't safe.

Charley ignored the ominous warning and charged forward without a second's hesitation.

CHAPTER SEVEN

Charley approached the house as if invited. She gave a glance at a newspaper on the picnic table, but what really caught her eye was a bird cage hung on a hook attached to a second story beam. The bird inside chirped a nervous greeting. Charley turned to Rachel and said excitedly, "I know this bird. I saw him yesterday on my side of the hedge. He invited me here."

"Come on, Charley. We should go," said Rachel as she tried to pull Charley away.

Charley resisted. "But the bird... I know him."

Rachel grew agitated, motioning Charley to come along. "That's nice, say 'Hi' and let's go."

Charley ignored her. She spoke righteously and loudly with the authority vested in her by herself.

"Well, he shouldn't be caged. I'm going to free him."

Charley looked around for something to help her reach the cage while Rachel alternated between looking out for the owner and trying to pull Charley away.

Charley evaded Rachel's grasp. "Why don't you help me instead of getting in my way?"

"We're trespassing on the property of someone who obviously does not want visitors."

Charley gave up searching for a tool or a ladder and fished a stone out of her satchel.

"Charley, wait!" exclaimed Rachel.

Charley closed her eyes and held the stone with both hands near her heart. "I wish I was tall enough to reach the birdcage."

Charley collapsed immediately, falling on her backside and crying out in pain. As she sat, her legs extended like a climbing vine, her heels sliding and bumping along the ground until her feet were a good ten feet away. The rest of her body remained petite Charley-sized. She tested her legs and peered up at her friend with a worried look.

"You never listen. Remember? I said you have to be careful."

Charley kicked her feet to find out if they still functioned.

"I think it worked, though," she said sheepishly.

Rachel rolled her eyes. Charley made several clumsy attempts to stand. Eventually, she had to roll over and, with Rachel's help, scrambled to her knees. She crawled toward the house and used a wall to climb to a standing position. With one hand on the house for balance, she looked down on Rachel with a nervous smile.

"Good for you. Do you know how to walk on stilts?" asked Rachel.

"I'm going to learn right now. Watch me," said Charley.

She pushed off from the wall and initiated an awkward arm-waving dance as she grew accustomed to her newly elongated limbs. As she whooped and wiggled, the bird chirped along with her. Rachel tried to shush them both, but it was too late. The door to the house opened, and a figure emerged. Charley shuffled to a halt and leaned against a wall near the cage.

A man barely taller than Ordinary Charley scuttled out and sized up his visitors. He placed his hands on his hips and cleared his throat, as if about to say something important. He paused, attempting to create an even more splendidly dramatic effect. Charley and Rachel looked at each other and then back to the little man. They had time to look back and forth at each other one more time before, finally, in a high squeaky voice, he said, "What's going on here?"

From Charley's vantage point, the man was as intimidating as a bottle of milk. He had a mottled bald scalp except for a patch of sparse gray hair spanning the distance between large ears, too big for his head. He wore a black three-piece suit with a wrinkled shirt that may have been white originally , but was now the color of lint. He rocked back and forth on bare feet waiting for an answer, somehow able to stare them down from below.

Charley spoke up, emboldened by her new stature. "What's going on here is, I'm letting my friend out of this cage."

"Your friend?" said the man. "That's my bird. I found him. I caught him. He's mine."

Charley scoffed at him. "You can't own a free bird."

The man wasn't intimidated at all by Charley towering over him. He squared off and confronted her, his upturned face at Charley's knees.

"Oh, I can't? Are you an attorney?"

Charley bent down to shake her finger in his face. "No, but I know you can't put people in cages."

"It's a bird cage. He's a bird, you silly girl," countered the man.

Charley began to boil. "He's not just a bird. He's my friend."

The man raised his eyebrows in doubt. "Do you even know his name?"

Charley straightened and furiously twirled a lock of her hair, trying to remember if she had heard the bird mention a name in their previous conversation.

"Some friend," the man said. "His name is Cecil, and he's mine. If you want to buy his freedom, you can pay me three stones."

"I'm not paying you anything," argued Charley.

Charley lurched into motion. She took one step toward the cage and the man squeaked.

"Don't you dare! You will regret it, young lady. You might think you can steal from me, but you won't get away with it. I'll tell my brother, and he'll chase you down no matter how far those freakish legs take you."

To Rachel, the man said, "Talk some sense into your friend."

Charley stuck out her tongue at the man and opened the cage. The bird flew out and circled the scene before disappearing down the river bed. The man was hopping mad now. Rachel backed away from him, and Charley laughed.

Charley was gleeful over liberating Cecil and for successfully defying the old man. "I'm not afraid of you or your brother. You can yell and scream all you want, but Cecil is free again, and that's that. Come on, Rachel."

Charley walked away, taking long, confident strides. Rachel had to run to keep up. The man chased them on short, spindly legs for a while, but he soon tired and gave up.

When they were out of sight, they heard him call out. "You will pay! My brother will find you!"

They kept up their pace for a while longer until Rachel stopped running and called out to Charley.

"Please slow down! I can't keep up."

Charley had gotten the hang of walking quickly with legs ten-feet-long, but she had not practiced stopping. She looked back to see Rachel, huffing and holding her side as she struggled to keep pace.

Out of pity, she tried the first phase in the act of graceful, non-lethal stopping; the slowing down. The result was a spectacular three-stage tumble. She reacted instinctively by leaning forward and putting her hands down to break her fall, but the ground was considerably farther away than usual. All that did was set up the second stage of the tumble; the twisting and flipping. Once complete, all that was left was the landing on her back and the subsequent, inevitable whipping of her legs into the dirt. Charley executed the third stage perfectly and added a loud 'Oomph!' for good measure.

Rachel had missed it all. She was still bent over, catching her breath. When she straightened up, Charley was lying on her back with her arms and legs spread wide. She approached her slowly, looking for signs of life. She knelt beside her.

"Ouch," said Charley.

Rachel ignored her physical condition and asked about her emotional state of mind. "Are you happy now, Charley?"

Charley groaned and answered, "I am. I'm a little sore, but I'm happy."

"Because you got your way."

"Yes," Charley agreed with satisfaction, happy Rachel was finally seeing things her way.

Her forehead creased in concentration moments later. "No," she said, withdrawing her agreement and somersaulting back to belligerence. "Because Cecil didn't deserve to be in a cage."

"How thoughtful of you. It wasn't the least bit selfish, I'm sure."

Charley exhaled a long, frustrated breath. "Could you give me a break for a minute? I'm just going to rest for a little while. I'm not exactly the picture of health here."

Rachel stared her down. Charley closed her eyes to escape the girl's intense questioning glare.

"Okay, take your time, princess. We only have the old man's murderous brother to worry about. Maybe he's the sane one."

"Just one minute?" begged Charley.

She convalesced peacefully on her back, oblivious to Rachel storming about in a reenactment of the famous climactic scene from the unwritten play, *The Choking of Charley Stanton.*

CHAPTER EIGHT

A minute later, Charley's eyes opened. Rachel held out her hand to help her up. After reaching sitting position, Charley waved her off.

"No, I'm not going through that again."

Charley reached into her satchel for her last stone. She showed no sign of uncertainty. "I can't go back home like this. I look like a freak."

"Here, give it to me. I'll do it. You could end up inside out or worse."

Charley twirled her hair. She toyed with the idea of arguing, but she knew her friend was right. She handed the stone to Rachel.

Rachel muttered some words and waved her hands over Charley's legs, and they began to shrink to their normal length. After moments of excruciating pain during the transformation, Charley was delighted. She stretched tentatively and, feeling no pain, she jumped up and badly performed the beginning of a routine she started to learn in her three Modern Dance lessons from last Fall.

"This is much better, thank you very much."

Rachel smiled, but advised her, "I'm glad you're happy, but we still have a problem. We're going to be hunted like Bigfoots now. Who knows what his brother will do to us?"

At that moment, Cecil cruised into view and landed on a flat rock at their feet. He gave a formal chirp and what appeared to be a bow. Charley clapped and bowed in response.

"You're very welcome, Cecil. It was so sad seeing you in a cage. You should stay far away from that awful little man. In fact, you should stay with us."

"Charley, remember, we're wanted criminals now."

Charley cut her off. "You're such a worrier, Rachel. If you want, we'll find three stones and pay him. Then you can stop being such a wimp, and we can get around to looking for a way home."

"I don't think we should go back there. That man is dangerous."

Charley laughed off her warning. "Make up your mind, Rachel. He's just a weird little guy. We'll give him his three stones and be on our way. Cecil, do you want to come with us?"

Cecil took off and circled them twice before alighting on Rachel's shoulder. Charley's face betrayed her with a disappointed look.

"Cecil, why don't you fly around and search for stones for us? You'll find them faster flying than we will walking around. Even better, why don't you just bring them to us?"

Cecil and Rachel exchanged a look.

"You want Cecil to find the stones to pay your debt?" asked Rachel. "Cecil, you don't have to do what she says."

Cecil answered her with two chirps and a cock of his head. Rachel shook her head in agreement. Charley looked at them both, exasperated.

"Well, he does owe me for rescuing him, doesn't he? Go ahead, Cecil. We'll be waiting right here."

Cecil shrugged his wings and took off upstream with a squawk which sounded authentically resentful despite coming from a bird. Charley sat with her arms crossed over her knees and a smile of self-satisfaction. She was also oblivious to the tone of Cecil's parting words and the reproach in Rachel's expression.

"Rachel, can I have something to eat now? I'm starving."

"What happened to your lunch?"

Charley shrugged her shoulders.

"I told you to make it last!"

Instead of showing remorse, Charley opted to go on the offensive. "You are so selfish. A real friend would share."

Rachel shook her head and tried to de-escalate the rising tension. "Don't be like that, Charley. I suppose I could split my sandwich in half..."

"That's better. If you think about it, it's kinda your fault. You should've packed more this morning."

Charley accepted the sandwich and peeled it apart for inspection. "A cheese sandwich? Really?" She gave one slice of bread and half the cheese back to Rachel. She folded her slice around the cheese and chewed away in ungrateful disgust.

"We'll need to find something more to eat along the way," said Rachel.

They dined in near silence, save for Charley's smacking and barely audible grumbling about cold cheese on stale bread. When finished, Rachel walked up the bank and stood with her back to Charley

From the riverbed, Charley called out, "Rachel!" only to be ignored.

She called out again, "Rachel!"

This time Rachel turned to face her. "What?"

"I wanted to say I'm sorry..." She was interrupted by a chirp from upstream. "Cecil's back."

They turned to look, as Cecil swooped in unsteadily clutching a stone in his right claw. He released the stone mid-flight, and it clattered to a stop close to Charley's feet. Cecil wheeled and landed on the ground, obviously tired.

"Well done, Cecil. Only two more to go. That didn't take long. If you hurry, we can be on our way before supper."

Cecil responded with a single loud questioning chirp even a selfish, inconsiderate child would interpret as a protest. Charley did not pick up on it. Instead, she smiled sweetly and nodded at Cecil as if to say, 'Run along'.

Rachel skipped back downhill to rejoin Charley.

"You know we could always look ourselves."

"We could, but I don't want to get farther away from the little old man's house. Happy hunting, Cecil. Don't be too long."

Cecil cocked his head and blinked.

"What are you waiting for?"

Cecil paused for another moment before angrily taking off again. He quickly flew out of sight.

"I can't believe you sent him to find stones for you."

"We wouldn't owe the stones if it weren't for him," protested

Charley.

Rachel sputtered in disbelief. "But you. You caused all of this."

"Some people might see it that way," said Charley with confident defiance. "I saved him. If it was up to you, he'd still be swinging in that cage. He's free now, thanks to me."

"So now you think you can order him around. How is that better than being in someone's cage?"

Charley's mouth opened and snapped shut again without a word.

Rachel swung her backpack onto her shoulders. "Let's start back now. It will give me something to do besides be angry with you. Cecil will find us. We might as well be close to the house when he does."

Charley moved to follow, but a spell of dizziness slowed her down. Her face flushed as a downpour of anxiety and worry dampened her good spirits. She struggled to keep up with Rachel's pace and didn't even make an attempt to search for stones. To take her mind off the rising panic, Charley attempted to start a conversation.

"Rachel, how long have you been here?"

Rachel kept on walking, making Charley wait for her eventual answer.

"A long time, I guess."

"Do you wish you were home?"

"Sometimes. It's lonely when there's no one to talk to."

Charley continued her barrage of questions to wear her friend down and hopefully slow her pace. "Are there any normal people here? Like us?"

"Ha! I haven't met any normal people."

Charley felt it was a good time for sincere and heartfelt honesty. "Then I'm glad I rolled down the hill where I did."

Rachel stopped and turned around. She decided it was probably about the best apology she was going to get out of Charley.

"I'm glad too."

She held out her hand, and Charley accepted it. The cool touch soothed her fears, and she sighed in relief. They walked together in silence.

CHAPTER NINE

"This is close enough. Now we wait for poor Cecil." Rachel kicked off her shoes, lay down on the bank, and began to hum.

Charley continued to watch the hedges, hoping to find a break she missed when she was moving through the valley in the opposite direction. Tall trees loomed over the hedge on both sides here, providing plenty of shade. She climbed the bank to investigate the mysterious, impenetrable hedge.

The branches waved in the wind, and a kindly male face appeared. He stared at Charley with a bemused smile. Her curiosity led her to draw on something from her favorite class in school, Science with Miss Hailey. She boiled the scientific method down to the one step she remembered, the experiment. She stepped to the side and made a move to part the branches to the right of the man's face. The green visage frowned and moved with her. Charley sidled far to her right to avoid him and stopped short. A different face stared back at her, the suspicious face of an old woman. The pair were determined to prevent her from passing between. Wiggling through the hedge had been unpleasant enough on the way in. Charley shuddered at the thought of squeezing between the eyes of a green ferny face.

She turned her back on the hedge and walked downhill. Halfway down, she stopped and sprinted up again, hoping the faces of her jailers had given up. They were indeed gone. She gave a whoop and leapt at the hedge with her left hand held out straight to slice a path. Her hand did indeed pass through without resistance, but the rest of her body slammed against the branches so hard she bounced and fell to her back at the crest.

Rachel had waited with her arms crossed at the floor of the ravine to watch Charley's clumsy escape attempt. She climbed uphill and helped Charley to her feet.

"You can't go home yet Charley."

"Who says?" said Charley defiantly.

Rachel pointed to the hedge. "They do."

Charley stood and brushed herself off. "Who do they think they are? They can't tell me what to do."

Rachel uttered a brief pfft and said, "It sure looks like they can."

Charley's eyes narrowed. "Are you telling them to keep me here?"

"No, Charley. You can't talk to them. Some of them seem friendly, and some of them are scary, but they don't do what anybody says. At least not for me, and obviously not for you either."

Charley accepted that Rachel was not involved in the conspiracy. They settled down on the bank and stretched out on the grass. Birds soared high overhead and bees zipped past on their never-ending hunts.

"So, what did you do here before I showed up?" Charley asked out of the blue.

Rachel ticked off her favorite pastimes on her fingers. "Exploring, picking flowers, bird-calling, chasing butterflies..."

"I don't have time!" Charley broke in. "I have to get home."

"What is the big rush...?"

Rachel rose to rest on one elbow, and Charley sat up to look in the same direction. Cecil was coming in low, laboring, with a stone clutched in each foot. He released the stones separately, throwing himself off-balance. He pulled up barely in time to avoid a beak-first landing in the dirt. As it was, he did not have the energy to keep his feet. Rachel ran down the hill and lifted him.

"Are you happy now?"

Charley switched instantly back to aggressively defensive mode. "How did I know he was going to try and carry two at the same time?"

Rachel slapped her hand to her own forehead in exasperation.

"He shouldn't have had to carry stones at all, Charley. You should have done the work yourself. Go ahead. Pick them up."

Charley seethed. She gathered the stones and put them in her satchel.

"Are you alright, Cecil?"

Cecil gave Charley one sharp, angry chirp followed by a series of soft piping trills; possibly the avian equivalent of muttering. Rachel took charge, placing Cecil on the ground.

"Let's go. Cecil, why don't you rest here? Charley, do you know what you're going to say to him?"

Charley gave no thought to the question before answering.

"I'll tell him I have the three stones and Cecil belongs to me now."

"Cecil is free now," Rachel corrected.

Charley nodded. "That's what I meant. I'll say we're all square and he can tell his brother to leave us alone. And Cecil too."

She squatted down next to Cecil and patted his feathered head. "Get some rest. We'll be back soon."

Cecil raised one wing and waved before settling down, exhausted.

Rachel asked, "It's time to face the music. Are you ready?"

"Why are you always so melodramatic?"

"I learned from you," responded Rachel. "Let's go."

CHAPTER TEN

They approached the area of the house with caution. As the man's lair came into view, they fell to their elbows and knees in an area of tall grass and crawled forward like salamanders. From this direction, the house looked much bigger. What previously looked like a shack on the verge of collapse now appeared to be larger than Charley's house. It was still in desperate need of paint and carpentry, but it looked stable.

The little old man had been joined by dozens of other little old men. Apparently, their rescue of Cecil earlier had taken place while everyone was on a break. A crowd of men dressed in similar three-piece suits of varying degrees of black now milled about. It was impossible to guess their exact number as they came and went from the house like identical drones from a hive. Either they were setting up for a picnic or doing a bee waggle dance.

Charley and Rachel looked at each other.

"What do you think?" whispered Charley.

"I don't like the odds."

Rachel's militant attitude surprised Charley. "We're not attacking or anything, right?"

Rachel was still assessing the situation for any kind of tactical advantage.

"I guess it could be okay. We could run away at any time. I doubt any of them could keep up. Okay. Let's do this," she said gravely as she rose.

"Wait," said Charley, pulling her down. "We should have a signal."

Rachel nodded in agreement. "Okay, good idea. But don't make it something that will make them suspicious."

Charley thought about it. "How about this? If either one of us thinks we should run away, we'll say the word, 'escape'."

"No, that doesn't sound suspicious at all."

"How about 'rhinoceros'?" Charley offered.

Rachel frowned at her. "Charley, it has to be a word that might come up in ordinary conversation."

Charley nodded sagely, "Ahh… like 'and' or 'the'?"

Rachel rolled her eyes. "It's going to be hard to have a conversation without using the words 'and' or 'the'."

"Alright, then you decide."

"If either of us senses danger, we should say the word, 'hedge'."

Charley mulled it over with a sullen look on her face. She didn't want to admit Rachel was the least bit clever, but she had come up with an appropriate code word. She nodded with reluctance. "Okay, 'hedge' it is."

They rose to their feet. Charley tugged on Rachel's sleeve again before they took a step. "We should use fake names, so it will be impossible for them to find us later. You be Kate, and I'll be Abigail."

"Okay, Charley. They'll never be able to tell us apart from all the other girls walking by."

Charley missed the sarcasm and started off. Before they had taken more than a few strides, the men scurrying around the house noticed them and stopped their buzzing. They stared at the pair with furrowed brows and expressions of disdain or contempt. Rachel and Charley continued their approach into their midst without pause, holding hands and unsuccessfully trying not to appear nervous. They stopped when they reached the picnic tables where the little old men crowded around them, whispering to each other. It turns out, some of the men weren't old at all. There were young men too, imitating their elders by wearing old-fashioned glasses on the end of their nose and shaving all but a strip of powdered white hair around the back from ear to ear.

Without moving her lips, Charley whispered to Rachel.

"Hedge, Kate?"

Rachel shook her head, no. There was a pause until a familiar man emerged from the house. He looked around, angry and bewildered.

"What's going on out here? Why aren't you working?"

He spied Rachel and Charley standing shoulder to shoulder. "Oh, it's you," he said with an evil grin.

The man looked them up and down. "I don't see my bird, girly. Wait until my brother hears about this."

At that, the circle closed in, and the expressions on the faces of the men turned malicious and threatening. Charley sidled even closer to Rachel and whispered, "I don't think we can hedge right now."

"Show him the stones, Abigail."

Charley spoke up. "I don't think you have a brother."

She looked around at the group surrounding them. "At least any brother big enough to scare us," she said, hoping bravado would strengthen her resolve and weaken that of the angry mob surrounding them.

It didn't work. The man sneered at her. "Oh, I have a brother, all right. Twenty feet tall, stronger than a tidal wave, and meaner than a box of scorpions. You'd wet your pants if he so much as looked at you."

Charley shivered and squeaked out, "Whatever. We're here to pay you for Cecil."

She reached into her satchel and fished out the three stones. The man ignored the stones and continued to stare up at Charley, making her cower.

"That was the old price. Now it's four stones."

"But I just let him go an hour ago."

The man fished a handkerchief out of his vest and used it to wipe a monocle attached to a chain.

"Markets fluctuate. You're only a little girl. You don't under-stand finance."

"That's not fair."

"It's business. *I* am a businessman," said the man without a speck of compassion for the pain on her face.

"It sounds like cheating to me," bleated Charley.

"It might seem like cheating to a little girl," he said, smirking.

The group of men and boys laughed at her.

Rachel said, "We only have three stones. Take it or leave it."

Charley, feeling Rachel at her back, found her nerve. "Yeah. Take it or leave it."

She held out her cupped hands with the stones, and the man slapped them up from below. The stones jumped out of the bowl of her hands. With swift moves of his gnarled fingers, he plucked the stones - one, two, three - from the air.

"I will take the principal, but you still owe us the interest. Say one stone per day, until the debt is paid off in full?"

Charley looked at Rachel with a look of disbelief on her face. Rachel leaned in and whispered in her ear.

"I'd take the deal, Abigail. But make him put it in writing."

Charley whispered back. "I'd rather just hedge away from here, Kate."

Charley turned back to the businessman with her hand extended. "We have a deal. Shake on it."

The man shook his head hard enough for his ears to make loud flapping sounds against his skull.

"No, child. We do not shake on matters of finance. Come inside, and we will fill out the proper forms."

He waved to one of the other diminutive businessmen.

"Mr. Bitterman, get me a Form 220J and bring it to my office."

Bitterman sprinted toward the building while the rest of the men returned to their mysterious duties. Charley and Rachel followed the leader inside the house.

"We'll stop at the vault first. Follow me."

CHAPTER ELEVEN

Once inside, Rachel and Charley listened to his footsteps as he walked away. They remained rooted, wondering how to reconcile the ramshackle exterior outside with the grand interior in which they now stood. Their mouths hung open, taking in a large circular room with five hallways leading away like fingers on a hand. The floors were polished green marble and torches held by golden sconces were spaced at regular intervals on the wall. The torches lit four of the hallways as far as they could see. The fifth hallway, the thumb, was dark, and the top of the archway at its entrance was far above their heads. Words in an unknown language were inscribed as a warning, or possibly an epitaph.

They shifted their eyes away from the yawning tunnel and looked upwards together from the palm of the floor to see a large chandelier suspended on a chain hanging from the peak of a dome. It was lit by dozens of candles and festooned with hundreds of strands of glowing stones glittering from the candle flames. The dome was painted with a circle of green hedge around the bottom, topped by gray mountains, and crowned with a deep blue sky.

They stood with their necks craned and their mouths agape for a few moments until the sound of the man's shoes returning broke the spell.

"Shall we?" he suggested.

They followed him. He walked no more than a few feet down the index finger and stopped. Fishing a large key out of his jacket pocket, he inserted it into a tall, heavy-looking door. The door opened silently and smoothly, and they found themselves blinking in sunlight.

"I must caution you not to speak when you pass this threshold." The man took a step outside the hallway and stopped.

"Perhaps caution is not the correct word. I must insist you... No, make that warn you... Just keep your mouth shut, or else."

"But..." interjected Charley.

The man muttered a few words and a group of his minions appeared out of nowhere to surround them. In seconds, the girls found themselves gagged and bound at the wrists.

He led them toward a low brick wall. They stepped up to look over and see it formed an oval, enclosing an atrium the size of a hockey rink. Three large fountains in the shape of dragons were partially buried and happily spitting water on an enormous collection of thousands of red glowing stones piled high and spreading from wall to wall.

The man casually tossed the three stones he had taken from Charley over the wall. He turned and ushered them back inside. The door closed with a deep, resounding thud. More of the man's flunkies came out of the shadows and released their bonds.

Charley stammered, "Wait, wait! You have all those stones. What do you need mine for?"

"I don't understand your question," he asked as he locked the door.

"There are thousands of stones out there, maybe millions! We don't have any."

"Yes. You are correct on both counts," agreed the man, leading them away.

Charley continued, "So why are you threatening us over three stones?"

The man looked at her dumbfounded, as if she had said something incredibly confusing. "You owed us three stones for releasing Cecil from the cage."

"Okay, I got that, but why do you need three stones when you already have so many?"

The man was still confused by Charley's question. "You owed us three stones," he repeated.

Charley looked at Rachel. Rachel shrugged her shoulders. Charley looked back at the man and stomped her foot in frustration.

"It's not fair. You shouldn't have put Cecil in the cage in the first place."

The man held up his hands to stop Charley's tirade. "That was my business and none of your concern. When you made it your business and let him go, it became my business to be reimbursed for that bit of funny business. You came here, I presume, to get this business over with in order to avoid any nasty business with my brother. Fair does not enter into the equation. It's business. Do you understand now?"

Charley put her hands on her hips and steamed like a teakettle.

The man appeared satisfied that Charley was sufficiently befuddled and bothered by his lack of customer service. He gestured away with the back of his hand and told them in an authoritative voice, "Now, if you'll follow me to my office, we can fill out the paperwork, and you may be on your way."

They returned to the rotunda and walked on into the middle finger. They passed several doors on either side with the names of the occupant stenciled on frosted glass. At the end of the finger hallway, they passed through an open door into his office. Charley made a point to look at the door and found the name, Mr. Yink Giggleton.

Mr. Giggleton waved his arm toward a chair. "Please have a seat." He circled a grand wooden desk, obviously too large for a man of his small stature. He slid papers around in search of something.

"Ah, here it is. Bitterman has found the form. Excellent!"

He placed two paper forms on the desk in front of them.

"This form stipulates that you, the criminal, will pay interest of one stone per day until such time that the new initial principal of one stone is repaid in full."

He pulled a fountain pen from his pocket, dipped it into an inkwell, and leaned across his desk, handing it to Charley. He sat back into an oversized high-backed leather chair and steepled his fingers.

"Sign both copies at the bottom, please."

Charley and Rachel looked it over. The title of Form 220J was a work of art. The letters and numbers were large, colorful, and beautifully illustrated. The body of the document itself, however, consisted of two poorly hand-scrawled lines followed by one long paragraph in much neater and much smaller print.

The hand-written lines read:

Little Girl Thief owes one (1) stone as compensatory interest on damages incurred.

Interest shall be one (1) stone per day until debt paid in full or death, whichever comes first, beginning on this day, September the 21st.

They had to lower their faces to inches away in order to read the small print. This paragraph, if it could be called that, was made up of recognizable English words, seemingly spilled randomly, and re-sorted back into sentences. The only sentence making any sense at all was one at the end ending with, 'or stepped on by the Chief Executing Officer, resulting in death.'

Giggleton reclined in his chair, twiddling his thumbs, and swinging his feet.

"I don't want to sign. It sounds fishy. What do you think, Kate?"

"I don't think he'll let us go until we sign."

Charley pointed to the gibberish on the form. "I don't even know what this means."

Giggleton assumed an air of superiority. "It's standard boilerplate language. You must sign the form. Our business cannot be concluded until final restitution is made."

Charley made no move at all, holding the pen and chewing her lip. Rachel shrugged her shoulders, unsure of how to proceed.

He continued, "Since you are currently unable to pay your debt, we must make sure the proper forms are filled out, so both parties are protected. This is our policy."

Charley made a counterproposal. "Why not let us leave? We'll go out and find a stone and bring it back? Or better yet change your policy so everyone is happy?"

"That is not acceptable," declared Giggleton.

Charley asserted herself, "Well, I find being stepped on unacceptable."

66

Giggleton smiled at Charley. "That clause won't apply if you pay back the stone you owe us."

He motioned for Charley to sign the form. She sighed and signed her name at the bottom of each form. Giggleton jumped out of his chair and climbed up on his desk to snatch the pen from her hand. He turned the papers around, signed them himself and then handed one copy to Charley.

"This is your copy," he said in a dismissive manner. "Show this to any of my people when you return with the stones you owe. They will know what to do. Thank you. Could you see yourself out? I am extremely busy."

He climbed down to return to his chair and made an exaggerated point of shuffling papers around and stamping forms randomly, hoping their business was concluded.

Charley said, "We'll be back before you can say Yink Giggleton."

They burst into giggles and hurried out the door. As they walked down the finger, many other office doors opened, and a stream of little old and young men emerged in a torrent. Every one of them carried briefcases in their right hand and held umbrellas, pointed to the ceiling, topped with fedoras in their left. Rachel and Charley were swept along by the marching crowd until they reached the rotunda where still more businessmen streamed out of the index, ring, and pinky fingers. They waited patiently, plastered against a marble wall, as the crowd exited through one revolving door.

When only a few businessmen remained, Charley approached one of the younger men and tugged on his sleeve.

"Where is everybody going? We need to find a stone and come back to pay off our debt."

The old man-boy stole furtive glances down every finger. "We're going home. It's quitting time. The bank is closed for the weekend."

Charley groaned. "Weekend? That's not fair. We have to wait around here for three days?"

Seeing no one left in the rotunda, the man turned to them with a genuinely sympathetic expression. "Could I take a look at your contract?"

Charley handed him the document. He scanned it over, front and back. Then he held it up to a torch to see if there were hidden clauses. His frown was tell-tale.

"I'm sorry. You got Yinked, fair and square. The old man is tricky. He didn't get where he is today by letting helpless little girls get the better of him. I'd be careful if I were you."

He pulled his arm away from Charley and hurried to the door. Pumping his umbrella quickly with an upward motion, he sent his hat into the air. He took one step forward and let the hat settle on his head. With that moderately entertaining but thoroughly under-appreciated trick, he hopped into the spinning door leaving Charley and Rachel alone in the rotunda. The only sound was Charley, muttering to herself. Rachel walked slowly toward the thumb and stopped.

"Charley come here," she insisted in an unintentionally loud echoing whisper.

Charley joined her, and together they took a few more steps toward the thumb. It appeared to be more of a cave or tunnel than a hallway like the others. It was impossible to tell how far it stretched. The light from the torches chickened out when it reached the entrance to the tunnel. A deep groan rumbled from the darkness. They both tore off, panicked for a few seconds at the revolving door, eventually squeezing together into one slice of the pie to rotate and pop out, hitting the ground running.

They ran for a few seconds until Rachel grabbed Charley's arm and stopped her.

"Wait a minute. Where are we going?"

Charley was nearly hysterical. "What do you mean? We're running away! Hedge, Rachel, hedge!"

Rachel tried to inject some reason into their panic. "We need to find a place to stay for the night."

"You're not suggesting we stay in there?"

"No, if we hurry, we might make it back to my place."

Charley chose another option. "No, we need to go downstream. Remember?"

"But we can't go far." Rachel grabbed Charley's hand, still holding the signed form. "We have to find some stones and then be here when they open on Monday."

Charley pulled her hand away and tore the contract in half. Her eyes were wide with recklessness.

"There. Now we can leave. We never have to come here again."

She nodded with a knowing look. "They'll be looking for a girl named Abigail Chickenfingers.

Rachel groaned in disappointment. "I wish you hadn't done that."

Charley was in action mode, which meant any rational discussion was out of the question.

"I'm sorry, Rachel, but that wish isn't coming true. No one named Yink is going to bully me. Let's go meet Cecil and get far away from here."

Charley began to run again. After a few strides, she stopped and turned to see Rachel standing still.

Charley called and waved Rachel on. "Are you coming or are you waiting around for someone to step on you?"

Rachel hesitated, biting her lower lip. With a sigh, she stumbled into motion. Charley waited for her to catch up, and together they set off at a trot downstream. When they reached the spot where they had left Cecil, he was nowhere to be found.

Charley called out, "Cecil! Where are you?"

Rachel hushed her. "Charley, don't yell. You're going to let them know where we are."

"I'm not afraid. Why would anyone be chasing us? They won't be expecting us until Monday. And another thing, I doubt there even is a nasty brother. That cave with the smoke and the smell and the groaning is probably just for show."

Rachel was not entirely convinced, but she conceded, "You

might be right."

Charley scoffed at Rachel's weakness. "You worry too much," she proclaimed with all the confidence in the world.

"One of us has to. We don't have a place to stay tonight, remember."

"Don't worry. I have a plan," stated Charley. She immediately began thinking of a plan.

"Oh, good. What a relief. Let's hear it."

Charley hesitated, causing Rachel to lower her expectations regarding the efficacy of the soon-to-be-revealed 'plan'. After a full minute of fits and starts, Charley's plan was hatched.

"I watched my Dad build a doghouse once. We can make something like that."

"Charley..."

"No listen, we find two stones. I'll wish for a saw and a hammer."

Charley walked up the slope and slapped a tree. "Then we cut down this tree. We cut it up, and then we nail the boards together. Wait, we'll need three stones. We'll need some nails."

"Charley! Stop!"

Charley reluctantly asked, "Okay, what's your idea?" She secretly hoped Rachel's idea was as ineffectual as her own.

"Let's keep hurrying downstream. There are cabins like mine all along the river. If my memory serves, I think it's not so far to the next one."

Charley twisted her lips into a pretzel shape to avoid commenting.

"Do you have something to say, Charley?"

Instead of answering, Charley put on the angry face she learned in the third and final acting class she had taken the past Spring.

"Let me guess. You're hungry, and your feet hurt, and you think I'm the meanest person you ever met."

"You are!" Charley blurted. "Why can't we do what I want to

do?"

"Your plan would take hours and probably hundreds of stones. You remember the monsters and wild animals from last night, don't you? They live all the way up and down the river. We need to find something safer than a doghouse made from sticks, and we need to find it before the sun sets."

Charley relented quickly out of expediency, but she was by no means content with the arrangement. She said tersely, "I'll go, but I'm not going to talk to you."

Rachel picked up her backpack and slung it over her shoulder. She closed in on Charley and smiled the biggest fake smile she could muster.

"Fine with me."

Charley sniffed and set off ahead of Rachel, taking control back from the older girl. Rachel shook her head and followed.

"You know we're going to pay for tearing up that contract," Rachel said to Charley's back.

"I'm not talking to you, remember?" answered Charley.

Rachel's answering gesture was pointed and unladylike. Charley called without turning, "You're going to pay for that when it's time to eat again."

"I'm not listening to you," responded Rachel, thereby sealing a pact of non-communication that would last for the better part of an hour.

CHAPTER TWELVE

The better part of an hour later, Charley spied a glowing stone on the ground. She stole a glance at Rachel and smiled smugly as she gathered it and dropped it into her satchel. She turned her back once more and continued walking.

"If we were on speaking terms, I'd suggest a better place to put that stone," said Rachel to her back.

They left behind the familiar maples, birches, and ashes they had become used to seeing on their journey to enter an area of the river valley closer and more heavily shadowed by pines. Banks were covered with a thick layer of needles and hundreds of pinecones made for some dicey footing. It seemed the hours Charley had spent watching online instructional ninja videos would come in handy. She slipped only once, but it was breathtaking. The poor girl pulled off a rare Trip, Slip, Flip, and Split usually only attempted by trained professionals. Rachel was unable to contain herself, and a chuckle escaped. That small giggle at her expense was enough to send Charley into a rage.

For the next minute, it seemed the spirit of an ancient mariner possessed Charley as a torrent of curses and expletives in a language not spoken in ages spewed from her mouth. Rachel shuddered and flinched in defense. She had to duck more than once to avoid being struck by solid physical manifestations of psychic force. The last twenty seconds were in English though. Rachel recognized personal insults regarding her own appearance, her heritage, her body type, and the general way she breathed in and out while taking up space on Earth.

Unsurprisingly, Rachel took offense. It is only natural to have hurt feelings when someone you count on as a friend curses at you in Phoenician and makes fun of your freckles. She sighed yet again at Charley's immaturity. Without a word, she spun and began walking downstream.

Charley recovered from her fall and subsequent possession. She hid her remorse down deep right next to where she stored her self-awareness and shame. She was about to speed-walk ahead of Rachel when she noticed another glowing stone at her feet. She picked it up and waved it triumphantly at Rachel's back. It disappeared quickly into her satchel without Rachel's knowledge.

Charley lagged behind for the duration of this new cold war. Rachel made no effort to communicate at all. She strode away with a purpose to put distance between herself and Charley. Charley busied herself with watching for stones and wondering what had come over her friend. She told herself it was important one of them at least was looking out for the lifesaving wishstones.

Luckily, this area of the riverbed was littered with them. She found two dozen in a short span of time. As she stooped to pick up her latest find, the weight of her satchel caused her to lose her balance, and she tipped over. Rachel turned to find Charley lying on her side. She came back and helped her to her feet. Charley tried to hide the fact that her satchel was now heavy enough to make her shoulder raw and cause her to lean as she stood.

"Would you like me to help carry some of those?"

"No, there are only a few. It's not heavy," lied Charley.

"You must have about twenty in there, Charley. I'm not stupid."

"You saw all those stones, and you didn't pick any up for yourself?"

"I thought you were picking them up for both of us. You aren't going to share?"

Charley hadn't considered it to that point, but now it would be selfish not to share.

"Of course, I'll share some with you... if you're talking to me again."

Rachel frowned. She knew Charley's offer meant four things. First, she had only offered to share some of her stash. This could mean half her hoard or one, with the formula more likely resulting in a number closer to the lower end of the range.

Secondly, by qualifying her offer, Charley had added a stipulation that Rachel would accept sole responsibility for the last hour of silence. Thirdly, her own offer of help thereby dissolved the no-communication pact adding to Charley's tally on the scorecard that she was, no doubt, keeping in her head. And fourth, Charley could be a selfish brat.

Rachel relented, "Yes, I'm talking to you again."

Charley smiled, forgetting the fact her actions had initiated the whole break. "Good," she responded. "I'm glad that's settled."

The afternoon wore on for another hour as the pair followed wiggles in the river's course. They chatted occasionally on mundane topics such as the pointlessness of making one's bed and why food that is good for one's health often tastes like dirt. Their energy was flagging however and the sense of urgency to find shelter grew.

"We should stop for dinner," declared Charley.

She sat right down with her back to a pine tree and fished through her satchel.

Rachel disagreed. "You shouldn't sit there, Charley."

Charley was resolute. "I can do whatever I want. If I want to sit here and eat, I'm going to sit here and eat."

"You're right. You can sit there, but you're probably going to regret it."

"Are you threatening me?"

"No, I'm pointing out to you that by now, you're covered with pine sap." She smiled in pleasure at the way this confrontation was turning out.

Charley sighed and struggled to detach herself from the tree. She got to her feet and looked back to find two streams of sap running down the trunk. She stretched and reached to her back and came away with sticky fingers. Her shoulders slumped, and her head bowed in defeat.

"Could I get any dirtier?"

Rachel nodded with genuine empathy. "You could be as dirty as I am."

Charley smiled at her friend. "We're both pretty ripe. I'm going to wish for a bathtub and soap next. After dinner, though. We've got lots of stones. Let's have a feast."

She clapped her hands together, resulting in a muttered curse and a few moments of difficulty spreading them back apart. She reached for her satchel, but Rachel was still opposed to halting.

"We need shelter more than food, Charley. There could be a cabin right around the next bend."

Charley stood with a stone in her right hand. She bit her lower lip while deciding what to do. Rachel waited patiently, knowing Charley was bound and determined to make a wish. Rachel studied Charley's face and knew instinctively the moment she had made up her mind.

"We'll wait for dinner, but I want to make one wish now. I haven't wished for anything since I wanted to be taller."

"If you have to, but try not to make a wish you can't undo if it goes horribly wrong."

"Don't be ridiculous. I have the perfect wish," said Charley with a suspiciously cunning look.

"Oh no," replied Rachel, gritting her teeth in skepticism and doubt. She backed a few steps away for safety.

Charley closed her eyes and gripped the stone with both hands. "I wish I was the most beautiful girl in the world."

Rachel relaxed and rolled her eyes. Charley opened her eyes slowly and looked down at the stone. Its glow was fading, meaning something had happened. She looked to Rachel with eager anticipation.

"Well? Am I? I don't feel different. I mean I'm still dirty, but am I beautiful? Rachel?"

She reached up to feel her face and succeeded in smearing dirty sap onto her cheeks. Rachel hesitated and made a show of studying Charley's face. This pause caused Charley's expression to turn from expectant delight to disappointment.

Rachel nodded slowly. "I see it now. It's hard to tell with all the dirt and this dim light, but you're definitely prettier. Definitely. Oh, yeah. The change is remarkable." She was nodding like a chicken now.

Her nod was so emphatic and so sincere that Charley's smile returned, bigger than before. She fell to her knees and reached into her satchel, clutching for another stone. "I'm going to wish for a mirror."

Rachel reached down to stop her. "Come on, Charley. You said one wish. We have to go now."

Charley reluctantly stood and assumed an air of regal bearing. It was the one skill she had learned from her experience at last year's Bi-County Fair as a contestant in the Perfect Little Miss Beauty Pageant - Junior Division. She ran a hand through her hair but only succeeded in getting her pine-tarred fingers stuck in the snarls. She growled and pulled at her hair with her free hand, finally extricating herself. She grumbled under her breath and bent down to pick up her satchel. The sun was sinking lower in the sky and darkness was not far off.

CHAPTER THIRTEEN

They set off again at a good clip, keeping an eye out for shelter on either side of the riverbed. The river bent sharply to the left and they found themselves standing at the edge of a wide plain. The hedges stretched out of sight to the left and the right. There were no trees or distinguishing features. The entire plain was a sea of tall reeds with no end. The previously singular path of the river was now a network of many channels winding off in all directions through the grass beginning at their feet. They were standing at the entrance of what appeared to be a gigantic maze.

"We'll never cross before dark," stated Rachel flatly, slowly shaking her head at their predicament.

Charley stood beside her, nodding in agreement. "We're in big trouble."

Turning in unison to look back upstream, they had to raise their right hands to shield their eyes in a salute to the low-hanging sun.

Rachel looked at Charley. "What do you think? Backward or forward?"

"Can we wish for more time?"

"Points for creativity, but I doubt it would work. I think if we had torches, it might keep any monsters away, at least for a little while."

"It seems like a waste of stones just to wish for sticks to burn."

Rachel was patient but insistent. "Charley, we're running out of time. We can keep going downstream, or we can go back. Those are your choices."

"Fine, we'll make torches and get lost in the maze. I hope we don't set fire to the whole place and us with it." She reached into her bag.

"We don't need the torches yet, Charley, but it might help to have walking sticks. It might be swampy, and we can use them to test the ground ahead of our steps.”

“Good idea,” agreed Charley eagerly, but her excitement was due more to being able to make any wish at all than appreciating the actual usefulness of owning a stout walking stick. She reached into her bag and pulled out two stones. She handed one to Rachel and set her mind to crafting her wish. She muttered, starting and stopping many times before settling on her wish.

Rachel stood to the side and held out her hands with the stone laying in the palm of her right. She whispered a few words and a long, straight wooden pole appeared, balanced perfectly on her left hand. She gripped it and turned it to tap the ground at her feet twice. The stick was about eight feet long and as smooth as an icicle. She dropped the stone and looked at Charley, ready to go.

Charley stood looking, eyes flicking back and forth between Rachel’s handiwork and her own walking stick. She held what appeared to be a thin twig fallen from a birch tree. Charley did not take kindly to Rachel’s frown. She threw her twig away and reached into her satchel again. She pulled out another stone and squeezed it as hard as she could, thinking applying pressure to the rock would make it more obedient.

Rachel intervened before all of Charley’s considerable fury was brought to bear on the stone. She covered Charley’s hand gently with her own free hand. Charley’s eyes flashed, her lips ready to unleash a wish that might set off an earthquake.

“Would you like one like mine?” she asked in a soothing voice.

Charley’s expression softened from a grimace of rage into a sneer of spite. She relaxed slowly and turned her shaking hand over to drop the stone into Rachel’s palm. Rachel repeated her previous whispered wish with a slight alteration for size. A solid stick stood balanced on its end in front of Charley.

Charley immediately forgot her anger and embarrassment. She grasped the staff and stepped back, twirling it like a weapon. After narrowly missing caving in the side of Rachel’s head, she brought the end of the staff down to the dirt with a two-handed thud and shouted,

"You cannot pass!"

Rachel clapped. "Very nice. You're terrifying."

"And beautiful?" asked Charley.

"Definitely. You are a fearsome Amazon warrior."

Charley beamed. "You mean it?"

"Definitely. Can we go now?"

They shouldered their bags and set off confidently into the unknown. They chose a path winding to the right and in no time at all they were in another world, the tall grass blocking the waning sunlight. They looked up to find a full silver moon had appeared, resulting in a positive development. They were able to pick out several directions to travel. On the other hand, they were able to pick out several directions to travel.

"Stay close to me, Charley. We can't get separated in here."

"Agreed."

"Keep your eyes peeled. We could be surrounded already."

"That's reassuring. Thanks."

They resumed their journey, outwardly confident, but inwardly terrified. They took one step and immediately froze in shock at the sound of a roar like thunder. Booming sounds caused by the stride of something enormous followed. Charley let out a shriek and covered her ears, dropping her walking stick.

"It's a T. Rex! Grace is here! Run!"

She grabbed Rachel's arm and spun her around, not knowing which direction to run. Rachel used her staff to stop the merry-go-round. Charley maintained her grip on Rachel's sleeve as she bent down to pick up her fallen staff. The booming stopped and the only sound to be heard was Charley's whimpering as she hid behind Rachel.

They remained frozen still for five tension-filled seconds.

Charley whispered, "Do you think it's gone?"

A deep, echoing blast answered her.

"CHICKENFINGERS! I COME!"

Charley fell to her knees, covering her ears. Rachel turned

around and tried to pull her to her feet. She spoke in a hushed tone. "Dinosaurs don't talk, Charley. I think someone's here to collect a debt."

Charley's eyes widened, and she sprang to her feet. Without a word, she retrieved her staff and dashed away down a dark path. Rachel was forced to follow. For a while, she was able to keep Charley close by, thanks to periodic shrieks and yelps from her young friend, but the dinosaur-sized man was also able to pick up on their location using Charley's unintended help.

A voice amplified to loudspeaker volume emanated from somewhere within Rachel to distract him and hopefully allow Charley more time to escape somewhere, anywhere. "HEY, GIGGLETON! OVER HERE!"

The booming stopped for a second and the only sound was the tall grass rustling in the wind. Charley had finally stopped screaming. Another explosion of "CHICKENFINGERS!" rocked them both and Charley let out another involuntary squeak. The massive man lurched toward the sound. Rachel also headed her way and eventually ran into the path of crushed grass left in the monster's considerable wake. She followed the trail with caution.

Charley stopped, afraid and unable to decide on her next move or stop herself from crying in terror. The stomping footsteps of the monster were coming closer, zeroing in on the sound of her cries. She looked left and right and up to the moon for guidance. She took a big gulp of air and tried to hold back her sobbing. This turned out to be a lucky stroke when a hand reached out from the tall grass behind her and covered her mouth. The arm attached to that hand pulled her backward into the cover of the grass. Charley sat still, not minding the hand on her mouth at all, knowing someone was protecting her.

The sound of the monster approaching grew louder, and Charley used her hands to cover her ears. When the thunder roll of its strides stopped a few yards away, it roared again, "CHICKENFIN-GERS! WHERE YOU ARE?"

This time, with no sound to home in on, the monster turned

away and continued its harmless trampling of the vast grass plain.

Her rescuer's hand remained firmly on her mouth. A man's voice whispered in her ear, "Girl, not a sound, you know what I'm saying?"

Charley nodded, and the man released her. She hesitated, afraid to move without direction from her rescuer. She slowly spun to face him. Even kneeling on one knee, she could tell he was tall. Young and athletic, he wore spotless tan work boots, black jeans, a black tee shirt, and a black football jacket with gold sleeves. He stood and held out his hand to Charley, helping her to her feet and back into the clearing.

The man's face was serious but not frightening. "Follow me. I know where it's safe."

Charley hesitated. She almost cried, thinking about the monster tracking her and the other possible dangers lurking in the grass. She also thought about Rachel out there somewhere, hopefully safe.

The man was impatient. "C'mon girl. There's some nasty vermin hereabouts you don't want to meet." He walked quickly toward one of the many paths leading out of the clearing.

Charley was torn. Rachel was her only friend. She should search for her. Charley was about to call out when Rachel miraculously appeared from an opening. Charley jumped into her arms. Rachel looked past her toward the man disappearing down the path behind them.

"I heard a man's voice and followed it here. Are you alright?"

"Yeah, he saved me when the monster was about to get me," exclaimed Charley with exaggerated breathlessness and heaving shoulders.

"How did he do that?"

"He held my mouth so I couldn't make a sound."

"I'll have to remember that trick if I need to rescue you in the future. Or just get some peace and quiet."

"Okay," said Charley, missing her sarcastic tone. "Come on. He says he can take us someplace safe."

The young man returned to the clearing and this time his face was frighteningly serious. He showed no surprise at the sight of Rachel standing by Charley's side. "Hurry up. It's gonna get crowded out here real quick. It's not far. C'mon. Get moving."

Rachel handed Charley her walking stick and they followed the man to what they hoped was safety.

CHAPTER FOURTEEN

Night settled over them like a cold, wet bedspread. Almost immediately, as if sprayed with a hose, they were drenched with dew. They watched the walls of tall grass for any sign of enemies, staffs gripped tightly in both hands. Their new friend moved swiftly and surely, choosing his path with no hesitation as they weaved through the maze. They ran hard to keep up, the rhythm of their feet squishing on the soft, muddy turf and the huff of their labored breathing the only sounds to be heard. He moved so swiftly they lost sight of him. They turned a corner and found themselves at a fork without their guide.

They stopped and listened in vain for the sound of his footsteps. Charley looked around, her eyes wild with fear. Rachel stood calmly, poised on the balls of her feet with her staff at the ready. Charley tried to imitate her friend, but her arms shook, and her legs wobbled as she stood.

"Keep your back to me, Charley. He'll come back and get us soon."

Two paths led forward into darkness. She fought the urge to race blindly ahead. Instead, she did as she was told, and an electric trickle of courage crept up her spine. Her grip on her staff relaxed and she took a deep breath to calm down.

In front of Charley, a dark shape poked out from the base of the reed curtain eliciting a scream of terror. She dropped her staff and spun to hide behind Rachel. It attacked with a rattling hiss, coming at them low and fast. Rachel reacted by thrusting her staff to jab down at the creature. The stick bounced off its scaly hide causing her to lose balance. She fell to one knee but managed to swing her staff around to poke it into the creature's jaws. It clamped down on the stick and wrenched it from her grasp. It swung its head from side to side, breaking the staff in two and giving Rachel a chance to stand.

Charley was so frightened by the scene before her she didn't notice two more of the creatures emerging from the grass behind her. With a loud bellow, their guide returned, jumping to a stop, one foot on each wedge-shaped head. He hopped off and swept Charley up, swinging her toward the open ground near Rachel. He picked up Charley's staff and immediately whacked the two newcomers.

He pointed at the path they should take and shouted, "Run! Run until you see a wall!" He jabbed at the first creature to keep it at bay. "Climb the wall. I'll be right behind you! Run!"

They took off, sprinting for their life. They arrived at a stone wall, half as tall as Charley and quite out of place in a swamp. More of the creatures emerged from the grass, padding quickly on short legs. Rachel scrambled up first and reached back to help pull Charley to safety as the creatures massed below, thwarted by the low wall. The moonlight reflected off a dozen pairs of glowing green eyes and rows of pointy teeth lining long snapping jaws.

The girls peered down the path, hoping to see their rescuer. They heard him before they could see him. He came, screaming a warbling war cry as he closed in on the safety of the higher ground. They both yelled a warning.

"Stop!"

"Watch out!"

He almost lost his balance as he jumped to a stop. Twenty-four eyes oriented on a new target. Instead of moving into a defensive posture using Charley's staff as a weapon, he charged them. Taking advantage of their inability to organize and coordinate, he planted the staff into the ground directly in their midst and vaulted up and over them to land on the ground between Rachel and Charley. He got up and looked down at the swarm of creatures below and laughed at them. Rachel and Charley stood side by side, amazed, with their mouths hanging open. He looked at them and laughed again.

"What's the matter with you? No applause?"

They each clapped twice slowly, still unable to believe what had happened. He snapped his fingers in their faces.

"Follow me. The gators aren't the only things we need to worry about."

They followed him away from the ledge, winding their way through shrubs and bushes arranged and aligned in an orderly fashion but growing wildly out of control. Stone benches covered with leaves and vines waited, ready for occupants, here and there on the path. Fruit trees lined the way, many of them split and choked by poison ivy. All were stunted, but some overripe crabapples still hung on branches. The effect was one you might find walking the grounds of a long-deserted country estate.

They caught glimpses of the full moon as they hurried along the path. It cast an eerie glow on the landscape, contributing to the feeling of dread and danger pressing on them in the near-dark. They reached the edge of the stand of trees and shrubs to find the moon shining down like a spotlight on a house in the middle of a clearing.

Their guide stopped and stretched out his arms, holding up the two friends. They followed his gaze to the sky. Silhouetted against the silver circle of the moon, several large, winged creatures wheeled high above, surveying the plains for a meal.

The three-story house standing alone in the center of a large lawn looked like nothing more than a thin, crooked tower with three one-room stories all askew. From this distance, it had the appearance of a pile of blocks built by a toddler. A spire rose from the top block to poke at the moon's face.

"Are you ready for the last dash?" asked the young man. In the moonlight, his eyes were sparkling, and his toothy smile was a brilliant white. He appeared to be enjoying himself.

Rachel looked at the house and frowned. "That's sanctuary?"

Charley shoulders were slumped, and she didn't look capable of a stroll, let alone a dash. "Why do we need to run? Can't we circle around?" she asked in a whining tone.

"No time. The boogers will start roaming the woods right about now. We'd never make it. See those birds flying up there? They're like F-35's with claws. I've seen them swoop down and carry off gators. Do you think they'd have any trouble with a little girl?

"What's a booger?" asked Charley.

"They're bad news. That's all you need to know. We got one chance-- a full sprint to the tower. You ready?"

Charley looked both left and right to see humanoid figures emerging from the bordering woods and spilling onto the perimeter of the plain. She spun quickly to scan the way they had just come, expecting a zombified booger to be shambling towards her with arms outstretched. She was close to hysterical, but the young man took pity on her.

"Let me carry your bag. What've you got in there anyway? Bricks?"

Charley clutched the strap and turned away from him.

Rachel scolded her. "Let him carry the bag, Charley! He's not going to steal it. You're too tired to run with ten pounds of stones."

Charley reluctantly turned to face the man. He was watching her with suspicion. She bent down and slipped the strap over her head, dropping the satchel to the ground. The man stepped forward to grab the bag.

"Wait a minute. What's your name?" asked Charley.

"You want to stop for introductions? Now?"

"Just in case we get separated, I'm going to come looking for you," said Charley in as menacing a tone as she could manage.

The man's eyes twinkled as he suppressed laughter. "You think I'm gonna steal it? Alright, girl, you can call me Chilly."

Charley dug in deeper. "That's not your real name. We're not going anywhere until you tell me the truth."

"That's what I'm called. Take it or leave it, but I'm running like mad to that house. You can try dragging your bag of bricks across the open field, in the moonlight, by yourself, with those giant birds up there just waiting for a little mouse to scamper by."

Rachel prodded Charley again. "Charley, let the nice boy carry your bag."

"Alright," she said with too much anger in her voice. "But be careful. It's heavy."

He lifted it up, surprised by its weight. "Holy... Do you have gold bars in here?"

Charley's rare smile was mischievous. "Better."

He laughed at her. "You're crazy. Just like everything else in this place. You ready?"

They nodded. He tucked the bag under his arm and turned toward their destination.

"1-2-3."

He took off with a whoosh across the lawn. Charley and Rachel ran in his wake. He was far ahead, almost at the house, when Charley felt pain in her side. She looked up frantically to see if they had been noticed, but her clumsy running made her head bob wildly. She told herself to run faster. Rachel tried to help by pointlessly telling her to run faster. They were halfway there themselves when Chilly came back into view, running back toward them at locomotive speed and waving his arms. He didn't slow down at all as he closed the gap between them.

He hollered, "Split up!" but there was no need. They had already veered apart and hit the grass to avoid his hurtling form. From the turf, they could see a Pteranodon-sized shape drop and adjust its flight to make a grab for Chilly with its talons. It came away empty-clawed as he slid feet-first beneath it. The raptor's powerful wings beat the air to regain altitude with a furious, frustrated, piercing caw. They scrambled to their feet and ran for the house once again. Chilly slowed his pace to follow them intentionally, watching the sky in all directions.

They reached the house and found the relative safety of a small wooden front porch. Rachel took a step off the porch to look up and scan the night sky. Charley leaned out to see without leaving the safety of the porch. The tower of blocks swayed slowly back and forth, the spire scraping the night sky.

Chilly joined them and noticed their apprehension.

"I know. I know. It makes some crazy noises, and it looks like it's about to tumble down, but it's better than getting eaten or carried off to some nest to be fed to their babies. Come inside."

Charley looked at Chilly. "Wait. Where's my satchel? What did you do with my bag?" she asked in a panicked voice. Chilly pointed to the porch. Charley's bag was leaning against the wall.

"I left it there before I came back to save you. Again," he said with a scowl on his face.

Charley's face flushed. In order to avoid the uncomfortable truth about her accusatory tone, she changed the subject. "Did you know most birds can't smell?"

Rachel looked at her with her customary bewilderment. Chilly's confused stare added to her embarrassment.

"I learned that in school," she added in a whispery voice.

Rachel punched Charley on the shoulder with gentle, yet appropriate force. Chilly shook his head and his stare melted into a smile.

"You got a strange way of saying, 'Thank you', girl," he said. "Come on, let's get inside.

CHAPTER FIFTEEN

He turned his back on them and walked toward the door. Charley gave Rachel a dirty look and a second later remembered to rub her shoulder in mock pain. As they followed Chilly, they conducted a silent argument, their eyes flashing and mouths twitching angry words back and forth.

The door resisted his efforts. Another screeching caw from just overhead split the night and the girls crowded closer to Chilly. He pushed and twisted and the study wooden door finally gave in, creaking loudly. He pushed it open and disappeared into the dark. The girls took a look around for alligators, spiders, or snakes before entering themselves. When the door closed with a satisfying bang and click, they felt relieved and when a heavy deadbolt slid and locked, they felt at ease. Finally, when a match was struck and a fire began to pop and crackle, they felt safe.

They huddled together, barely inside the door, as their eyes adjusted to the gloom of the room. Their host moved about, arranging furniture.

"Have a seat. They're a little dusty, but they're comfortable."

They climbed into wooden chairs apparently built for giants. Each seat was covered with multiple cushions and sheets making them ideal resting spots for petite young ladies, or perhaps large hounds. They both perched at the edge of their seat with feet dangling and hands gripping the arms.

Their host finished his business and reclined in his own chair. The room was barely larger in area than Charley's bedroom at home and it had the same sink and pump as Rachel's cabin though the ceiling was higher. It also had the same level of dust and cobwebs. The other obvious difference was steps leading up out of sight. Someone had made a weak effort to make the room cozy, hanging dingy lace curtains and a few poorly painted watercolors of flowers haphazardly on the walls.

The man looked at them with expectation. "Relax. You're safe now. Nothing can get in here."

The girls both presented him with their politest smiles. "It was real nice of you to help," Charley said. "I don't know what would have happened if you hadn't come along. Thank you."

The man waved his hand. "I didn't get a good look at the dude chasing you, but he was a big boy."

Rachel spilled down from her perch, walked to the window, and pulled the curtains aside. Charley relaxed in her chair. "You're not from around here, are you?"

The man sat up at that. He looked hard at Charley. "Just where is here?"

"Don't ask me. I just got here yesterday."

She looked around to see Rachel climbing the stairs to take a peek at the upper floor.

"I ran away from home, and now I can't get back. I guess we're supposed to keep walking 'til we get to the end of this river."

"River? Do you see any water around here?"

"No, so far, it's been dry as a bone. But until we got here it sure looked like a riverbed. Nonnie said the river is meant to be traveled."

Chilly relaxed again. "Who's Nonnie?"

"She's this funny old lady that lives in the valley. She talked a lot but didn't say much. Typical adult."

Rachel reappeared from the staircase. "Show him Butter."

Charley pulled the scabbard out of her overalls, "Oh, yeah. She gave me this." She slid the knife out and held it up.

Chilly leaned forward to examine the knife and smirked. "That might protect you from vicious cucumbers, but it wouldn't be much use in a real fight."

"I know," Charley admitted. "I told you she wasn't helpful."

Rachel stood, leaning against the back of Charley's chair. "My name is Rachel."

Charley remembered her manners. "Oh, and my name's Charley. Well, it's Charlotte, but you can call me Charley. Your real name isn't Chilly, is it?"

"My Ma named me Achilles, after the Greek hero in the Iliad. She used to read me stories when I was growing up. He was pretty badass, but I got sick of explaining the whole story all the time to my friends. It's easier to go by Chilly in my neighborhood."

Charley's mouth opened and closed, and she blinked twice. She didn't want to sound stupid, so she settled for looking that way instead.

Rachel helped her out, whispering in her ear, "Achilles was a warrior in Greek mythology. *The Iliad* is a book about Achilles and the Trojan War."

Charley snapped out of her stupor. "Achilles sounds like a cool name to me."

"Thanks. You can call me Achilles then. It's not like I'm gonna run into anybody I know."

"Where do you come from, Achilles?" She shook her head. "Nope, I'm going to call you Chilly. Achilles is too hard to say."

Chilly grinned. "No problem. I live in Alabama, but I don't think I'm anywhere near Double Springs anymore. I was doing home-work at my desk three days ago, and I remember feeling sleepy. I blinked and the next thing I know I'm looking out on a huge field of sawgrass and stepping into... mud."

He looked surprised and thoughtful. While he paused, Charley looked back and up at Rachel. "What's up with him?" she whispered.

"I think he believes you now, about the river."

"Oh!" Charley pretended to understand.

He stood quickly, surprising both girls. He waved his arms around, indicating their surroundings. "I get it! Man, this isn't a river, though. It's like a swamp, but dry. It's like we're sitting on an island in the middle of the Everglades," he said, the excitement rising in his voice.

"I thought I was stuck here for good. But you're saying we're supposed to travel on the river. That means there's a way out, a way home."

He bent down and grabbed both arms of Charley's chair and shook it. Charley pulled up her knees and hugged them along with her satchel.

"Do you get it? I can get out of here! I've been going in circles and damn near getting lost out there, but there's a way out."

Charley smiled and relaxed, sharing in his excitement. "Of course we can get out of here. Tomorrow, though, right?"

"You saved me!" he exclaimed, taking Charley's hands, and pulling her up. He bent down and hugged her. He let her go and spun around, kicking a chair over. "This is my last night here," he said to the ceiling with relief.

He spun around to face the girls with a worried look on his face.

"On this river, is there anything to eat besides these rotten apples?"

He pointed to a bowl on the table. "I bit into a worm yesterday, and I can't eat another one."

Charley started to speak, but Chilly interrupted her.

"Of course not, the river's dry. No fish," he said, answering his own question.

The girl tried to speak again, but he interrupted her again, talking to himself. "Maybe there are some nests with birds' eggs." He looked at the girls with a strange and serious expression on his face.

"On the river, are there trees you can climb? With birds' nests?"

Rachel crossed her arms and rolled her eyes. Charley opened her mouth to speak and shut it immediately when Chilly closed in on her.

His eyes were wild. "Are the birds normal-sized?"

Charley imitated Rachel and added a 'Tsk' for good measure.

"Are they?" repeated Chilly.

"Are you done?" Charley responded, full of her customary sass..

Chilly straightened up and shook off whatever had come over

him. He returned to his normal cool demeanor.

"Are you hungry?" Charley asked.

"I could eat," Chilly replied casually.

"I bet you could," retorted Charley with another ration of impudence. She looked pointedly down at her satchel.

He grew curious. "Are you telling me you have food in that bag? It's not filled with gold bars?"

Charley turned around and placed the satchel on the chair. She opened it up and stepped back. Chilly closed in, one small step at a time. The stones inside gave off a glow rivaling the light from the fireplace. Chilly's eyes widened, looking back and forth between Charley and the stones.

He reached toward the bag and paused, turning to Charley. She nodded. He picked out a stone and looked it over. "I saw a stone like this the first day I got here. It didn't glow like this."

"They don't shine so bright in the daytime. You only found one?"

"I only saw one. They're unusual, but so what? You can't eat 'em."

"Show him, Charley," said Rachel.

Charley held out her right hand, palm-upward toward Chilly. He dropped the stone into it and she closed her eyes to make the effect more mysterious. She held out both of her hands But, not wanting to embarrass herself again, she settled for something safe, something like what had worked before.

In a loud voice, she said, "I wish I had an orange! No, a bunch of oranges! Aww, not again!" She uttered an inappropriate word out of anger and frustration and slapped a hand over her mouth.

A single orange appeared on her left hand, which she promptly dropped. Chilly, in a moment of weakness, uttered his own inappropriate word and bent down to quickly pick it up for her. When he rose, he shrugged sheepishly and gazed in wonder at the orange fruit. He uttered the same inappropriate word again as he stared at it. He nodded in apology to the girls and returned to staring.

"Go ahead, you can eat it," said Charley.

Chilly wasted no time in peeling it down and taking a bite. He ignored the girls as he relished the fruit, savoring every chew. Rachel took the opportunity to give Charley a backhanded slap to her shoulder.

"You really need to use your imagination, Charley," she said. "You have a lot of stones, but it's going to get boring eating one fruit at a time."

"I know! I know! I'll get the hang of it. Just stop hitting me!"

Chilly returned to Earth. "This is delicious. Thank you."

He held out his hand, and Charley handed him the stone. He held it up to his eyes and watched it dim.

"Can you wish for anything?"

"I'm not really clear on how they work yet."

"I'll say," said Rachel. Charley glared at her and received an artificial smile in return.

"I wasn't always this pretty. I did get that wish right," she said with pride.

"You wished to be pretty?" asked Chilly.

Charley boasted, "Not just pretty, the most beautiful girl in the world. Now, when I get home, I'm going to become a famous actress and model and singer and..."

Chilly turned his back on her. He added another log to the fire, fiddling for a little longer than necessary, waiting for the urge to laugh out loud to pass. When it did, he stood and turned to Charley with a polite smile on his face.

"Anyway, the stones are tricky."

"You should read the directions," Rachel told her with a straight face.

Charley grabbed another glowing stone out of the bag and examined every centimeter of it.

"There aren't any directions on them!"

"Uhm... right." Chilly approached her in a kind and gentle manner. "Can I try?"

She hesitated for a second, before sighing, "I suppose. You did save my life." She reluctantly handed the stone to Chilly.

"Just think about what you want and ask for it, but be as specific as you can," she instructed him. "And don't make it complicated. Sometimes the stone gives you something you didn't ask for."

Chilly nodded and closed his fingers around the stone. The glow from the stone intensified, seeping out from his grip to light up his face. He closed his eyes and concentrated. Charley looked at Rachel who was as surprised as she was. The stones had never shined so brightly when they held them.

Chilly walked to the bowl of crabapples and picked it up. He scooped the apples into the fire. Handing the bowl to Charley, he asked, "Wash this for me, okay?"

Rachel watched him while Charley did as she was asked, without complaint for a change. Chilly paced about the small room, his hands clasped behind his back, nodding as if in conversation with himself. Charley returned with the bowl, and he motioned for her to place it on the table. He faced the table and held the stone palm-down over the bowl. His expression was deadly serious and intent.

"Don't wish for vegetables," Charley blurted out.

Chilly's concentration was broken. "For real, girl?"

Charley's face turned red. Rachel, standing behind Charley, poked her with a finger in the back.

"Wish for whatever you want. Sorry." She held up her hands. "I'm not even here. Forget I said anything."

"What is wrong with you?"

Chilly's tone and expression were intimidating, but his eyes were twinkling with humor. Charley locked her lips and stared at the ceiling as Chilly got to business. He bent over to get low enough to put his hand directly above the rim of the bowl.

With a deep, ominous voice, he said, "I wish for a bowl of hot and spicy worm casserole."

Charley gasped and slapped her hands on the table to peer into the bowl. It was empty. Her eyes darted back and forth between the bowl and Chilly's face. Rachel joined her at the table to look in the bowl.

"Why? You can't waste wishes like that!"

Chilly maintained his expression for a few seconds more while Charley sputtered. She looked to Rachel for support. Rachel had a confused, but suspicious look on her face. Charley reached to touch Chilly's hand holding the stone. He opened his fingers to show he held nothing in the palm of his hand. His mouth broke into a wide grin.

"You faked it?" Charley was more embarrassed than angry. "That wasn't funny."

Chilly walked to the fireplace to retrieve the stone he had hidden on the mantel. He showed the stone to the girls, holding it between his thumb and index finger.

"Let's do this again," he said with a smile. "I wish for a bowl of hot and spicy chili."

A steaming, reddish-brown concoction of peppers and large chunks of beef filled the bowl, saturating the room with a smoky, succulent aroma. Three faces closed together to peer into the bowl, their mouths slightly open, drool welling at the corners.

Their smiles turned to thoughtful expressions as they contemplated how to eat the hearty stew. They looked at each other.

"Bread," said Rachel.

Charley popped up and retrieved another stone from her bag. Rachel told her, "Wish for a long loaf, like the staffs we made before."

"That you made before," Charley muttered to herself.

"What did you say?" asked Chilly.

"I said I should wish for a lot of bread."

"Hurry girl. The chili isn't getting any hotter."

"Don't rush me. The chili isn't getting chilly, Chilly."

He gave her a withering look of irritation. Charley held up her hands to Chilly. "Chill," she said with impertinent boldness and a wink.

"You done?"

Charley smiled proudly. "Yes."

Rachel said, "Well?"

Charley tried to focus. She did not want to embarrass herself again. She copied the method Chilly had used.

"I wish for a five-foot loaf of fresh crusty Italian bread," she said with one eye open. She was rewarded with a five-foot long loaf of crusty Italian bread on the table next to the bowl of chili. They all clapped and shouted in celebration. Before Charley could break off a hunk to dunk in the chili, Rachel stopped her.

"Shouldn't Chilly get the first bite? It is his chili."

Charley disagreed vehemently, but she kept her feelings to herself. She was starving, and the aroma of the chili was making her mouth water. She was ready to fight an alligator for a bite.

She looked up at Chilly and said, "You first, Chilly. You deserve it. You did a good job for your first time."

Chilly shook his head. "No, guests eat first. I insist."

Charley forgot about her recent intense feelings of craving and greed that had almost resulted in a brutal and primal struggle for life-preserving nourishment. Without even a thank you, she tore a chunk of bread from the loaf and scooped a mouthful of chili out of the bowl.

"I hope it tastes as good as it looks," said Rachel. Chilly followed Charley's lead and spooned out his own first bite. He closed his eyes and savored it. Rachel spooned out her own next. The trio stood taking turns for a good long time, but the bowl was still half full when the girls gave up and staggered to chairs. Chilly lifted the bowl and the left-over bread and placed it on the floor near the fire. He continued to eat while the girls held their bellies and moaned.

"That was soooo good, Chilly. Just spicy enough," exclaimed Charley. Rachel said nothing. She sat back with her hands on her belly and groaned, adding an unrepentant burp as an exclamation point. Charley shook her head, unable to determine whether she really had just seen steam escaping from Rachel's ears.

"Thanks, Charley. I just pictured the chili my Ma makes." He took a bite. "I wonder what else I could wish for." He gazed at the ceiling, wondering as he chewed.

"You should sleep on it and think of the perfect wish. Then, when you find a stone of your own, you can wish for it."

Chilly ignored Charley's thinly veiled self-serving suggestion. He continued his assault on the bowl of chili.

Rachel groaned and rose to her feet. "Charley, do you want some water? I'm gonna fall asleep soon and my mouth... is on fire."

Charley rolled herself off her own chair and followed Rachel to the sink. Together they worked the pump and swallowed several mouthfuls of water. They also made a weak attempt at washing their faces and hands. Chilly walked toward them and pumped some water of his own as the girls returned to their chairs.

By the time he settled into his spot near the fireplace, they were both asleep. His mouth twitched. Discussion on the topic of tomorrow's journey would have to wait. He placed the bread in the bowl on top of the remaining chili and carried it to the table.

He walked to the front door and exited the house, closing the door as quietly as possible. At the edge of the porch, he looked up to see the gigantic birds still circling. Sitting down on the step, he stretched out his long legs and rested his weight on his elbows.

"Giants, and little princesses, and wishes that come true? Where am I?" he asked the moon.

Rachel poked her head out of the door. She silently slipped out and padded a few steps away and tossed the used stones out into the yard. Chilly was still reclining and taking in deep breaths of the fresh outdoor air. She returned to her spot on the threshold and listened to him continue to talk to himself.

"I'm not lost anymore. Tomorrow, I'm leaving this swamp behind."

He stood and walked out into plain view of the circling birds, raising a fist to the sky.

"You aren't taking me! I got a plan now."

The birds apparently conceded the point. They ignored him. Chilly laughed at them and spun around to return to the house.

Rachel ducked inside, glided to her chair, and watched Chilly re-enter and close the door behind him. He checked on the dying fire and took another drink. Unlacing and removing his boots, he settled back with a sigh of comfort and fell asleep. Now that everyone was safe and comfortable, she was able to rest herself.

CHAPTER SIXTEEN

The next morning began with a shout from Rachel. Charley jumped up, bewildered and dazed. Chilly snored on, oblivious to the ruckus from the girls.

"Charley, we slept late! We need to get going! It must be noon."

Charley rolled her eyes. "Is that all? I thought alligators were attacking."

"Do you want to be stuck in the middle of this swamp tonight?"

"You're right. You're right. I know you're right."

Charley left Rachel to fill the canteens. She walked over to Chilly, tapped him on the shoulder, and leaned over his face. The only muscles he moved were those controlling his eyelids. He used his eyeball muscles to focus his gaze at Charley. Her face was inches away, her expression a mixture of curiosity and silliness. Still, Chilly lay still.

"That is some powerfully bad breath, girl. Are you sick?"

Charley maintained her position, her noxious exhalations ready in case her quarry tried to make a break for it.

"I used to be. You wanna duel?" she said, challenging him.

"You best take that dragon breath away from my face before I blast you with a burp that'll set your nose on fire."

Charley grinned and backed off. "We slept late. We need to get going. It must be noon."

She left him alone to count the stones in her satchel. Chilly nodded and stretched. He walked around Charley to pump water, filling the basin. Chilly took some sips and then bent down to drown his face in the sink. He came up sputtering and smiling. Rachel waited by the door with her backpack and Charley joined her at her side while Chilly walked leisurely to his chair and sat down to pull on his shoes.

"We out? Which way?"

Charley looked up to Rachel for guidance.

"We've always had the sun at our back, remember?"

Charley assumed the special air of know-it-all-ness Rachel found so annoying. She told Chilly, "We need to see where the sun is. Then we'll know which direction to go. Don't worry. I'll get us out of here."

Rachel pretended to slip her hands around Charley's neck while Chilly finished tying up his laces. He gave a short snort of laughter, apparently accepting Charley's confident assurance. He stood and surveyed the room one last time for anything that could be of use. He made sure the fire was out and picked up the bowl of last night's dinner. It didn't look nearly as appetizing, but he offered it to the girls anyway. They both crinkled their nose and shook their heads.

"We'll leave it for the mice." He dropped it on the table and clapped his hands. "Lead on, Princess."

Charley looked at Rachel and then pointed to her own chest. "Me?"

Rachel laughed. "Well, he's definitely not talking to me. You're the most beautiful girl in the world."

Charley did remember, her smile spreading from ear to ear.

"Allow me to get the door, your highness."

Rachel was mocking her again. Not wanting to appear like a spoiled brat in front of Chilly, Charley ignored her and opened the door herself. They all filed out onto the porch and off into a beautiful sunny day.

Chilly closed the door and turned to face them. "Which way?"

The girls looked at each other and then to the sky.

"You have no idea which way to go, do you?" asked Chilly.

"The sun is right over us. I can't tell…"

Chilly interrupted her. "It's okay. I remember where you came from."

He pointed in the direction of a stand of trees far away. "Look familiar from last night?"

Both girls nodded.

"So, we go that way?" he asked, pointing in the opposite direction. "I have an excellent sense of direction. I might not know where I am all the time, but I never get lost."

He strode confidently away from the house, and the girls followed. Before long, they came to the end of the raised plateau that was their island in the swamp. Chilly jumped down, followed by Rachel. Charley remained on top as a fit of coughing shook her. Chilly came back and helped her to the ground below.

He cautioned them, "I'm gonna set a good pace, but I won't leave you behind. If you can't keep up, let me know. Ready?"

Rachel was raring to go. Charley adjusted the satchel strap on her shoulder. She couldn't find a comfortable spot due to soreness from carrying so many stones yesterday. She slipped it around to the other shoulder.

Chilly asked, "Do you want me to carry it for you?"

"I could help," offered Rachel.

Charley bit her lower lip. "No, this feels okay. Let's go."

They set off with Chilly in the lead, Charley in the middle, and Rachel trailing. They made good time, weaving, but maintaining a fairly straight line through the plain. Charley's initial fear of waking sleeping alligators faded quickly as the pain on her shoulder grew worse. Chilly looked back from time to time to take a peek at the sun which had begun to dip in the sky.

Rachel noticed Charley flagging as the afternoon wore on. She walked beside Charley and said, "Let me help."

Charley whimpered and coughed, but remained defiant. She stopped walking and hissed at Rachel, "No!"

Chilly stopped. He took one look at Charley, walked over and reached out to take the satchel from her. She backed away and started to sob.

"They're my stones. You can't have them."

His eyes flashed with genuine anger. "What kind of man do you think I am? I'm only going to carry them for you. If I wanted the stones, I'd take them and go."

Rachel tried to calm Charley down, but she was out of control. "I don't know. You're just a kid, anyway. A really tall kid, but you're still a kid. You could be a really tall thief. How do I know?"

Chilly took a deep breath. "You're a scared little girl. I'll let you slide. You don't need to be afraid of me. Gimme the bag."

"Give it to him, Charley," said Rachel.

With a grimace of pain, she lifted the strap over her head and let Chilly take the bag. She turned away to hide her tears. Rachel made a motion to put her arm around Charley's shoulders but thought better of it. Instead, she stroked her tangled hair and patted her back.

Chilly waited patiently for Charley to regain her composure. When she turned back around, he said, "You know, the prettiest girls in the world shine from the inside out. C'mon, dry those tears. ."

Charley smiled weakly at first, but eventually, she turned red from embarrassment and broke out her beauty pageant smile.

"Oh, brother," said Rachel.

Chilly took it as a sign that it was time to move on again. They set off again at a slower pace in deference to Charley's condition. She spent the next hour making soft noises which were noted and duly recognized by her friends. The conversation in that hour consisted mainly of 'How's it going back there?' and 'It can't be long now'.

The latter turned out to be true. Chilly, being almost a foot taller and yards ahead of the girls, had a better view of what lay ahead. He made a yelping sound causing the girls to form into a defensive posture, back-to-back.

He called out, "I see trees ahead. We must be out of the swamp."

The three friends rushed forward, and now the girls could see that indeed they were coming to some boundary. They rounded a bend in the path and found themselves in front of an imposing wall of elephant grass seeming to stretch forever in both directions.

Charley stiffened so suddenly and completely that she began to shake and tremble in anger. She was able to utter a long, guttural, gargled sound of frustration, punctuated by a choked and unintelligible curse intended to rid the world of every phyla of the plant kingdom. Rachel stood at her side and sympathized in her own way. "Well, that's disappointing."

Charley looked sideways at her friend and sighed, defeated. "It's the hedge again."

"What hedge again?" asked Chilly.

Charley's temper rose to a boil. "There's a hedge on both sides of the river that won't let you get through and out of this place! Now there's an even taller wall around this swamp. It's everywhere. There are stupid faces in the stupid hedge, and I hate it!"

She stomped around the area, kicking up dirt.

Chilly tried to reason with her. "It's only tall grass, Charley. We can..."

Charley sprinted between Rachel and Chilly to throw herself at, and hopefully through, the barrier separating the swamp and what lay beyond. The grass was no match for a small girl hurtling through the air at a high rate of speed. She disappeared from view and landed on the other side with a bump and a tumble.

CHAPTER SEVENTEEN

Charley looked around to find herself in a familiar valley lined by trees and the detested hedge. She looked back at the wall she had come crashing through to see Chilly's hands appear, spreading the grass apart, followed by his face. He stepped through, closely followed by Rachel. They both had concerned looks on their faces which was a relief to Charley. She had expected to be teased mercilessly by her older and so much more mature friends.

They approached her and Chilly helped her to her feet. "Are you alright?"

In a dignified tone, Charley said, "Yes. Thanks for asking." She dusted herself off and turned to survey the river ahead.

"It's better to look before you leap," said Rachel to Charley's back.

Charley's hands balled into fists and her face twisted in fury.

"Thanks, Charley, for saving us a lot of time," Rachel added.

Charley took a deep breath and relaxed. She turned around slowly and took a bow.

"Can we go now?"

Chilly and Rachel shouldered their burdens and followed Charley. The hedges stood tall and resolute. The course was wide and relatively rock-free. There were no abnormally huge birds circling overhead. The only other creatures in evidence were ordinary run-of-the-mill insects, scheming their tiny schemes for taking control of the world. The valley ahead lay in a straight line all the way to the horizon.

"The good news is it doesn't look like we're going to have any surprises in the near future. It looks like clear sailing for a while," said Rachel.

Charley nodded as her friend joined her to walk side-by-side on the gently sloping bank. They ambled confidently, comfortable in familiar surroundings. Chilly was less so. He picked his way down the center, stumbling on the rocky terrain. He looked around with trepidation and fell behind the two friends despite his longer strides.

"Wait up!" he called.

They stopped and turned to see Chilly hobbling along. "Get out of the stream, Chilly," suggested Charley. "Honestly, do you want to sprain your ankle?"

"Hey, I'm new here."

Chilly made his way to the grass and joined them. "Are we safe here at night?"

Charley's face turned nervous and twitchy. "No, there are bears, and wolves, and giant spiders, and who knows what else."

"So, we need a place to crash tonight?" Chilly surmised.

"We have a few hours to find a cabin," said Rachel.

Charley added, "It won't be dark for a few hours. Relax."

"In that case, what do you say about eating something?"

Rachel nodded, and Charley shouted, "Great idea!"

He slipped the strap of the satchel over his head and laid it on the ground at Charley's feet. She knelt to fish out a stone. He pointed to the hedge. "Is that the hedge with the faces?" he asked.

"Yup."

"It doesn't look special to me."

"Other than faces staring at you and the fact that it's impossible to cross, it isn't that special. It's like a big green guard rail."

"Do you know what guard rails are for, Charley?" asked Chilly. "They keep people from driving off cliffs or into oncoming traffic."

Charley pondered Chilly's words. She had not given it much thought since the sum total of her driving experience consisted of sitting in the back seat hearing her mother complain about her father's driving and vice-versa. It seems her mother was a danger to everyone else on the road and her father drove like a maniac.

"Okay, I guess that makes sense."

"He makes a lot of sense," agreed Rachel.

The girls looked at the hedge in a new light. Chilly walked up the slope to test the hedge himself. He tried to squeeze through but had no more luck than Charley. He backed away a few paces and looked in both directions. When he looked straight ahead again, a breeze swept through the valley, and a face appeared in front of him. He backed away quickly, losing his balance. He half-slid and half-rolled all the way down to where the girls were standing.

They both chuckled at his clumsy retreat and the stricken look on his face. He lay on the ground, flat on his back, pointing up the slope where the face smiled, winked, and disappeared.

"What the...?" he finally choked out.

"She told you," said Rachel.

"You didn't believe me?" asked Charley as she lent him an ineffectual hand to help him up.

Chilly was still shaken. "You didn't tell me the face in the hedge was going to be my uncle. That face looked exactly like my Uncle William."

"I've seen lots of different faces in the hedge, Chilly. They don't all look like your uncle," said Charley.

Chilly was adamant. "That didn't just look like my uncle's face. It was my uncle's face. This is not right!"

Charley tried to calm him down, but he ignored her. He strode up the bank and looked around for more faces. He swept his hands furiously, along and through the branches of the hedge. The girls climbed the bank to stand on either side of him while he tried to bring his uncle back.

Charley tried again to calm him. "Chilly, I don't think they listen to us."

He swung around angrily to face her. "It was my Uncle William. He's been dead for three years. What is he doing in this crazy bush?"

"I believe you, I guess. Some of the faces look familiar to me too," said Charley.

Chilly calmed down enough to be led downhill, and they resumed their march in silence. Before long, a strong breeze swept past them on its way downstream. As one, they lifted their faces as if a message were being carried along by the wind. Dozens of green faces appeared on both sides of the valley to look down at them with serious expressions of warning. A cacophony of squawks and caws rose around them as birds flew off for parts unknown. Silence followed as even the insects hid from what was approaching.

A booming sound behind them made them all turn at once. Charley panicked at the sound of heavy footsteps growing louder. She grasped Rachel's arm.

"What do we do? It's Yink's brother again!"

Rachel looked around. "There isn't any cover. There's nowhere to hide!"

"That giant? How did he find us?" exclaimed Chilly.

Rachel shouted at Charley. "What about the stones? Give him the stones."

"He'll probably still stomp us to death," cried Charley.

"What did you do to make him so mad?" asked Chilly.

"CHICKENFINGERS!" rolled and clattered downstream like a boulder-sized gutter ball.

"There's no time to explain," insisted Rachel.

The faces in the hedge looked frantic as the booming footsteps were closing in on them. Chilly pushed Charley toward the riverbank.

"Go up and hide in the hedge as best you can. I'll climb up the other side and distract him."

Charley followed his directions immediately, sprinting up the hill. Rachel paused to watch Chilly climb his bank and take a position at the top. She smiled and waved to him and then joined Charley, who was looking for any small gap at all to get out of sight.

Chilly took a break from keeping one eye out for the lumbering giant to look across at the girls. They stood with their backs to the hedge, nowhere near hidden. To his amazement and relief, the girls were absorbed by the hedge until only the toes of their sneakers were visible. The faces on the hedge disappeared as the giant came into view.

Their gigantic and pungent pursuer lumbered into view. He was at least twenty feet tall. His massive body was topped by a grotesque, humanoid head. His face was pale and the skin, waxy and pebbled. A single bloodshot eye recessed beneath a bony eyebrow searched the ground below. His only clothing was a dangerously loose-fitting loincloth that might have been the sail of a schooner at one time. His arms and legs were thicker than most trees.

The giant slowed to a halt upon seeing Chilly waving his arms. He raised his long bulbous nose to snort and sniff the air. Chilly shouted at him, and he brought his heavy, dull concentration to bear on the young man.

"Hey, big guy! Look over here! Who let you out of your cage?"

Chilly's weak taunt had the desired effect of drawing the giant's attention without enraging him to the point of murderous stomping. The giant surveyed the valley once quickly with a sweep of its head and then turned back to focus on Chilly.

"Hey, One Eye! Your diaper's slipping."

The monstrous brute lifted his head to the sky, and a bellow of volcanic proportions erupted from his throat. The echoes eventually finished reverberating, and Chilly recovered his balance. The giant stood in the middle of the valley facing Chilly while the stricken faces of the two girls peeked out of the hedge on the opposite side.

Chilly lost sight of them when the monster turned to face him, spread its feet, and bent forward, placing its hands on its knees. Chilly shook with revulsion as the giant's breath washed over him, coating him with stench. He closed his eyes and forced his knees to stay locked. He swayed but remained upright.

The giant sniffed at Chilly and focused his eye on him. He roared, "CHICKENFINGERS?" into his face for good measure. Guessing the monster was not one for conversation, Chilly simply pointed downstream. The giant's eye followed his gesture and then returned to focus on the nervous young man. Chilly's eyes burned, and he struggled to stop from retching. He pointed once more, nodding like a woodpecker as he held his breath. Apparently satisfied, it stood abruptly and stomped away downstream leaving behind a trail of footprints and a visible cloud of greenish yellow reek.

Chilly fell to his knees and buried his face in the grass to smell the sweet scent of dirt. When he looked up again, the giant was out of sight, and only a trace of his essence remained. Birds returned to their roosts and other avian pursuits. The insects resumed plotting. Chilly rose and staggered downhill.

On the opposite bank, Rachel was leaning over Charley lying on the grass. She slapped Charley's face gently a few times until her eyes fluttered. By the time Chilly arrived to join them, Charley had risen to rest on her elbows.

"I was able to distract him. I thought he was going to bend down and bite my head off," he said. "Man, it smelled like a dumpster was throwing up on me. What happened to you?"

Charley shot back. "You're lucky. While he was bending over to face you, this side of the river got the bad end of the deal."

"Oh," said Chilly sympathetically.

They all shuddered. Charley remembered she held a stone in her hand.

"Does anyone want to eat?"

Rachel and Chilly both shook their heads and patted their stomachs.

"I can't eat anything yet," said Chilly.

"Me either," agreed Rachel.

"We can walk a little bit farther, but then we eat, okay?" asked Charley.

Either her stomach was not as delicate as her friend's, or her nose had a shorter memory. In either case, she was up and ready to go. Her friends were still a little green, but evidently passing out had prevented Charley from getting as strong a dose of its poisonous gas. She skipped down the hill, leaving them behind. However, her two weeks of classical ballet training in January hadn't improved her balance and poise enough to prevent her from falling to her hands and knees, skinning them all in the process.

She blew out a huge breath like a train whistle and took in even more air to fill the vacuum. Rachel hurried downhill to help her, but before she could get there, Charley let loose with a wordless blast of agony and anger, sending birds flocking to the sky for safety.

Rachel clapped her hand over Charley's mouth. Charley breathed in angrily through her nose while struggling to escape Rachel's hold.

"What's the matter with you? Do you want to bring that walking garbage truck back here?" scolded Chilly.

Rachel released Charley. "Hey, that does work."

Charley stuck her tongue out at Rachel and showed them her hands and knees.

"This hurts, you know. I can scream if I want to."

She almost screamed again to show them she could, but cut it short, realizing they were right. Filthy, embarrassed, and scraped bloody, she stormed off downstream to head off any chance for her friends to make fun of her.

They walked for a while in silence with Charley in the lead and Chilly bringing up the rear. The valley no longer stretched ahead of them in a straight line and without a distant horizon ahead, they all shared the feeling that something new-- fair or foul- could be around the next bend. The vegetation also changed-- towering trees crowded over the hedge on both sides bringing closeness and shade, adding to a sense of uneasiness for them all.

Rachel decided to distract Charley. "Let's eat."

Charley turned to Chilly and asked him, "Can you eat now?"

"Sure. Let's eat. What's for lunch?"

"Pizza?" suggested Rachel.

Charley shrugged her shoulders.

Chilly put in his order, "How about pasta?"

"I think I could do that," Charley said without complete certainty. "Wait, we don't have a bowl or plates or silverware."

"Alright, then wish for something we can carry with us, like ..."

Charley interrupted, "Like a stick of cookie dough?"

"I was thinking something more like beef jerky," offered Chilly.

Charley turned up her nose.

"His idea is better, Charley. We can eat and walk," said Rachel.

Charley's facial muscles twitched, trying to refrain from pouting at her friends to get her displeasure officially on the record.

"I've never had beef jerky, Chilly. You make the wish," she said through clenched jaws.. She tossed him the stone.

Chilly nodded, caught the stone without looking, and began preparing his wish. Charley took the opportunity to try amending the menu.

"Can we have the cookie dough for dessert?"

Chilly gave her a weary stare, which predictably got Charley's back up. "I was just asking, Achilles."

He placed the satchel on the ground and opened it wide. He knelt with his hand over the bag.

"I wish for three pounds of beef jerky wrapped in a napkin."

Charley peered in to spread the napkin on top of her pile of stones and found the dried meat stacked neatly in thick strips.

"You caught on almost as fast as I did."

Rachel made a sound which may or may not have been a snort. In any case, Charley was more interested in a snack than a snort. She accepted her portion of the jerky from Chilly and bit off a piece.

"It's not bad," she said, surprised.

"Let's see if we can make this last a few days, alright," warned Rachel.

Chilly pulled out a strip of jerky and stuck it in his mouth like a meat cigar. He pulled it from his mouth like a character from an old movie. "I like my jerky a little spicier, but I made it mild just for you."

Charley laughed. "Thank you, sir. You're a gentleman."

Chilly reached down and pulled out the canteen. While he drank, Charley walked over to Rachel and offered her some jerky.

"I don't like how this place feels, Rachel," Charley whispered.

"I know what you mean. It feels like we're being watched."

"It's good we have Chilly with us," said Charley. "He's been good luck so far."

"Let's hope our luck holds, Charley. We need to start looking for shelter for the night."

"You know, you always take the fun out of everything," whined Charley.

"Survival is kind of important, you know."

Chilly approached them and handed Charley the canteen.

"Here, drink up. We need to start looking for shelter for the night."

Charley threw up her hands.

"You're all so weird. I don't wanna grow up. You forget how to have fun."

Rachel opened her mouth to scold Charley, but Chilly beat her to it.

"You wanna have fun? Like playing tag with a bear or outrunning a pack of wolves? That kind of fun?"

"I'm just sayin'," muttered Charley.

"You can stop sayin' and start walkin', Princess," said Chilly as he set off. Rachel gave Charley a smug look and followed, turning her back and walking away. Charley gave them both a sarcastic salute and matching their pace, settling in a few steps behind.

Half an hour later, the uneasy feeling the girls had experienced was still with them. Charley spent much of her time looking up at the trees and catching fleeting glimpses of faces in the hedge. Oaks and cypress grew in front of and beyond the hedges, many of them sporting heavy beards of wet Spanish moss in the thick and humid air.

The river bent left, obscuring the future. Without a clear view of the stream ahead and the closeness of the atmosphere, one could easily mistake the moss for webs or ghosts. Charley's imagination turned the harmless plants into the nesting place of an army of ghost spiders. She lengthened her stride to close the gap between the older teenagers and herself. Not watching where she was going, she crashed into Chilly and looked up to find both of her friends staring ahead.

She pushed in between them to get a glimpse of what had stopped them short. As the bend in the riverbed straightened out, they were able to get another good look at the terrain ahead. Not far, but close to another jog to the right in the river's course, a trio of people walked.

Chilly looked down at Charley, standing at his right hip. "Should we try to talk to them?"

Rachel said, "They look normal."

Charley didn't know what to think. Now that Chilly was with them as protector, her first instinct was to avoid any more contact with strangers.

"We don't need them," she decided.

"There's safety in numbers, Charley. I'm going to go talk to them. Wait here," said Chilly.

This blatant dismissal of her decision did not sit well with Charley. Her usual course of action, in cases where her directives were disregarded, was to raise her voice in volume and pitch and demand obedience from everyone within earshot of the resulting shrill, piercing shriek. She was even now preparing for such a shriek.

It's possible an epiphany of realization occurred to Charley at that point. Those two instincts put together may have a lot to do with why she had no friends. It's also possible Rachel's dirty hand clamped over her mouth had something to do with her decision not to call out after Chilly as he dropped the satchel and sprinted away. She trembled, holding her anger in as he ran on. When Rachel saw that Charley's rage had subsided she released her.

"You know, I'm really getting tired of your smelly hand on my face," she growled.

"You know he's right, Charley. If they're travelers like us, we might be able to help each other. I'm sorry about the hand on your face, though. When something works, you stick with it."

"As long as I don't have to share any stones with them," groused Charley.

She bent over and pulled the satchel open to look inside. "I'm running low."

Rachel looked for herself and found about 15 stones remaining in the bag along with two pounds of beef jerky.

"We should probably wrap that jerky better before it gets dirty and gross."

"I don't care. I think it's gross already."

"That's not very nice, Charley. Chilly had a good idea."

Charley was still angry about him running off against her wishes. She pointed toward him as he ran to catch up with the newcomers.

"Yeah, he's full of good ideas, like his idea to chase down those people."

The valley weaved right, and the group passed out of sight. Chilly continued to yell and try to wave down the strangers. He continued pursuit until the girls could barely make out his voice calling. Disappearing from view, Chilly left the girls alone in sudden silence.

The riverbed was uneven and rocky here, stretching almost from hedge to hedge. The girls looked at each other and came to an immediate and silent agreement that they should not have let Chilly out of their sight. They hurried after him, stumbling and staggering over the treacherous terrain. By the time they reached the point where they had last seen Chilly, there was no sign of him, upstream or down.

CHAPTER EIGHTEEN

Rachel and Charley searched desperately for Chilly, calling for him until their throats were sore. He and the people he was chasing were gone. This stretch of the river was a straight shot for a long distance. They should be there, but they weren't. There was no explanation for their mystifying disappearance and Charley was now frantic.

"Do you think they kidnapped him? Do you think he's okay? Do you think they were all taken by giant birds?" she guessed, hoping her fears were unfounded. She scanned the sky for marauders but found only gray clouds and a setting sun.

Charley trembled with worry. Rachel hurried to her side and threw an arm around her shoulder.

"We'll find him. He could be hidden from our view. Don't worry."

Charley was having none of it. "He's like eight feet tall, Rachel. Look around. If he were around here, we'd see him," she said in a shrill voice.

"Still, we shouldn't give up. Come on."

The riverbed was now a basin and so wide at this point it could be properly called a lake. It stretched all the way to the horizon. Charley had no choice but to follow Rachel. She couldn't take the chance that her only remaining friend might also disappear. They trekked across the lake, keeping up their desperate search until they reached a raised mound perhaps twenty feet in diameter. On the crown of this island, it appeared someone had built a shelter. The partial shell of a rowboat rested on the ground nearby. The girls stepped up onto the small plateau and circled the shelter, eyeing it with sadness and pity.

The rustic cabin was a five-foot cube with three walls and a roof made of irregularly shaped wooden slats. The whole structure was held together by chicken wire. It was difficult to tell whether it was constructed by design or formed by litter thrown together by the wind.

The architect of this minimalist shack had chosen to integrate the natural landscape into the design as much as possible. Ventilation was provided by the broad gaps between the slats. Natural light was abundant thanks to multiple jagged skylights in the roof. The yawning missing side was partially blocked by a filthy flapping cloth that functioned as a loud, welcoming invitation to enter. The actual landscape of stones and dirt made up the floor of the doorway. Pieces of wood left over from construction were scattered around the plateau.

"It looks more like a box than a cabin," said Charley in a dejected voice.

Rachel walked toward the opening. She called inside. "Is anybody home?"

No one admitted to being in residence. Rachel pointed to a piece of wood on the ground near the entrance. She picked it up and showed it to Charley. Burned into the wood was the name, 'Spike'.

Rachel gave Charley a wry smile. "It looks like a doghouse, Charley. Someone else stole your idea."

Charley was in no mood for teasing.

"Mine would have been better." She looked around. "Why would someone build this in the middle of nowhere?"

"Maybe they used to fish from this spot when the lake was full," said Rachel. "It doesn't matter. Looks like we have no choice. We're staying here tonight."

"Here? What about Chilly?"

"Charley, Chilly's a big boy, and he can take care of himself. He's got to stop for the night too. We'll start looking again tomorrow."

"But..."

"No buts, Charley. The wind is picking up, and it feels like it might rain. We can try to make this place a little bit sturdier. Who knows what kind of creatures might be prowling around out here?"

"You're getting bossy again."

"You're getting whiny again."

Seeing Charley's eyes flash, Rachel softened her next statement into a request.

"Charley, why don't you think of a wish or two that might make this box habitable?"

Charley frowned, obviously unenthusiastic about using her wish stones on the renovation of a dilapidated pile of planks, turning up her nose at their home for the evening.

"A dog wouldn't bother to raise its leg to pee on this thing," said Charley.

She gestured to the ground around them and suggested, "If you don't want to use stones to make a wish, why don't we at least stack these stones up around it to keep anything from crawling under?"

Charley didn't like that idea much, either. She dropped her satchel and pulled out some beef jerky. She sat down with legs crossed to consider her options. When she looked up at Rachel with an expression of defiance, the older girl came close to losing her temper. Instead, she dropped her own backpack to the ground and began gathering medium-sized stones. She took an armful and dropped them next to the side of the shack facing the wind. She arranged them along the wall and set out again to gather more stones. After fifteen minutes of strenuous activity, Rachel had worked up a sweat by forming the beginnings of an actual wall to partially block the wind from whipping through the slats.

Charley watched her while she ate. She did feel guilty about not helping, but she pushed feelings aside to make room for the comfort of self-pity, her oldest best friend. Though it was comforting to wrap that blanket of misery around her psyche, it did not do an adequate job of keeping her warm.

"Rachel, I'm cold."

Rachel replied in a clipped tone through gritted teeth. "You could help."

Charley did get up and collect some stones, but she couldn't carry many at a time, and her heart wasn't in it. She knelt at the wall Rachel had started.

"How about you bring the stones over and I'll stack them?" she offered.

"It's a deal but keep thinking of what we can do with a wish or two."

Rachel set about gathering stones again while Charley knelt and stacked the stones from her last load. She looked to the sky and estimated there was an hour or so before darkness fell, and the night-time denizens came out to play.

On the next trip back, Charley made a suggestion. "Rachel, do you think a fire would keep the monsters away?"

"A fire might help, but it also might attract attention from night creatures too. Anyone around could see it for miles."

"So, do you think it's a good idea or a bad idea?"

"There isn't a lot of wood to burn around here, but if it would make you feel warmer or less scared, then I guess it's a good idea. Go ahead."

The overcast sky helped to hasten the onset of dusk. Charley left her job building the wall to enter the shelter and look around while there was still light. She made several trips outside to gather some of the driftwood lying about and bring it inside. With the matches from Rachel's backpack, she lit the wood. It ignited immediately to brighten the small hut as well as her mood. She smiled and warmed her hands on the merrily burning fire. Her smile melted quickly however as her campfire was not going to last more than an hour with the paltry supply of fuel by her side. She sat back on her heels and gnawed anxiously on some beef jerky. To pass the time, she dumped her supply of stones on the ground to count them.

Meanwhile, Rachel continued her labor, building up the wall and setting stones all the way around the perimeter. She gave up her efforts when the darkness prevented her from seeing any more stones. Charley had settled into their cozy nest some time earlier, leaving her to do all the work alone in the wind and darkness. Rachel walked around the shelter, searching for any signs of danger from marauding monsters. She looked up to the sky as well to see if there might be any threats from above. As far as she could tell, the only danger they were currently facing was the danger of the shelter collapsing in the wind.

She pushed the curtain aside and prepared to let Charley have the piece of her mind she had been saving and clearly Charley was in no shape to refuse. She had wrapped Rachel's thick woolen blanket around herself and was now laying in a fetal position with her back to the wall against the stone windbreak outside. The fire was already guttering and dying out but there was enough light from the embers to allow Rachel to see Charley's teeth chattering as she shivered uncontrollably.

Rachel ducked her head and crawled inside and pried, open Charley's clawed hand to take a glowing stone. Charley shook her head and stammered, "N-n-n-no!" but Rachel ignored her. She also pulled the blanket free from Charley's grasp and took it outside with her along with the stone.

A loud cracking sound in the darkness frightened Charley. More snaps and claps followed, increasing her anxiety, and making her wonder whether Rachel was doing the cracking or getting cracked herself. Her whole body jolted with every crack and bang until the noises ceased. She shivered through an excruciatingly long minute with pressure throbbing in her ears until the gusts no longer whipped through the gaps in the wall. The buffeting from the wind's fury had died down considerably. Barring any precipitation, their night in the shelter may be bearable.

Charley crawled to the doorway and yelled out, "Rachel, are you alright? Where are you?"

A voice outside answered her, but she grumbled and scowled, unable to make out what Rachel said. She poked her head out and looked left and right. She staggered to her feet with her arms crossed around her chest in the cold.

"Rachel!" she cried in her loudest voice.

Rachel's voice answered deafeningly into her right ear, "What?"

Charley jumped and covered her ears. "Why would you scare me like that?"

Rachel was holding broken planks and two long poles. "I didn't think you would hear me if I whispered. Do you want to let me back inside?"

Charley allowed Rachel access to their comparatively cozy shelter and followed her in. Rachel deposited her wood supply next to the fire and sat down without saying a word against the opposite wall. The cold had taken its toll on her as well. Her lips were trembling, and her hands shook as she picked through the remains of the rowboat, arranging the wood on the fire. Charley grew impatient waiting for an explanation.

"Well, what did you do?" she asked.

Rachel didn't take her eyes off the fire. "You're welcome."

Charley beat the ground with her fists. "Why do you have to try and make me feel guilty all the time?"

Rachel slowly raised her eyes to meet Charley's angry stare. "If you feel guilty about something, you should get it off your chest."

"I didn't say I feel guilty..." Charley's voice broke.

Rachel waited for her to continue and then resumed tending the fire. Charley shook her head in frustration, and a short stalemate ensued.

Rachel finally relented and spoke, "I wished for the blanket to be longer and then I wrapped it around the outside of the hut. The wind is basically holding it on. No big deal."

"Oh Good thinking."

"Thanks."

The fire was now giving off enough heat to melt the shivers out of the girls. Rachel stopped paying attention to the fire and reached for Charley's satchel. She pulled out some jerky and settled back to eat.

"It's much warmer in here now," Charley ventured.

Rachel smiled, "You're welcome."

"Thank you."

"Did that hurt?"

"I'm sorry. I'm not as strong as you, Rachel," Charley admitted. "I'm not as smart as you either," she added in a whisper.

The fire crackled, greedily consuming the bone-dry wood. Charley sniffed and wiped her nose with her sleeve.

"Charley, I've only known you for a few days, but I can tell you are strong, and you are smart."

Charley looked at Rachel with a small, brief, sad smile. "Can I tell you a secret?" she asked.

"You can tell me anything, Charley. We're best friends."

Charley paused. "I have something wrong with me, Rachel."

From the look on her face, Rachel knew this was no time for a joke. She simply asked, "What's wrong?"

"I have a genetic disorder. From the time I was a baby, I wasn't normal. I was always small and weak. Nothing worked like it's supposed to. I was always seeing doctors and going to emergency rooms. They didn't think I'd live very long."

Rachel blinked back tears and sniffled. Charley turned her back for a little while.

"Then they started trying different treatments, and I started improving and getting stronger. Anyways, a few years ago, my doctor told us there was a good chance I could live a long life."

"That's great news, Charley. I had no idea. I'm sorry I was mean to you."

"Don't be stupid, Rachel. You're my best friend. I know you're just kidding around."

"Still..."

"I mean it. If you start treating me different, I'm going to kick your butt."

"Now I'm scared."

"You should be. Anyways, because I was getting better, my mom and dad thought it was okay to treat me like a slave and make me join clubs, and play sports, and try all these new things. They signed me up for everything, music lessons, art classes, sports. And just like school, everyone always treated me like the sick weirdo.

"You haven't taken your medicine while you've been here, have you?" asked Rachel.

"No. I haven't. And I don't know how to wish for it."

"I had a feeling something was wrong. That's why you weren't helpful, isn't it?" ventured Rachel.

That stung a little. Charley felt like crying because Rachel's remark bothered her. Those familiar feelings of doubt and defensiveness swept over her. She almost resorted to her customary reaction of an immediate, full-frontalscathing attack, but she knew in her heart she could have been more helpful when Rachel was rock-hunting and wall-building. She nodded and gulped in air to prevent the tears from coming.

Rachel nodded and smiled in sympathy. "All the more reason to get some sleep then," she said in a soothing tone. She sat back and added more wood to the fire while Charley composed herself.

"My doctor says I'm a medical marvel."

Rachel stared at the fire. "So, they found a cure, and now kids like you will survive. That's great news."

"It is great. I'm always going to be small, but at least I'm beautiful, right."

"I'm happy for you. Really I am."

Charley smiled. She felt better, but Rachel was still focused on the fire instead of looking at her.

Rachel continued, "You're also rude, ungrateful, and immature sometimes."

Charley gritted her teeth and held her tongue.

"The thing is, you're just a kid," said Rachel.

"I'm doing pretty good out here on my own."

Rachel lifted her eyes from the dancing flames and stared at her in disbelief. Charley stared back, unaware of how unaware she was. She was so confident in her ludicrously erroneous stance she was prepared to spend the night locked in ocular combat with her friend. After two seconds, Rachel blinked in surrender, allowing Charley to win the shortest staring contest ever.

Rachel pulled out her canteen and took a swig. She added

more wood to the fire and settled back to lean against the wall, retreating from the light. "Get some sleep, Charley."

Charley was disappointed over Rachel backing down so quickly. In order to punish her for spoiling her improving mood, she decided to disregard Rachel's subtle attempt to assert her dominance. Instead of settling down for the night, Charley reached for a stone.

She had fifteen stones at her disposal, and her mind raced at the possibilities.

"Charley, what do you have in mind?"

"I'm going to try something. Wish me luck."

Rachel gave her the silent go-ahead face.

"I wish I was back home on my front porch."

The stone zapped her hand, and a puff of acrid smoke rose from it. She dropped it like it was a lit firecracker. The remaining stones flickered briefly in sympathetic concert with their blown-out cousin.

Rachel shook her head as Charley looked at her cache in panic.

"You didn't really think that would work, did you?"

Charley ignored her to inspect her palm for burnt skin. Seeing none, she squatted to pick up another stone. It still glowed red, allowing her to breathe in relief. She looked at Rachel for guidance.

"I should probably test one, don't you think?"

"What we should be doing is getting some rest while we have a fire."

"I know. Rachel, do you want a new outfit? I'm gonna wish for new clothes."

"If you want to waste stones, go ahead."

"Come on, we both could use some clean clothes. How many weeks have you been wearing those jeans? And that tee shirt tie-died a long time ago."

Rachel was not in the mood for Charley's nonsense. "Go to sleep, Charley. If we get up early, we might catch up to Chilly."

"I'm changing, Rachel. I'll give you a stone for nothing if you want to change too."

Rachel held out her hand, and Charley dropped a stone onto her palm. She closed her fist around it, and her lip curled into a sneer.

"For nothing? How generous."

Charley ignored her. For a moment, they pondered all the possibilities. Rachel was the first to decide. She closed her eyes and began to mutter.

"You know, I am kind of crusty," admitted Rachel.

"Wait, I'm not ready," Charley shouted, interrupting Rachel's wish.

"Why do I have to wait for you?"

Charley's voice trailed off as she spoke, "I want to do it together."

Rachel threw up her hands, "Charley, hurry up. We're not putting on a fashion show."

Charley closed her eyes and screwed up her face to get down to business searching for the perfect ensemble in her mind.

"3-2-1. Wish!"

They both spoke to their stones, and a second later Rachel was wearing a new, clean tie-dye tee shirt and spotless, well-pressed skinny jeans. Her holey sneakers had been replaced with a new gleaming white pair.

Charley opened her eyes to find her stone had made some modifications to her specifications. She was clad in the jeans and hooded sweatshirt she had in mind, but her stone had chosen a psychedelic tie-dye pattern like Rachel's for her hoodie.

"Oh..." said Charley.

She cast the stone away in disgust and disappointment.

"That's not what I wished for," said Charley.

"We're shirt sisters," laughed Rachel.

Charley sighed with the weariness of a runner who had run a marathon with a piano on her back.

"Can we sleep now, Charley?"

Rachel arranged her backpack as a pillow and lay down. Charley gave up on trying to understand the stones. They were reasonably safe and reasonably warm on a cold, windy evening in the middle of a dried-up lake. They had food and water. They would survive the evening.

"Rachel, why did Chilly leave?" she said with a hint of sadness in her voice.

From the other side of the fire, Rachel answered reassuringly, "We'll ask him tomorrow when we see him."

"I kinda liked having a big brother," admitted Charley.

"I guess they would come in handy sometimes," agreed Rachel.

Charley sighed in contentment. She had never gotten so much exercise before due to her condition, and it was catching up on her. The heat from the fire added to her drowsiness. The howling of the wind still rose and fell outside all around them, but it wasn't loud enough to keep either awake.

CHAPTER NINETEEN

Charley awoke with a start and raised her head, leaning on her elbow. She saw Rachel kneeling, alert and erect, across the fire. Rachel saw Charley staring at her and raised her index finger to her lips.

"What is it?" Charley whispered.

"Something's out there," Rachel hissed in warning.

"It's morning, isn't it? Maybe Chilly found us."

Rachel shook her head. "Charley, look up through the roof. Look at the fire. It's still the middle of the night."

Charley looked up hoping to see a gray morning sky. Her head sank after seeing nothing but inky blackness. The fire still burned brightly. She had barely slept at all.

Both girls' heads lifted in response to a flapping sound overhead.

"Just a bird," said Charley with hopeful optimism. They both craned their necks, alert for any indications of danger. When the only sound to be heard was their old friend the wind, they both relaxed. Charley settled down to sleep.

Suddenly, a riotous flurry of hundreds of flapping wings swept over the shelter. Rachel and Charley reflexively ducked to the ground and looked up through the skylights. The flock veered away and returned again and again while the girls grew more and more frightened. Rachel crawled around the fire to lie next to Charley. Then, as abruptly as the swooping squall began, it stopped.

"At least they were normal-sized birds," Charley said, relieved.

Rachel was still alert for their return. Instead of the sound of wings, the girls were dismayed to hear the howl of a wolf, close by. Answering calls echoed from every direction. Both girls looked at the flimsy cloth serving as the door to their suddenly not so cozy shelter. Rachel seized a broken oar handle and thrust it into the flames. It caught immediately, and she rose to her feet, stooping to keep from getting her hair caught in the low ceiling.

The howling wolf orchestra was closing in on their location. Deeper bellowing growls from some other creatures joined the symphony. Rachel looked down at Charley, cowering on the ground over her stones.

"Bears and wolves? I don't think we're going to get much sleep tonight, Charley."

Charley grabbed a stone and tried to concentrate on a wish that might protect them. Her voice trembled, "What do we do?"

A terrifying new sound reached their ears. What sounded like a conversation of chittering clicks was taking place right outside. The girls stared at the entrance with dread. The sharply pointed, jointed leg of a gigantic crab brushed the curtain aside for a moment causing Charley to gasp.

The birds returned for another pass to investigate the commotion in the center of the lake. Charley had to yell at the top of her lungs to get Rachel's attention over the wind and the din. "Rachel, do something! They're right outside!"

Rachel bravely advanced to the entrance and knelt. Charley crept up behind to lean against her back. Rachel slowly reached for the curtain and pulled it aside. She thrust the burning oar out first, and it struck right between the eyestalks of a crab the size of a small car. Both girls screamed in fright and fell back while the crab scuttled away in pain.

The girls continued to scream when the walls of the shack started shaking. Growls in the dark responded to their calls of primal fear. They fell to their knees. Rachel held the burning oar above her head while Charley wrapped her arms around Rachel's waist.

The blanket wall of their shack was pulled away, and the wind increased its relentless attack. The flames twitched wildly in the center of what was now their cage. Golden ravenous eyes from many shapes and species stared at them from outside the flimsy walls. Having screamed their voices raw, the girls watched in silent horror as they realized that flock of birds was not a flock of birds. Hundreds of pairs of tiny claws clutched onto the chicken wire, followed by small bat faces thrusting inside to get a look at the girls in a cage.

More hoarse shrieks erupted from the girls. Rachel reached as far as she could in an arc to wave her sputtering oar at the grinning bats. Tall, shaggy shapes in the dark bellowed and rocked the shack back and forth. Charley fell to her knees and picked up a stone, frantically trying to make a wish, but she was too hysterical to come up with something that would help in this dire predicament.

Suddenly, a gigantic crab claw burst through the roof, smashing and stabbing into the ground right next to Charley. Rachel whacked it with the blackened former torch to no effect. The claw rose, almost lifting the whole shack off the ground. Charley crab-walked to hide behind Rachel before the pinching claw could clack shut on her leg. Rachel thrust her club into the soft muscle between the pincers. The crab pulled out its claw and Rachel's club with it, leaving them unprotected.

The shack was falling apart around them, the walls about to collapse. Bats squeezed through and flapped wildly inside the crumbling cube. Bears on each side took turns rocking the structure off the ground.

Rachel picked up two planks from the boat and started whacking bats out of the air. Charley cheered whenever she struck one, but dozens of the flying mammals had found their way inside the shack. Charley took up a plank of her own and flailed wildly, almost striking Rachel with one unbalanced swing.

For a second, the rocking stopped and the bats streamed out of the hole in the roof. The howls also trailed off. The only sound was the cold air whistling through the gaps in the walls. Rachel and Charley looked at each other with relief.

Something determined and heavy landed on the roof, crunching and cracking what little structural integrity was left to the pitiful little shack. Charley and Rachel were flung to the ground by the force of whatever fresh horror had now descended upon them. Charley was able to roll over and see huge scaly yellow claws gripping what was left of the roof above her.

The sight of the giant talons petrified the girls as they lay on the ground. They were soon treated to a more close-up glimpse as the roof collapsed still further under the weight. Before they could scream one more time, the force of the monstrous creature's wings beat the air, and the girls were no longer in danger of being squished by the roof. It rose up and away from them slowly. A tremendous rush of air blew sand and sparks into the confined space causing the girls to cough and sputter. To the girls' dismay, the roof continued to rise, and half of the shack soared away with it. The girls were left with one wall leaning on Rachel's back next to a dying fire, surrounded by enemies. The remaining wall was their last flimsy layer of protection between them and the horde. The girls were like marshmallows in a s'more as the beasts pressed down on the wood.

The stones gave off more light than the flames, and Charley's attention was drawn to them. The girls scrambled and crawled desperately to the stones, Charley reaching them first. The growls and roars resumed and the bats returned to swoop and dive at any hands or feet that poked out from beneath the wood The pincers of more than one crab clacked on the ground all around them. Charley desperately racked her brain for some device or weapon to wish for as the monsters closed in. In the end, Charley began to cry from panic. She grasped Rachel's hand with her left hand and lifted a stone with the other.

Their heads were battered by the host of creatures on top of them. The light from the stone in Charley's fist shone bright red through her hand. Charley's hand dipped to tap the pile of remaining stones. She shouted, begging the stones, "I wish they would all go away!"

Her wish touched off a crimson fountain of force that threw the remnants of the shack up and off into the night. At the same time, an expanding ring of energy swept the monsters away and spread over the surface of the lake until it crashed up onto the shores in a perfect circle in all directions. An aurora of rusty red light shimmered in the sky around and above them like a dome.

Charley and Rachel lay face down with eyes closed, holding hands. The stones on the ground pulsed, fading in blue synchronicity. Rachel was the first to raise her head to survey their surroundings. She supported herself on her elbows and looked up. The air was still under a false morning sky.

"Charley, open your eyes. You've got to see this!"

Charley blinked and opened her eyes, but they were unfocused and glassy. Her right hand unclenched, and the stone dropped onto the pile. The fingertips and palm of her hand were red and raw but she did not seem to be in pain. Rachel stood and tried to help Charley into a sitting position.

Gradually, Charley roused and responded to Rachel's soothing words and gentle, but insistent, slaps to the face.

"Enough. You can stop hitting me."

"You did it, Charley. You saved us!"

"What happened? What did I do?"

"You wished for all of them to go away; all of the bears, and the wolves, and the bats, and the crabs, and who knows what else. They all disappeared."

Charley was confused. "I did that? The last thing I remember was seeing a giant claw come crashing through the roof."

"Yes, it was you," laughed Rachel. "It was amazing! We were done for. Then, all of a sudden, everything exploded! You must be in shock still. It'll come to you eventually."

Charley looked up then, and her jaw dropped. The dome above them was pink like a sunrise with streaks of orange falling to earth like rain on a windowpane. She noticed her hand for the first time and flexed her fingers, expecting to feel pain. She shook it frantically as if a spider had dropped out of the sky onto her palm.

She looked down to see her potent treasure of wishing stones was now a pile of cold, worthless, pale blue rocks. She fell to her knees, lifted her face to the heavens, and uttered a desolate and mournful cry.

"NOOOooo...!"

"Charley! Come on. We're still alive."

Whoever was responsible for the sheer epic magnitude of her crippling loss received one more blubbering protest of ingratitude from Charley.

"NOOOooo...!"

Rachel shook her by the shoulders.

"Stop it, Charley. There will be more stones. Get a grip!"

Charley rose and spun to face Rachel.

"You don't understand. I was going to use those stones when I got home. Now I won't have enough to wish for everything I need."

"What you need or what you want?"

"What's the difference?" countered Charley.

Rachel crossed her arms into what Charley had dubbed her Miss Perfect pose. "There's a big difference. Why can't you be satisfied with what you have? We almost got crushed, torn apart, and eaten, and now it looks like we'll make it till morning."

Charley picked up one of the spent stones and threw it as far she could. It landed twenty feet away, clattering to rest like one of the thousands of ordinary stones surrounding their lonely island in the center of a lonesome lake.

"So, what now?" Charley asked with little enthusiasm.

"Why don't we try to get some rest? I think this dome will hold till morning. We'll get moving again when the sun comes up."

"I don't think I can sleep," complained Charley, turning to face her friend.

Rachel had already laid her head back down on her backpack. She closed her eyes and suggested, "Why don't you try counting stones?"

"Are you trying to be funny?" said Charley as she clenched her fists. She muttered to herself, wishing that she hadn't told Rachel not to treat her differently.

CHAPTER TWENTY

The sun peeked over the horizon and burned away Charley's dome of magical protection while she tossed and turned on the cold hard ground. Morning had arrived long before Charley was ready to receive it. Consequently, she was not her usual cheerful self when Rachel shook her by what happened to be her sore shoulder. She groaned and slapped Rachel's hand away.

Rachel tried rousing her by shouting in her ear. "Charley! Charley! Get up!"

Charley clamped her eyelids tighter and willed herself back to sleep. It wasn't because she was keenly interested in returning to a dream. Her reticence for waking stemmed from an intense desire to ignore the dismal prospects of facing another day filled with mortal enemies and narrow escapes.

Rachel insisted. "Charley, wake up."

Rachel pulled the satchel from beneath Charley's head, succeeding in her efforts to open Charley's eyes. The bounce of her head on the ground was the impetus Charley needed to climb to her feet and greet the new day. She started her morning routine by facing Rachel in Warrior pose. Rachel nonchalantly handed her the satchel and walked away.

Charley's mood did not improve now that Rachel had backed down from a confrontation. Nothing left her more frustrated than an undetonated tantrum. She ran to step in front of Rachel after gathering her things.

Rachel sighed. She straightened and leaned over the younger girl, spoiling for a fight. "Charley, I'm not interested in your foolishness. We have to go. You have to get up. It's that simple."

"Foolishness?" Charley sputtered. "I've had a rough few days. I thought you understood. I'm sick, you know. I need my rest."

"I didn't forget. I want to get you home. Sooner or later, we're going to run out of luck and you're going to get badly hurt or worse."

Charley looked at Rachel with suspicion. "I could have slept a little more. What's another hour?"

Rachel waved toward the sun. "The end of this river might be just out of sight. Don't you want to find out?"

"Sort of. I kinda like being on my own." She chewed her lower lip. "Except for the monsters."

"Well, I'll remind you again. You're not on your own. I'm here too, lucky for you."

"What do you mean, lucky for me? I'm the one that saved us last night. Chilly saved us the night before."

"I give up. You're on your own." Rachel shot back, throwing up her hands. She started walking off in the direction of the rapidly rising sun.

"Fine!" Charley shouted after her.

She bit her knuckle and twirled her hair, standing alone next to the scraps of their shelter and the ashes of last night's campfire. Her eyes darted back and forth, indecisively, as she contemplated her next step.

Rachel reached the edge of the island and turned around.

"Charley, are you coming?"

Charley wasted no time in scooping up her satchel and trotting toward her.

"You're a giant pain you know," Rachel informed her.

"So are you."

They stepped down onto the lakebed and walked in uncomfortable silence toward shore. As they approached the beach, they found this part of the lake bounded by what may have been the taller and more forbidding cousin of their friend, the hedge. Firs, hemlocks, and cedars grew tightly together on the sharply rising slope, and the gaps were filled by thick patches of thorns and bramble. Any hope of skipping out on the rest of their river journey was dashed.

The girls came upon a long pier jutting out into the lake and headed for it. They climbed a ladder onto the dock and stopped to turn and take a look at the lake, side-by-side.

"I bet it would be nice here." Charley looked up at Rachel. "I mean with water."

Rachel nodded. "Speaking of water, we need to find some somewhere, or we're going to die of dehydration."

"We can stop for breakfast," Charley said hopefully. "What do you think?"

Rachel turned her back on the lake. "You know what I think, Charley."

Charley did indeed know what her friend thought. "Never mind. Let's go," she said.

"You're not going to argue? Not even a little?"

"I don't abide mocking."

"Look who's all mature," said Rachel.

"I'm saving my energy for later."

"Thanks for the warning."

She smiled at Charley and Charley smiled back. As long as Charley remained in good spirits, this day might actually be pleasant.

They stepped quickly down the sun-bleached planks of the pier, careful to avoid gaps, loose boards, and exposed nails and screws as they walked. Shore birds circled overhead calling forlornly, perhaps in despair over the long-ago disappearance of their aquatic food source or the lack of discarded trash to pick through.

At the end of the pier, they found Rachel's decision to walk directly toward the rising sun had paid dividends. A path leading to a gap in the encircling trees ran away from the base of the rickety pier.

Charley stopped Rachel with a hand on her arm. "Do you think Chilly's alright?"

"I do," said Rachel with confidence. "He did a good job taking care of us. I'm sure he can take care of himself."

Charley smiled and nodded. "You're right, Rachel. He's probably saving someone else right now."

Rachel put her hand on Charley's shoulder. "I wouldn't be surprised. Shall we go?"

"Okay. Let's get back on the road. Or river in this case."

The girls strode into the river valley with a spring in their step. Steep banks topped by the hedge bordered the wide course of the river here. The terrain in this stretch of the river, from the hedge to the narrow watercourse was covered by a dark green carpet of short, thick sod. They had grown used to picking their way over rocks and stones in the flats beside the river. The girls looked at each other and smiled, hatching the same idea at the same time. They dropped their bags simultaneously, hopped on one foot and pulled off a shoe, then a sock. When they each put their foot down in unison, they both uttered the same shuddering, delighted squeal. The other shoes and socks came off in no time, leaving the girls standing barefoot in cool, soft bliss.

They purred like cats getting scratched behind the ears as they wiggled their toes for a long, long time, lost in stress-free reverie. Surprisingly, it was Charley who spoiled the vacation from their journey.

"My toes have decided to stay here."

Rachel stood still with a dreamy, faraway expression on her face.

"Rachel, snap out of it!"

Rachel's eyes fluttered open, and her head turned to face Charley. She muttered something inaudible.

Charley stood on her toes to shout in Rachel's ear. "What did you say?"

"I said you should let your toes make all your decisions."

"Really? Well, my toes are telling me to kick you in the shin," her eyes signaling her anger pilot light was about to reignite.

Rachel showed no signs of being afraid of Charley's threat. "That would be dumb, Charley. You'd break your toes. I only meant that I agreed with your piggy toes. I could stand here all day."

Charley's rage subsided after accepting Rachel's explanation for the egregiously offensive comment. She bent down, picked her shoes and socks off the ground, and stuffed them into the satchel. Rachel did likewise, and they shouldered their burdens together. They set off once again humming softly and stepping lightly on the springy carpet of grass.

136

"Rachel?"

"Ye-e-e-s-s-s, Charley," Rachel droned sarcastically in response.

"How much farther do you think?"

Rachel shrugged her shoulders. "Not far, I think. At least I hope it's not much farther because it's going to be a long walk home for me."

"You don't have to walk all the way back to your shack."

"Hey, that's my house you're calling a shack," said Rachel with pretend indignation.

"Seriously, Rachel? It's going to fall down in the next storm."

"It's sturdier than it looks."

"No, you're coming to live with me. That's final."

Charley's certitude made Rachel smile; a small, sad smile, but still a smile. Charley held out her hand.

"We'll see, Charley." Rachel accepted Charley's hand, and they walked that way for a long time in silence.

The river valley narrowed in front of them. The luxurious lawn continued while the river was now a five-foot path of dark brown soil snaking through the green. This morning on this stretch of river had been a welcome relief from the treacherous and troubled terrain of the past few days. The girls were relaxed and carefree until they negotiated a bend at midday and felt the smooth, soft footing replaced with irritating weeds. They were forced to stop and don their socks and shoes again, grumbling about injustice and discrimination all the while.

When the stream straightened, they encountered a group of four young adults seated on the grass on the opposite side. They were less than fifty yards away and their chattering voices stopped abruptly at the girls' arrival.

The girls stopped and looked at each other, uncertain as to how to proceed. Two young men and two women observed their approach, their heads perked and alert.

Rachel whispered. "Don't make any sudden movements. You don't want to spook them."

Charley nodded, freezing in place.

The two young men slowly rose to take positions in front of the women. Rachel and Charley held up their hands to show them they meant no harm. They stepped slowly toward the group. As the girls neared the center of the river, the men shifted to keep themselves between the two dirty vagabonds and the proper women seated primly on the crabgrass. They stood, ready for action, with matching serious expressions designed to intimidate.

"We come in peace," said Charley.

The young men looked at each other and laughed. The taller of the two said, "As if it matters. What could you do? Overpower us with your smell?"

"Good one, Tucker," said the more tanned of the two.

Charley's low tolerance for snobbery set her off. She prepared to jump the divide, but Rachel held her back.

One of the young ladies called to them. "Tucker, please. You're going to pick a fight with a little girl?"

She got to her feet and walked to the riverbank. She wore a white dress and a pink sweater with matching flats. She crouched gracefully down to Charley's level with her hands on her knees and asked in a little girl voice, "Are you one of the... local tribespeople?"

Charley looked at her as if she were insane. She looked at Rachel and then back to the young woman.

Charley attempted to be civil. "I'm not sure what you mean. We're all traveling downstream, right? If it's alright with you, we could travel together. There's safety in numbers."

The woman considered Charley's proposal but looked dubious. "Yes, well, we haven't exactly..."

The other woman chimed in. "We're going to stop here for a while."

"You can go on ahead, and we'll catch up later," said Tucker. The others nodded their heads vigorously in agreement.

The first woman straightened and brushed her hands together to clean them off despite not having touched anything. "You see we're having a quiet picnic and we only have enough food for four."

Charley looked past her to see the other woman with her back turned, actively blocking Charley's view of what was certainly an imaginary picnic lunch. She called out as she mimed placing settings.

"Brynn, the brioche and tea are getting cool. We should dig in."

Brynn looked down at Charley and bestowed a false, sickly sweet smile on her. "If you'll excuse us. We should dig in."

Tucker approached and put his arm around Brynn's shoulder, leading her away from the girls. Rachel and Charley were left staring at the ugly, grinning face of the shorter young man.

"What's your name?" asked Charley. "Dopey?"

"Run along, you dirty little freak," said Dopey with more than a hint of malice in his eyes. Charley stepped back in shock and fright. The others had turned their backs on the girls and huddled together. Charley held back tears and leaned into Rachel who comforted her.

"Let's go, Charley. I don't want to travel with them anyway. They're horrible people."

She led Charley away. Charley turned once to see them all laughing and the memories of many a day in school came flooding back. She refused to cry, but her eyes rebelled, and the tears flowed freely.

Charley sniffed periodically as they hurried away from the picnicking travelers. Rachel tried to cheer her up by imitating all their voices performing a dramatic scene from the never-produced movie, Uncontrollable Farting.

'Tucker, my dearest. I can't *fart sound* live another day without you.'

'You are my *fart sound* world, Brynn.'

'I am going to *fart sound* leave Dopey for you. It's always been *fart sound* you, Tucker, my love.'

'And you for me, *fart sound*, Brynn. But what about *fart sound* Brioche? She will be *fart sound* devastated.'

Charley's dour expression broke and a smile appeared on her face. She added more farting noises of her own as Rachel continued

the sad saga of the smelly love square until they left the flatulent teenagers far behind.

CHAPTER TWENTY-ONE

They passed into more familiar terrain and abundant greenery. They were in good spirits again. Charley's mood brightened considerably when she found a glowing stone directly in her path. She didn't bother to put it in her satchel. She held it tightly in her right hand and licked her lips in anticipation of a tasty lunch.

Rachel held up a finger in warning. "Be careful with your wishes."

"Oh, I'm going to take my time. I won't make any more mistakes."

In keeping with her serious tone, Charley walked in near silence. She muttered to herself, and Rachel watched her intently for any sign of weakness or the expulsion of an impulsive wish. The ambiance of the riverbed grew somber and considerably darker. It wasn't until Charley climbed atop a boulder in the middle of the missing stream that they stopped and made a complete inspection of their surroundings.

Tall sycamores loomed over the hedge, and large spider webs spanned many branches on both sides of the river. The air was still, moist, and heavy. Charley jumped down and joined Rachel as close to the center of the valley as possible. Several faces wavered briefly in the hedge, wearing expressions of concern and urgency.

The girls resumed their journey without discussion. They picked their way along the rocky course with deliberate, but hasty steps. They peeked up at the trees from time to time for signs of the spinners of those giant webs, but for the time being the eight-legged horrors remained hidden. A misstep from Charley resulted in a minor clack of two rocks which resounded with deafening volume, echoing back and forth across the valley. The girls huddled together in fear, awaiting the attack of a swarm of chitinous arachnoid warriors. Nothing happened.

"Be more careful, Charley. One of those webs up there might

have your name on it."

"I will" she replied.

The girls continued downstream, even more cautiously. The sheer number of massive, complex, and sturdy webs kept them in a constant state of creepy. They scanned the trees continuously for furry multi-eyed beasts ready to swing down in a moment's notice to wrap them up and take them away.

They were so concerned with the trees on the banks they did not see the thick strands of a web spanning the entire river valley directly in their path until their faces were almost trapped in it. Charley inhaled sharply and fell back and away to avoid it. Rachel helped her to her feet, and they limboed beneath it, scurrying forward to safety. The trees were close, the overcast sky a gray streak above the narrow valley. The banks were steep and thick with vegetation all the way up to the hedge.

The footing was treacherous here with smooth rocks piled on top of other smooth rocks. The girls concentrated on each step, windmilling their arms often to maintain their balance. Charley was especially tipsy as she still refused to put the stone into her bag. She clutched it close to her body and stumbled frequently.

Rachel stopped on flat ground and turned around to wait for Charley to catch up.

"Charley, why don't you put it away? You're going to drop it."

"It's a good luck stone, Rachel. We got past the spiders, didn't we?"

Rachel rolled her eyes. "We did that by walking."

"So? We had good luck."

"That doesn't make sense. Let's sit for a minute. My feet hurt."

Rachel collapsed with a groan and Charley crumpled to sit beside her. While Rachel massaged her feet, Charley fiddled with the stone in her hand, rocking back and forth.

"I can't take it anymore, Rachel. I'm sick of being dirty. I'm sick of being hungry. I'm sick of being mad, and I'm sick of being sick."

"I'm sure if we think, we can…"

Charley exploded again. "And I'm sick of you being such a know-it-all!"

Rachel fought hard to master her own temper. Her lip curled, and her voice lowered an octave.

"I've about had it with you."

Charley backed away from her to a safe distance. "Me? What did I do?"

"You're kidding me, right? That's a joke?"

Charley tried a double back-flip complement with a half-smile twist. "You have to admit; you have an answer for everything."

Rachel wasn't falling for it. "Some people might call that being smart and then listen to me because I might say something important you can learn from."

Charley tossed the stone between her hands. She let Rachel's words dissipate without a response. When a sufficient time had passed, she changed the subject.

"Why did that grinning dope call me a freak? I mean I'm the most beautiful girl in the world. Why couldn't he see that? I'm not that dirty."

Rachel picked up a stick and drew in the dirt at her feet. "People who are ugly on the inside can't see beauty. And, if they can see it, they want to destroy it."

Charley scooted over to sit next to Rachel. "Who would want to destroy something beautiful?"

Rachel continued to stare at the ground. "They hate anything that shines a light on how ugly they are themselves."

"Are there many people like that?"

"Too many. Stay away from them. They'll only infect you with their disease."

Rachel rose and kicked at the dirt, erasing what she had drawn before Charley could see it.

"How will I know who's ugly on the inside?"

"The ugly people will be the ones who put you down and try to take what you have away from you."

Charley nodded. "So, the ones who give me things are beautiful?"

"It's more complicated than that, Charley. You'll see as you get older. Just don't turn ugly yourself."

Charley flipped her tangled hair. "I don't have to worry about that," she bragged.

Rachel sighed in frustration. "On the inside, Charley. On the inside."

"Okay," said Charley with an exaggerated eye roll and head shake.

They continued for a ways until Rachel stopped short. Charley halted and followed Rachel's gaze to take in their surroundings. They had arrived at a fork in the river. A large boulder rested directly between separate paths. Charley's frustration boiled over once again as yet another obstacle blocked her path. She chewed her hair again in distress. To this point, the choice of direction had been straightforward. She looked to Rachel for help, but Rachel was staring at her for a decision.

"You choose, Charley."

Charley's face was clearly agonizing over the options. "Aaarrgghh!" she whined. "Why is this so hard?"

"What's hard? Just pick one. All roads lead to the sea."

"Is that true?"

"No, it's an expression. Like 'All that glitters is not gold'."

Charley twirled her hair, unsuccessfully pondering the meaning of each of these statements. "I'm too hungry to think, Rachel."

"Which branch should we take?" asked Rachel.

"Nonnie said we should always take the right path."

"I think she meant it figuratively, Charley." Rachel granted Charley a reprieve. "We can stop and eat lunch while we decide."

"Good idea. Oh, look! Another stone. And there's another! And another!"

Charley's attention flicked away from the task at hand. She

tucked her lucky stone into her overalls and picked up the glowing stones from the base of the boulder. She clacked them together so hard they created a spark.

"I'm tired of jerky. We have three stones now, Rachel. We should have something delicious for lunch and a dessert."

Rachel sighed. "Do what you want, but it sounds to me like you are very tired. I'm going to rest over here in the shade. Why don't you join me?"

Charley stared at her stones as she dreamed about something simple and filling. Rachel lay on her back with her head resting on her backpack, waiting for Charley to make up her mind about anything. Charley paced, coming up with several ideas and throwing them out just as quickly. She finally stopped and ran over to Rachel.

"I've got it! Why didn't I think of this sooner?"

Rachel sat up as Charley knelt and pulled her canteen out of her backpack. She tossed one stone inside her satchel and placed it flat on the ground. Bending forward to rest on her knees and elbows, she held the other stone in her fingertips, inches away from the makeshift leather platter. She took a deep breath and closed her eyes.

She muttered, "I wish I had a six-layer chocolate cake with chocolate frosting."

Charley opened her eyes to find nothing. However, Rachel clapped in delight.

"Don't get up, Charley," she warned.

The exact chocolate cake Charley had in mind had appeared, resting on her back. Rachel made a mess of it, but eventually succeeded in sliding most of the cake from Charley's sappy back to the satchel. When the transfer was completed, and the satchel placed carefully on the ground, the two girls sat, taking turns grabbing handfuls with their dirty little hands and stuffing the moist and gooey treat into their mouths. They even scraped the filthy leather satchel clean and licked every bit of frosting from their fingers.

"Charley, you're a genius."

Charley's smile beamed through a ring of chocolate around her lips. "I know. I made us lunch and dessert with one stone."

Rachel applauded. "You're getting the hang of this."

Charley curtsied a thank you. "But I still don't get why my wishes don't come true exactly the way I want them to."

"I told you, the stones are tricky. I think they don't want to make it too easy. It's like they want you to think things through before you wish for something ridiculous. You have to be specific and precise."

Charley was more proud of herself than usual. "We don't have to worry anymore. We can wish for cake at every meal."

Rachel made a nauseated face and rubbed her belly. "I don't know, Charley. Let's keep our options open."

Rachel took a small drink from her canteen. She shook it, and a worried look crossed her face. Charley gulped and gulped from her own supply without a care. Rachel reached over and pulled it away from Charley's mouth.

"Charley, slow down. We're getting low."

Charley wiped her mouth with her sleeve and nodded in agreement. They both stood ready at the boulder.

"Which way?" Charley asked.

"You decide. Both directions look the same."

Charley crossed her arms and chewed her lip. "We'll listen to Nonnie and go right," she concluded. "What could go wrong with going the right way?"

"I don't think that makes much sense, but as long as we're together, we'll be alright."

"Hang on a minute," said Charley. Before Rachel could stop her, Charley whirled to hide from Rachel and spoke into her cupped hands.

Rachel exhaled a heavy sigh. "Charley, what now?"

Charley turned around and fixed Rachel in place with a piercing stare and a devious smile on her face.

"Did you wish to look like a crazy person?" asked Rachel.

"No, I wished for a present for you."

Charley opened her fist to let a gold chain with a small opalescent butterfly pendant drop to dangle from her middle finger.

"I know how much you like butterflies, Rachel."

"It's perfect, Charley. You didn't have to do that."

"You didn't have to cheer me up, either. I know I can be a pain sometimes. This is just my way of saying, 'I'm sorry'."

Rachel sniffed and wiped her eyes with frosting-smeared fingers.

"It's really beautiful. And you're sweet. Thank you."

"Here," said Charley. "I'm sure I'll probably do something stupid in the future, so put it on and don't get too mad when I do."

Rachel raised the necklace and settled it into place under her hair. As Charley bent to gather her satchel, the butterfly's wings fluttered twice before settling to rest.

Charley's eyes narrowed and she pointed at Rachel. "What was that? What just happened?"

"What do you mean?" asked Rachel.

"I could have sworn... Never mind."

Charley blinked and shook her head. "Let's go."

They took the first step in unison, and with light hearts, full bellies, and the memory of sweet chocolate frosting sticking to their teeth, they both felt confident they had made the right decision.

CHAPTER TWENTY-TWO

They left trees and grassy slopes behind for rock walls, sand, and cacti. A hedge of prickly cactus climbed both sides to stand atop the rock face, preventing any travel along the cliffs of sheer wind-worn orange sandstone. The riverbanks ahead closed in to form a narrow gorge. As they crept forward, they began to pass dark openings on both sides of the canyon leading to caves containing who-knows-what. The black holes dotted the walls ahead as far as their eyes could see. Charley and Rachel faced each other with worried looks.

"This is pretty creepy," said Rachel.

"Do you think it's safe?" asked Charley.

Rachel stepped toward the next cave on her right and leaned forward to peer in. After a very hasty peek, she pulled back quickly causing Charley to squeak and move to hide behind her. She clutched at Rachel causing her to turn and slap at Charley's hands. They both shivered and shook, eventually returning to normal teenage anxiety levels.

"Don't sneak up on people like that!" said Rachel.

"What did you see?"

"I didn't see anything. It's as black as night in there."

Charley picked up a pebble from the ground and attempted to toss it into the yawning cave. It struck the wall to the left of the entrance. They both turned and ran in terror until they left the narrow gorge.

Rachel slowed, grabbing Charley's arm to stop her. "Stop! Why are we running?"

She turned slowly to look behind, finding that nothing was chasing them. Charley was doubled over beside her, gasping for breath. Rachel rubbed her back until she returned to normal.

"We're being stupid," said Rachel. "Come on. Let's go back."

"I'll follow you," Charley nodded.

They walked slowly back into the canyon and approached the

first cave. Rachel held her finger to her mouth and whispered a quiet 'Ssshhh'. She crept forward and picked up a pebble of her own, gauging the distance to the opening. She threw the pebble into the cave as far as she could and listened for the sound of it striking an inner wall or possibly the thorny hide of a giant hideous carnivorous caterpillar. Hearing neither, she motioned for Charley to join her.

"It might go back a long way. Should we light a torch and investigate?" asked Rachel.

"Are you crazy?"

"I'm not crazy, I'm curious."

"We could get lost or trapped by a cave-in. Why don't we go back and take the other fork in the river?"

Rachel closed her eyes and made a snoring sound. "What about adventure? I thought you hated boring."

Charley took another cautious look into the cave. She turned to face Rachel and slowly shook her head.

"I'm not going in there." Her scared expression metamorphosed into her customary defiant glare.

Rachel gave it another try. "Maybe this is where all the stones come from? Miners might be in there right now, digging them out of the rock."

Charley gave her words some thought. The stones had to come from somewhere. She turned it over and over inside her head, weighing the chances Rachel was right against the possibility that this cave was one of many entrances to a fiery underworld of misery and horror.

"I think you're nutty. Let's go take the other fork."

"Alright, forget the cave. But we have to keep going forward, Charley. We'll never find shelter if we go back."

"What if we...?"

"No," said Rachel with finality.

Charley turned on her tantrum systems. Her fingers curled into fists. She planted her feet and stretched her neck. Her eyes began to water. She warmed up the muscles of her mouth, alternating pouts and frowns, and throwing in an occasional special glower she had only recently added to her repertoire.

"Stop that, right there! Are you going to waste your energy on whining and crying?"

Charley set her systems on standby but maintained her petulant stance. "I am."

"Fine," Rachel snapped. "You do that. I'll be on my way."

She straightened her backpack and entered the canyon, not looking back. Charley was furious. She kicked her feet sending a stone after Rachel to smack against the stone wall making a loud, echoing clack. She looked one more time into the blackness of the cave, half-imagining the sound of something stirring. She took off after Rachel, whispering as loudly as she could, "Rachel, wait."

She caught up and matched her pace. Rachel gave her one look and then stared forward. They kept up a brisk tempo in silence for a while. The girls looked closely at the openings as they passed for signs of life, but nothing bothered them. Charley looked up to see if the hedges were watching from above.

She remarked to Rachel, "It's weird, but I miss the hedge."

Rachel only grunted.

They passed dozens of caves as they hurried forward. Each black opening contained the infinite possibility of anything. Rachel seemed bound and determined, without any fear of what might be in front of them, or above them, or below them. She kept walking, staring straight ahead.

Charley edged herself closer to Rachel until they were walking almost shoulder to elbow. She tried to duplicate Rachel's courage, but a growing fear of the unknown was increasing with every cave they passed. So far, exactly nothing had happened but, in Charley's mind, each black, mysterious entrance was another chance for something from her nightmares to pop out and swallow them whole, or worse.

She grabbed Rachel's arm and whimpered quietly in order to avoid alerting any nightmare monsters to their presence, yet loudly enough to get Rachel's attention. Rachel stopped and gave Charley a hug which she returned gratefully for a few seconds.

Charley broke it off. "What was that for?"

"You're crying. I thought you were scared or homesick of something."

Charley scoffed, "No, I have some sand in my eye, that's all. I'm not crying."

Rachel smiled, not believing a word of it. She swung the backpack off and placed it on the ground. She unzipped it and reached inside to pull out the canteen.

"Take a drink. It's very dry here," said Rachel. "Just a small one, though."

Charley pulled out her own canteen and gulped until Rachel lifted her palm, signaling her to stop.

"Charley, don't you understand? We need to make the water last. We don't know how long we're going to be in this canyon."

Charley nodded as if she understood, but it remained to be seen to Rachel whether it would affect her water consumption rate. She stopped up the canteen but did not put it away. Rachel's warning left her head immediately.

"How weird is it that we're in a riverbed but there's no water?"

"It doesn't look like there has been any rain in this part of the river for a long time. People might have lived in these caves when there was water flowing by, but they look empty now."

Charley pondered Rachel's theory. If these caves were abandoned years ago, it would be a big relief. Charley's anxiety eased.

"Yeah, that's what I was thinking," Charley lied. She took another long swig from the canteen. "Are you ready to go on?"

Rachel was surprised by Charley's mood swing from tears to bravado. "I'm ready. Are you?"

They gathered their belongings and prepared to walk away. A movement to Charley's left caught her attention, and the jitters of fear returned at once. Rachel's eyes followed Charley's look. A shadowy silhouette detached from a cave and walked silently toward the center of the canyon. A translucent shade of a woman carrying a large jug knelt and filled it with non-existent water. She was dressed in simple old-fashioned clothing. She stood and carried the jug into the cave without taking any notice of the two girls standing with their jaws wide open.

They looked at each other. They emitted no sounds, communicating instead with wildly dilated eyes and the unsubtle facial and hand gestures one might use in a situation where one's hands are on fire. When they could speak, Charley blurted out, "Did we just see a ghost?"

"I think so," said Rachel.

Rachel grabbed Charley's hand and pulled her along. "Come on. Let's go."

Charley looked back as they hurried away. She crashed into Rachel when the older girl stopped short. Charley poked her head around Rachel to see two more transparent figures walking along the right side of the canyon. Two men carrying leather bags conversed as they walked. They took no notice of the girls. Rachel led Charley along, giving them a wide birth. They were now moving in a gait halfway between a confident rapid stride and stark raving panic.

They slowed down when they were sure they had left the ghosts behind. By this time, Charley had relaxed most of her facial muscles with the exception of the eye muscles she was using to maintain her mask of terror. Rachel shook her and looked deeply into her eyes, trying to get her to focus. When Charley blinked and looked back at her, Rachel relaxed and fished out the canteens again. She handed one to Charley and drank deeply from her own. Charley held the canteen but remained motionless.

Rachel tried to get her attention. "Charley, it's okay. They're not ghosts like in scary bedtime stories. They're like daydreams. They aren't going to hurt us. They must be the people who used to live here."

Charley took a small sip. "You're probably right." She shuddered and looked earnestly at Rachel. "It's kind of sad, when you think about it."

Rachel shook her head. "I don't think they're sad. This might have been a nice place to live when there was water."

They looked around. Charley now had the urge to find out what was inside the caves. She walked to the mouth of one and stretched out hand which passed with no resistance or sound through a ghostly woman leaving the cave. The woman continued on her way without stopping, directly into and through Charley. She paused upon meeting Rachel and looked around as if sensing something on the wind and then continued her trip to who knows where. Charley was paralyzed and, dropped her canteen at her feet. She hugged herself and shivered from head to toe, holding in a scream. Rachel hurried to her side and hugged her once again. After a few minutes of stroking her hair and patting her back, Charley's teeth stopped chattering. Rachel let her go and bent down to pick up the canteen to find most of the water was now gone. She put the stopper back in and returned both canteens to her own backpack.

Charley stood at the exact center of the canyon. She reached out her hand to Rachel who held it and used it to lead her along farther through the canyon. They passed more ghosts causing Charley to startle, but not panic. She appeared to accept their presence now as if she and Rachel were characters in an educational film about the culture of an early civilization.

The trip continued without further excitement from the ghosts of the canyon. However, the pair was now forced to deal with a more basic problem: they had run out of water and Rachel had given Charley the last mouthful from her own canteen. The heat and dry air of the canyon was dehydrating them. They were sweating profusely now, and each step was becoming a chore. Charley stopped and stooped over, her hands on her knees. She squinted up at Rachel, grimacing.

"How can there be no shade at all? It's so hot. I would go in a cave with the ghosts at this point."

"No, you wouldn't," said Rachel.

"Neither would you," said an annoyed Charley.

"You're right. Come on. If we stand here any longer, we'll dry up and turn into sand."

Charley was miserable. "I'm so thirsty. We're in big trouble. This canyon goes on forever, and it's going to get dark soon."

"Charley, you have stones, remember?"

"Are you kidding me? Why didn't you remind me sooner?" asked Charley, laying the blame on Rachel.

"I thought you were saving them for an emergency," snapped Rachel.

Charley had to concede Rachel had a point, but she was bent on deflecting the blame onto the older girl anyway. "And you thought dying of thirst wasn't an emergency?"

Rachel shrugged her shoulders. "I'm not dying of thirst just yet."

Charley snorted. She gave Rachel a disapproving look and muttered under her breath. She stored her lucky wish away and pulled the stone from her satchel. Without a single thought for the crafting of a suitable and appropriate wish, she lifted her canteen to the sky.

"I want water."

Almost immediately, clouds gathered, and the distant sound of thunder announced the impending storm. The sky grew very dark and very angry, very quickly.

Rachel sighed. "I think you may have made a profound and horrible mistake."

CHAPTER TWENTY-THREE

Charley became annoyed with the stone now. She held it up to her face. "Oh, come on! You know what I meant."

Huge raindrops began to fall, causing puffs of dust to rise from ground which may not have felt moisture in years. The downpour made a sound like microwave popcorn popping in its paper bag. The girls opened their mouths to catch some raindrops. They were coming down harder now though, and the occasional drop in the mouth wasn't worth the dozens painfully pelting their faces. Lightning flashed across the sky above the canyon. Even the cacti above them waved in the strong wind.

Rachel grabbed Charley's hand and pulled her downstream at a trot. They were running in mud, and the center of the canyon was now a channel of water. They were spared from the worst of the wind, but the thunder rumbled down the canyon pushing them forward. More lightning flickered, and yet another roll of thunder followed seconds later.

Rachel yelled above the storm's fury, "Charley! Run! We have to get out of here."

They both struggled to stay on their feet and cover as much ground as possible. Through the driving rain, they could see the end of the canyon ahead in the distance. Claps of thunder buffeted them incessantly as they scrambled and slipped forward. A wide muddy stream now covered much of the canyon floor, running swiftly.

Finally, after an exhausting slog through mud and mire, the canyon walls ended. They found themselves in a wide-open green riverbed. They were now on opposite sides of a swiftly running steady stream. The storm lessened now, though a steady rain still fell. The last rolls of thunder faded in the distance. The girls splashed around in the stream, relieved one difficult, dry, and dusty leg of their journey was at an end.

A continuous roaring sound reached their ears from upstream.

The girls stopped their playing.

"That doesn't sound like thunder."

"What is it?" asked Charley.

"I don't know," Rachel answered, looking concerned.

The roar grew louder, and the girls looked back into the mouth of the canyon. In seconds, the source of the roar came hurtling toward them. A wall of brown water taller than Rachel hurtled toward them. They each scrambled madly up their own bank. As the wave escaped the confines of the canyon, it sloshed and sprawled, losing height but widening like a pteranodon spreading its wings. Rachel climbed high enough to escape, but Charley could not. She lost her balance when the wave struck, and she fell with a scream. Rachel watched helplessly from her knees as Charley disappeared beneath the torrent.

Charley remained under water for far too long. Rachel picked herself up and ran along the bank above the crest of the flood. She gasped when Charley finally popped up again, flailing her arms as she was swept downstream, struggling to tread water. Charley was able to articulate an abbreviated shriek before she disappeared again over a small waterfall. Rachel windmilled her arms herself when her frantic chase led her over the steep unsubmerged portion of the same drop. She somehow managed to land on her feet and continue on. She ran for a couple hundred yards until the torrent slowed and she caught up to Charley. She was still being pushed along, but she was able to stay afloat without much effort until Rachel waded in and swam to meet her. She ducked her head under Charley's arm and together they staggered ashore and collapsed on the bank.

Charley lay back, taking deep breaths, while Rachel stood and surveyed the riverbed. The river still ran high with a swiftly moving current but breaks in the storm clouds upstream signified that the downpour was losing strength. Rachel looked down at Charley on her back, somehow still clutching her lucky stone.

"You don't have to say anything. I know," said Charley, embarrassed.

"You know what?"

Charley spat out the words as if they were a mouthful of vege-tables. "I should have been less ambidextrous."

"It's ambiguous," corrected Rachel.

"Now you sound like Miss Radhika, my English teacher," she said with a sneer. "She's a know-it-all too."

"Charley, just because people know more than you about a particular subject, it doesn't make them a know-it-all."

Charley had to accept she had made a mistake; one that had almost been disastrous. She examined her stone and marveled at its warmth despite being submerged. She rubbed it between her hands and it seemed to glow brighter, perhaps in anticipation of being acti-vated.

"This is a good one. I think you're going to like it." She closed her eyes and made her wish.

"I wish I was smarter."

Rachel rolled her eyes. "Me too."

"Find your own stone then."

Charley opened her eyes and tried to mentally self-gauge her IQ.

She looked down at the stone fading in warmth and inner glow. She looked at Rachel and asked her, "Do I look smarter?"

"Smarter than what?"

"What do you mean?"

Rachel gave her a reproachful look. "What exactly did you wish for?"

"I wanted to be super-smart."

"Everything is relative, Charley. You didn't specify what you wanted to be smarter than. Or how much smarter you wanted to be, for that matter."

Charley thought back and realized she had done it again. The stone had defied her. She waded into the water to stomp her feet in frustration using the splashing to add a more dramatic effect. After an uncharacteristically short and subdued tantrum, she sulked, knee-deep and facing away from Rachel. Her shoulders rose and fell. She

shook her head and eventually turned to look at Rachel with a sheep-
ish and defeated expression.

"So, I might be smarter than I was before or I might be smarter
than something else, like a toad or a rock?"

Rachel's jaw clenched as she thought carefully for a good long
time about her answer. "Let's hope it's both. Can we go now? We can
dry out while we make a list of all the things you're smarter than."

Walking along the receding river, Charley squealed when she
spotted another glowing stone barely submerged. She ran to the edge
and plucked it from the mud. Before she could store it away, a large
fish leapt out of the river and tapped the stone out of her right hand.
As it submerged, the glow from the stone disappeared from sight.
Charley fell to her knees and stabbed repeatedly for the stone or the
fish or both. She looked at Rachel, pleading.

"Help me, Rachel! That fish took my stone. I think it swallowed my stone!"

Rachel held out her hands, helpless. "Charley, what do you
want me to do about it?"

"Get in here! Try to catch it!" she screamed.

"It's gone, Charley. We'll find more."

Charley's eyes lit up. "Another stone! That's it!"

She looked around wildly and found another. She grabbed it
and put on her squinchy wishing face.

"I wish I could breathe underwater."

"Charley, no!"

Charley's eyes bulged as her wish came true. She felt a con-
stricting pain in her chest. Strange sensations caused her to reach for
her neck, and she gasped when she touched her new gills. She could
still smell the clean, fresh air of the great outdoors in her nose, but it
wasn't being supplied to her newly improved brain. Charley continued
to gasp unsuccessfully as her face turned blue. She discovered panick-
ing, crying, and running in circles did not do the trick either.

"The water, Charley!"

She dove in headfirst. Rachel threw up her hands while Charley swam below the surface, pulling oxygen from the water and looking for the fishy thief. She was soon out of sight in the murky water. Rachel filled the canteens and waited. She grew concerned for her friend as a long time passed without a ripple or bubble. The river's surface was serene and calm.

Suddenly, something broke water many yards away. It was actually many somethings. Charley's face surfaced for a split second, and her arms beat the surface in a frenzied, disjointed rhythm that bore a resemblance to swimming. She was heading slowly in Rachel's general direction followed by multiple forms, barely making a ripple in their pursuit. Rachel waded into the river to assist Charley as she scrambled to get out of the water.

Whatever creatures were following her broke off and disappeared beneath the surface. Charley stood and smiled triumphantly, holding up a glowing stone clutched in her hand. The smile quickly turned to panic as she, once again, gasped for air. She shook her fist at the sky and blurted out, "I wish I could breathe air again!"

The magic of the stones had apparently had enough fun tormenting Charley. After a moment of intense searing pain in her lungs, she was able to breathe normally again. She inspected her neck and found the gills had closed up, leaving no trace. She peered into her wrinkled hand and watched the red glow fade from the stone. She stood on the shore of the river, soaking wet, embarrassed, and consequently angry at the nearest person not named Charlotte Stanton.

"Now we don't have any stones!" She faced down Rachel. "You did nothing!" she said, hoping Rachel would mistake her shivering for uncontrolled rage.

Rachel scratched her head and turned her back on Charley. She was quite wet as well and in no mood for a scolding. She calmly walked up the slope and sat down on the wet grass. The storm clouds had rolled on by this time, and the temperature was climbing. Charley fumed as Rachel unlaced her sneakers and peeled off her socks. She wrung them out deliberately, one at a time and placed them on a rock to dry.

Charley relented a little. "Did you hear me? We need more stones. You're not helping."

Rachel reclined on the grass, her arms supporting her head. The rain had stopped now and what was left of the black, heavy clouds had rolled far away downstream.

She ignored Charley's pointed remark and instead asked her, "How was your swim?"

Charley proudly puffed out her chest.

"I chased that fish for miles. Just when I caught up to it, I was surrounded by a hundred otters. The fish spit out the stone and swam off. There was a whole pile of stones underwater, Rachel. The otters must hoard them. Anyway, I think I surprised them because I was able to grab a stone and swim away before they could get organized. Then I swam away fast, like a graceful dolphin. They couldn't catch me. That's when you saw me."

"So, after all that, you have fewer stones now than when you jumped in."

Charley growled, "You would have to throw that in my face."

"Well, I didn't lose the stones."

"Well, you didn't find them either," countered Charley. "I did. And I know where there are lots more."

"Do you mean the ones the otters are guarding?"

"I have a plan," whispered Charley so that the otters wouldn't hear her.

Rachel looked around conspiratorially to see if the coast was clear. "I can't wait to hear it."

"First, we get some more stones…"

Rachel interrupted. "Hold on, Charley. Just wait. I'm sure your plan would be so cunning that generations of otters would remember this date as a day of infamy for years to come. But think about this. You turned into a mermaid, sort of. You recovered your stone from them and escaped like a magnificent tuna. They're probably already ashamed enough. We should start walking now. It's getting late, and we need to find shelter."

Charley thought about it and smiled. "You're right. We don't have to rub it in."

Rachel tied her laces together and slung her shoes over her backpack. She set out barefoot while Charley still wore her sneakers. They walked together at a brisk, squishy pace until Charley stopped suddenly and turned to face Rachel.

"Where did the otters come from?" asked Charley.

"What do you mean?"

"I mean before the flood, this was a dry riverbed. There were no fish or otters or underwater pile of stones."

"That is a good question," admitted Rachel.

"Does that surprise you? That I asked a good question?"

"Not at all. It would surprise me if you had a good answer, though. We see unexplained things every day."

Charley scratched her scalp and made an attempt to arrange her hair. She pondered the mystery for a time, eventually shrugging her shoulders.

"Probably some kind of multi-dimensional time-space rip brought about by too many reality-defying wishes."

Rachel cocked her head and stared, wondering if her young friend's wish to be smarter was taking effect.

Charley tented her fingers and touched her lips.

"Something to think about while we walk. Let's get a move on."

Rachel shook her head and followed this new Charley at a vigorous pace. Ten minutes of silence later, Charley stated, "I was like a dolphin."

"I'm sorry, what?" asked Rachel.

Charley was adamant. "I swam like a graceful dolphin. Not a tuna. You said a magnificent tuna."

"You looked more like a tuna to me. Tuna are excellent swimmers, you know."

"Of course I know. I've been to Sea World. I know how dolphins swim," said Charley.

Rachel gave in. "Fine, you swam like a dolphin. I'm sorry."

Charley's face brightened at that for a moment, even though her clothes were damp and clingy, and her toes were probably pruning in her soaking socks and sneakers. She fell behind as she hopped from foot to foot taking them off. She popped them in the satchel and caught up to Rachel, who put her arm around her. They tramped forward, confident the worst part of the day was over, and a warm, welcoming shelter would be waiting for them right around the bend.

CHAPTER TWENTY-FOUR

They walked near the top of the bank to avoid the noisome mud left behind by the draining riverbed. The sun warmed their backs and baked the moisture from their clothes. If not for the odor of drying muck and the swarms of gnats circling their heads looking for a nostril to enter, it might have been a pleasurable stroll.

Wildlife took advantage of the return of water to the river. A pair of raccoons at the shore was engaged in some suspicious behavior and an otter kept on eye on the girls for a while, giving them a dirty look as he floated along on his back. Scores of birds came to gorge on insects in the aftermath of the flood.

There were signs of human habitation as well. They came upon the remnants of small ramps, built on both sides of the river, now ruined beyond repair. The remains of a cabin stood partially exposed to the elements. A portion of the roof formed a precariously balanced lean-to with a single standing wall. Further along, they found the missing walls of the cabin lying flat on the ground while assorted debris littered the ground. The girls looked at each other, realizing this might have been their last chance for shelter were it not for Charley's ill-conceived wish.

Charley tried to lift one wall, unsuccessfully. "Rachel, help me. If we can lean it up against the other wall, we can sleep underneath like a tent."

"Charley, it's too heavy to budge. Besides, we need more than two walls to keep the night creatures out."

"Well, then what do we do?"

Rachel was resolute. "We keep going. I'd say we have a couple hours of daylight left."

Charley looked to the sky behind them. "That's it?" she said, on the verge of tears. "Can we get one day of peace?"

"Are you feeling okay?" asked Rachel.

Charley sniffed and wiped her nose with her sleeve. "I'm fine."

Rachel put on a brave face despite her growing concern. "We need to pick up the pace, Charley. Can you handle it? While we're walking, look for a stone or something you can use to defend yourself."

"We're not going to make it, are we?" said Charley in a shaking voice.

"We'll be alright, Charley. We've got each other."

Charley took some small comfort in the knowledge. Her friend was resourceful and dependable. She gave Rachel a tiny smile and an appreciative nod. They set off at a hurried half-walking, half-trotting pace. The level of the river was dropping quickly without a new source of water, and the other remarkable thing about the scenery they passed was the increasingly frequent visits from the watchers in the hedge.

Charley scanned the ground around her as they ran. She skidded to a stop when she found a pile of wooden slats that had been part of a crude fence. Each slat had a pointed end, providing Charley with the weapon she was searching for. She twisted one free and swung it with both hands as if it were a broadsword and not a moldy, crumbling fence post.

"Okay, feel better?" asked Rachel.

Charley actually did feel better. "A little."

"And don't forget to keep your eyes peeled for stones," reminded Rachel.

Charley swung again, more confidently, and received a sliver for her effort. She cried out in pain and dropped the slat. She inspected her right hand and found a piece of wood embedded in the fleshy part of the thumb. She pulled out what she could, but a sliver remained in her hand along with substantial pain. Not wanting to rely on Rachel for help, she applied a kiss herself to make it better. Unfortunately, her attempt at field surgery and post-op pain management was not entirely successful. She shook her hand, hoping flapping it violently would cause the embedded splinter to fly out. Now she looked toward Rachel for help, her eyes full of tears.

"Let me see." Rachel took Charley's hand and made a motion toward the sliver with her fingers. Charley immediately snatched her hand away and wallowed into the mud flanking toward what was now barely a stream. Rachel followed her and pulled her back.

"Charley, don't. The water is muddy. Let me see if I can work it out."

Charley was not going to let Rachel near her hand. She made a show of ignoring the pain, even picking up the slat again to prove her toughness.

"It's fine. Let's go," she said, trying to be intimidating. She didn't wait for an answer and headed downstream. Rachel threw up her hands and followed her.

Charley switched the slat from her right hand to her left. She also began to glance furtively toward her injured hand while stoically bearing the throbbing ache in silence. They continued this way, not talking, for quite some time. Neither girl wanted to look behind to see the setting sun. Rachel reminded Charley, "This is the best time to find stones. You can see the glow easier."

They both lengthened their strides, hoping to get where they needed to be without the knowledge of how long it would take to get there, or even wherever there may be. Charley did spot a stone glowing in the mud, down slope. She scampered to it and picked it up with her left hand. In the dim light, her expression was a mixture of happiness and anguish. Her forehead glistened with fever sweat, and a tight-lipped smile framed gritted teeth. Charley was not pretending. She was in a great deal of pain.

"Don't worry, Rachel. I'm going to take my time and think of a good wish. I can do it. Remember the cake?"

Rachel nodded. "It was good cake, but I think you should wish to make your hand better."

"We have to have shelter first," said Charley, trying to maintain a brave face. "Let's keep looking for more."

She clambered up above the mud line to join Rachel near the hedge, her face set in a distinctly unbeautiful grimace.

"Let me look at it, Charley," pleaded Rachel.

"Shelter first."

The evening orchestra made up of crickets and katydids began warming up their instruments. If they had thought to look back upstream, they would have been treated to a breathtakingly beautiful sunset. Instead, they set out once again downstream. After traveling no more than a few steps, they almost ran over a boy who appeared out of nowhere. He was unremarkable in stature, but his clothes and bearing marked him as unusual, if not supernatural. He was dressed head to toe in black with leather boots and a heavy cape. He was clean and sweet-smelling, almost sickeningly so. His smiled was barely sincere enough to seem friendly.

"May I be of service?"

He waited patiently for an answer as the girls recovered their equilibrium. Rachel pulled Charley closer, her protective nature taking over.

Charley shook off the fever long enough to answer. "I'm in a lotta pain."

The boy's face expressed sincere concern. He approached Charley and placed the back of his hand on her forehead.

"You have a terrible fever. What has happened to you?"

Charley made the supreme effort to lift her arm up and showed him her hand. It had ballooned to cartoonish proportions causing Rachel to gasp at the sight.

"That is frightening. Although I am not a doctor, luckily for you, I am quite handy."

He waited for a beat, proud of his clever pun. Receiving no response, he placed one hand under Charley's and gently covered it with the other. He stroked it lightly with his fingertips. Charley sighed as he continued. To Rachel's great relief, Charley's hand seemed to shrink before her eyes. She didn't trust him, but there was no denying he was helping her friend. Charley's eyes closed as the boy's treatment soothed the fever and reduced the swelling. He kept up the treatment until Charley's hand returned to its pink, dainty, and dirty state.

When her eyes did open, she found herself staring into the boy's face, inches away. She drew back, snatching her hand away, as if he were totally unfamiliar. She felt a twinge of dizziness, but her hand no longer throbbed, and she could think clearly again.

The boy ignored Charley's disoriented condition and blithely said, "Allow me to introduce myself. My name is Stefano. I am pleased to have been of service."

He extended his hand again. Charley looked at her own injured hand with a stupefied look and allowed him to take it in his. The sliver remained, encased in healthy pink flesh. He shook her hand gently and then turned it palm upwards.

"Please relax. You won't feel a thing."

Charley showed no fear, allowing him to pinch the flesh of her hand and draw out the offensive wood. He tossed it to the ground without releasing her hand.

"You picked up a sliver somewhere, I'm afraid. No worries now. Good as new."

Charley blinked groggily. "Better," she said. "Now I remember. It was the wooden sword. It was filthy."

She looked at Rachel in accusation. As accustomed as she was to Charley's oscillating moods, Rachel was taken by surprise at her vehemence. A few minutes earlier, she was worried sick her best friend was in the grip of a fatal fever. Now, she was being accused of causing her injury. She steeled herself for a fight.

Stefano interrupted, "May I give you something?"

Charley looked at him and backed up a step to put Rachel between her and the boy. "Who are you again?"

Rachel declined as politely as she could manage, for both of them. "You've done enough. Thank you."

The boy lowered his voice as if to share a secret. "I want you to have it. I give one to everyone."

"That's so generous of you. Don't listen to my friend. She doesn't trust anybody," said Charley.

"Who could find me untrustworthy?" asked Stefano, feigning

disbelief.

"I don't. Why would you want to hurt me when you just saved my life?"

"Thank you…," said the boy, expecting a name.

"I'm Charley. And this is Rachel. We're looking for shelter. Do you live around here?"

"Indeed, I do," he assured her. He scanned their surroundings for anyone who might be watching as he reached inside his cape. He pulled out the strangest lollipop Charley had ever seen. "Here, take this."

Before Rachel could intervene, he handed the lollipop to Charley and waited. She held it in her hand while he nodded for her to go ahead and put it in her mouth. She took a sniff, smelling all her favorite flavors all at once. The head of the lollipop was a large diamond-shaped candy shell with pulsating colors twinkling and swirling inside.

Rachel studied it more closely and was disgusted to find lint, hair, and nail clippings stuck to the otherwise mouth-watering treat. Charley drooled, apparently unable to see the pocket flotsam coating the lollipop. She gave an involuntary shudder at her greedy desire for the sweet prize in her hand.

Still, she hesitated, remembering someone's warning about taking sweets from a stranger.

"Do you have one for Rachel?"

Rachel shook her head while the boy looked her over.

"Your friend isn't interested in my treats," he said without taking his eyes from Rachel. She wilted under his gaze for a few more seconds until he released her.

The boy pointed at Charley. "Are you going to taste it? I assure you this lollipop will be the most scrumptious treat you've ever had. You deserve it after the ordeal she put you through."

Charley looked the lollipop up and down again and scowled at Rachel. The colors pulsating inside mesmerized her. She shook her head to clear out the fog.

"You've been around here for a while, right?" she asked. "Do you know what happened to the people who come out at night? Why do they look like zombies?"

A flash of impatience crossed the boy's face. His tone became terse. "Some of the people who travel the river don't make it all of the way to the end. They get caught up wishing for their heart's desire. Now, try the lollipop."

"Are they like me?" asked Charley.

"Enchanting?" he said, making Charley giggle. "No. They are weak."

Charley smiled and pressed on. "Why don't the monsters attack them?"

"Because they decided to stay here and not move on. They are part of the River now."

"Are they like you?" Charley asked.

The boy made a derisive snorting sound. "No, the fools get so obsessed with stones and wishes they actually swallow a stone. They think they will be granted unlimited wishes and a lifetime of happiness. "Try the lollipop, Charley. You won't be disappointed," he prodded, his gaze softening.

"How...?" began Charley.

The boy took a step toward her and raised his voice, "No more questions!"

Charley flinched away, but the boy grabbed the fist holding the lollipop and forced it toward her mouth. She pushed it away with her free hand and Rachel added her strength to Charley's to keep the charm away.

"Just try it. You'll love it," he hissed through gritted teeth.

The girls succeeded in twisting free from him.

The timbre of his voice changed back, and he re-assumed the role of the kindly young gentleman. "As you wish."

He pocketed the candy and, with a swish of his cape and a lethal glare at Rachel, departed downstream.

Charley called after him, "Do you know how we can get out of here?"

He stopped and spun to face her. "Perhaps," he said with a sickly grin. He left without telling her more.

Charley set out to chase him, but Rachel held her back. Thinking better of following the strange boy, she sank back into the safety of Rachel's arms. Before he passed out of sight, Stefano turned once more and blew them a kiss.

CHAPTER TWENTY-FIVE

Disengaging from Rachel's protection, Charley declared, "I've got it. Why didn't I think of this earlier? I'm getting out of here!"

She pulled away from Rachel and turned her back to drop and root around in her satchel. Sensing disaster, Rachel sprinted to make up the gap between them. She arrived in time to grab Charley's hand before she could make a wish.

"Let go, Rachel. I'm leaving now. I will take you with me, but if you really want to stay you can find a stone and wish for a new friend."

Charley pulled her hand out of Rachel's grip and stepped away to make room.

"Charley— wait," pleaded Rachel.

Charley turned her back to whisper her wish. Rachel threw up her hands, hearing Charley clearly say, "I wish I could fly."

She winced and waited for the pain that had accompanied her previous physical transformations. Instead, a feeling of weightlessness came over her. Her spirits were lifted by a euphoria that erased all her usual feelings of doubt and fear. She spread her arms, but she was shocked to see snow white wings extending from her shoulders. Happy tears practically jumped from her eyes.

"I'm an angel," she said in wonderment.

Rachel attempted to get her attention, but Charley ignored her.

"Charley, think about this. You might…"

Charley raised and lowered her wings tentatively and experienced a lift that set her off balance. In addition to the wings, she was experiencing a kind of internal modification that made her feel lighter than air. She stumbled to deal with her changing center of gravity. A full beat of her wings sent her staggering backwards, almost falling.

Charley tried, again and again, and eventually got the hang of it. Before long she was skipping forward and leaving the ground for short hops. All the while, Rachel chased her around, trying to keep her grounded.

"I'll come back for you, Rachel! Don't worry!" shouted Charley, pulling away from her friend.

Rachel begged her. "It's too dangerous to fly."

"Everything's dangerous according to you." Her head bobbed dangerously close to Rachel's face.

"Don't do it, Charley."

"I can go home, Rachel. Don't you get it?"

She gestured awkwardly with her right wing. "I'm going to fly over that hedge, and you can't stop me. I'll get home and be famous, and everyone will be jealous because I'm beautiful and I'm a genius, and I can fly."

"You're going to regret it," insisted Rachel.

Charley had never looked more determined. Rachel bit her tongue as she waited for her friend to think a little longer about the possible ramifications of this decision. The young girl pondered her options for almost three seconds before running downstream at full speed. Rachel chased after her, watching as Charley got the hang of the rhythm. She was airborne for many strides at a time now, bounding farther and farther away from her.

Charley was now traveling faster than her legs could keep up. Liftoff was imminent. This was fortuitous because the path ahead was about to end. The familiar riverbanks topped by hedges marched forward and down into a sea of gray mist stretching in all directions. Charley panicked for a second, but there was no stopping now. She rose at first, letting out a triumphant whooping howl, but her exhilaration turned to hysteria as her inexperience betrayed her. She dropped into the mist and disappeared from Rachel's view as the older girl skidded to a halt at the cliff's edge.

"Charley!"

Down below, Charley was flapping for dear life, tumbling and careening like the leaf of an oak tree on a windy autumn day. She was able to pull out of her nosedive at the last possible second, avoiding a splattering collision with the rocky ground below. She climbed and rose, higher and higher, toward the murky gray sky. Her intended heading was the top of a spectacular waterless waterfall which dropped from the same general direction she had just plummeted. She entered the cloud and smiled broadly at Rachel's shocked expression as she rocketed past her to fly back upstream.

She called out, "Your turn, Rachel! Follow me!"

Charley climbed higher to get her bearings. She had subconsciously learned to coast on the air currents, allowing her to enjoy the exhilarating feeling of soaring with total freedom. She closed her eyes and imagined herself as part of a family of clouds, puffy and weightless, liberated from limits and boundaries. In this form, at this altitude, she was no longer a small girl with big problems. She shouted above the rushing wind, "This would be the perfect time for a song; like in a movie!" She floated on thermals for a little while longer until a change in the wind rocked her out of her reverie.

Charley flapped her arms to stabilize herself and looked down for the first time. A fleeting feeling of vertigo caused her to shiver. It was about time to head for home. With any luck, she'd be sitting down for dinner in no time. She surveyed the ground below, beating her wings and banking in wide circles.

"Now, which way is the farm?" she asked the wind. Her hair was streaming behind her, and her eyes squinted to search for landmarks. As far as her increasingly dry and itchy eyes could see there was only an endless forest with a dry riverbed running through it. No matter how far she flew over the vast green forest in any direction, there was only more forest; trees, trees and more trees. She dived down to fly lower over the riverbed, screaming in frustration.

Charley flapped furiously to level out as she flew at the level of the canopy. Birds squawked in surprise and gave her foul looks as she passed. She recognized a familiar beak heading her way. Cecil was flying toward her on a collision course. She lost her concentration and almost crashed into him. They each circled to pass again, and Charley heard Cecil cry at her with an angry tone. Charley wanted to find out what had gotten into her feathered friend, but she was too caught up in trying to stay airborne. Cecil turned tail and flew away.

Charley climbed skyward once again and was followed by a murder of crows emerging from the trees below. They cawed menacingly, and Charley flapped furiously to gain altitude, hoping to escape the angry birds.

Charley leveled off and flew upstream as fast as possible. The birds eventually lost interest in her, or possibly they were distracted from their pursuit by a dead squirrel.

Charley's muscles were growing tired, and her frustration was mounting. She swore at the trees, angry at the unfair, unsuccessful conclusion of her flight for freedom. She was not looking forward to seeing Rachel's smug face.

She wheeled in the sky in ever shrinking circles until dizziness almost forced her into a tailspin. She screamed in fury one more time like a three-wattled bellbird before heading back to Rachel and the captivity of the riverbed.

As she closed in on Rachel, an irritatingly common problem recurred. As usual, she did not know how to stop forces once she had set them in motion. She flapped awkwardly in what she hoped was reverse, careening and dipping. Rachel stood ahead looking out over the edge, unaware that Charley was about to touch down, or more accurately, crash down.

She tried to level off and execute a graceful landing, but that is a maneuver a recently-hatched birdgirl should practice from lower altitudes and with much less velocity. She failed to find the correct airspeed and angle of descent, and her landing gear was not in the proper position when she crashed, bounced, and cart-wheeled into the ground. She came to a stop in a bizarrely twisted jumble of wings and legs a few yards short of Rachel's feet.

She lay still with her eyes closed.

"Wow! I thought that would have hurt more."

She opened her eyes to see clouds rolling by across the sky. She flexed her fingers and wiggled her toes. She tried again. The complete lack of sensory response from her extremities alarmed her. She tried to raise her hand to her face, but nothing came into view. She could feel nothing at all. In her mind, she was slamming the ground with her heels and her fists but in reality, she was completely and utterly immobile. She sobbed and wailed as the gravity of the situation crushed the spirit from her shattered body.

Rachel's face came into view above her as she knelt at Charley's side.

"You're back! Are you okay?" Her face betrayed her concern. "Of course, you're not okay."

Rachel bit her lip as she looked over the damage. She knelt down close to Charley's face and whispered fretfully, "Charley, you're broken all over. I can't believe you're not screaming in pain."

"You'd like that, wouldn't you?"

Her voice sounded muted to her own ears. Rachel showed no sign she had heard her hurtful answer.

"I'm here to help you. Just like I've been here for you since you got here. I'll be right back. Don't' move."

A spasm of doubt rippled Charley's face. Rachel rose and disappeared from Charley's field of vision. Charley tried to shout at a volume Rachel could hear, but no sound escaped. She heard an echo inside her skull, and real fear crept into her internal voice. "I don't want to be stuck like this forever. I could get torn apart by wolves."

Hearing nothing from Rachel's direction, she raised her voice futilely. "I'm sorry, Rachel. Come back. You can't leave me like this.

Her desperation could find no outlet. Her body would not obey her commands. Even her mouth betrayed her. The frustration and anxiety that would have been conveyed by swinging fists and kicking feet half an hour earlier, was bottled and paralyzed.

She screamed at the top of her lungs, "Rachel, help me! You have to help me! Please!"

Rachel did return then to squat down beside her head. She looked deeply into Charley's eyes with sympathy.

"I'm sorry. I had to find a stone, Charley. I hope you know I would never leave you this way."

Charley tried to blink an answer. The futile fury in her broken body drained away to be replaced by shame and panic. Rachel stroked Charley's face with her hands. She knelt and made her best effort to wrap her arms around the young girl.

"Charley, calm down. Shhh. It will be alright. You'll be alright."

She raised her head to look down on Charley. Rachel's initial reaction on regarding Charley's face was an intense involuntary shudder. Her forehead was a mess of matted hair, her cheeks a smear of dirty tear streaks, and an oil slick of fluid pooled under her nose. Her lips were cracked and dry. Rachel opted not to get a closer look at the rest of the Charley's injuries and she quickly cleared her expression so as not to scare her further. Charley's breathing was becoming more labored and ragged. Rachel placed the glowing stone on her chest.

"You probably broke your neck when you came down," offered Rachel. "And your legs, too."

"... and your arms, I mean wings."

"... and your back."

"Might as well include all bones and organs, to be safe. This might hurt a little. I wish everything on Charley's body that is broken or damaged was fixed."

Charley sent her consciousness around to pick up status reports from all the various sensory stations in her body. In a rush, they all reported back simultaneously as an excruciating tidal wave of pain. She felt the shooting agony of a million pins and needles piercing every inch of skin on her body all at once. She cried out in pain and convulsed into a fetal position. As the pain subsided, she noticed her body had returned to life, and she smiled through gritted teeth.

She swallowed a lungful of air and then another.

"I don't know what to say, Rachel. You saved my life."

"The conventional response is, 'Thank you.'"

"That's not even close to enough but, thank you. For a second there, when you looked at me, I thought you were going to freak out."

"You had me scared, I'll admit. Human bones aren't supposed to stick through the skin."

It was Charley's turn to shudder. She looked down at herself to find blood stains in spots on her clothes. She gasped, but a brief survey of her limbs found everything in order. She smiled through tears.

"Am I still beautiful?"

"Of course, you are, Charley," replied Rachel, stroking her hair.

"I probably shoulda been more careful," she said between sniffs. Rachel nodded her head. "I probably shoulda listened to you. You always know when I'm about to do something stupid."

"Charley, it's not about me," said Rachel as kindly as possible. "You go and do whatever you want without thinking about the consequences. Life is a series of challenges. You need to learn sometimes you might not be ready for the challenge."

"So, I can never try to do something that's challenging?"

Rachel paused. "I said, sometimes. Sometimes the first step you take is the top of a staircase, and sometimes it's a cliff. I'm saying, think things through before you jump, so you don't break your neck."

Charley was calmer, but still in distress. "That sounds like something an old person would say."

"Of course it does. Young people who jump off cliffs without a parachute don't hang around long enough to say the opposite; even if they've somehow sprouted wings."

She was finally able to uncurl and stand with Rachel's help.

"Welcome back, Charley. You were almost a goner there," she said hugging the smaller girl.

Charley stepped back. "I'm lucky you didn't just leave me behind. I've been a real jerk."

"Friends don't abandon each other," Rachel said with finality.

"I guess I don't have any friends then. The girls at school wouldn't put me out if I were on fire," said Charley as she stretched and tested her muscles.

Rachel gave her a sympathetic look, "We can be stupid sometimes."

"Why are girls so mean to each other?" asked Charley with all seriousness.

"Sometimes, it's rivalry. Sometimes, it's jealousy. Sometimes it's both at the same time."

"Really?"

"You didn't know that? You think boys are competitive and bloodthirsty? Girls can be just as bad. Are you ready to start walking again, Humpty Dumpty?"

Charley thought about Rachel's words. "I guess you're right," she said. She looked Rachel directly in the eye. "Not all of us are, though."

Rachel understood what she meant immediately. She smiled at her and said, "No, not all of us are. Some of us will be there to put you back together again when you crack."

Charley beamed at her. Rachel put her arm around her shoulders, saying "And, of course, you'll help me get up again when I fall."

"You never do anything wrong, Rachel," said Charley without a trace of sarcasm.

Rachel scoffed. "No one's perfect, Charley. We all fall. Will you be there for me? Will you be there for the next girl?"

Charley was deadly serious. "I'll try, Rachel."

"Good, that's two less mean girls in the world," said Rachel with all the certainty of stating two plus two equals four.

"I'm going to leave the skies to Cecil. I think he's still mad at me." She jabbed a thumb at the sky. "I saw him up there, and he almost crashed into me.

She chewed her lip thoughtfully. "I think he might have sent some crows after me too."

"Do you really mean it, Charley?"

"You mean about Cecil?"

"No, about flying."

"Sure. It was amazing while I was up there, but it was kind of lonely too. It's nice to get away from things once in a while, but I guess you can't get totally away from your problems."

"Nope, they don't go away if you run and hide from them."

Charley nodded, considering that. "We should get going, I guess."

Charley cleared her throat. Without looking in Rachel's direction, she said, "I'm sorry."

"You really are," Rachel responded playfully with a smile. She was content with any apology, even if it was compelled by shame and a near-death experience.

"You're my best friend Charley, and I like you better every day," said Rachel.

Charley licked her lips. "Rachel, when you fixed me, you didn't unchap my lips."

"Sorry about that," said Rachel.

"Now I know why birds don't have lips," observed Charley.

Rachel chuckled. They collected their belongings. Rachel put her hands on her hips.

"Now, about this mist..."

CHAPTER TWENTY-SIX

The blanket of thick, gray, rolling fog was still there, stretching away to merge with the silver sky. The vista before them was a blank canvas. The trees and vegetation ended at the misty shore. Tendrils of vapor snaked onto the solid ground to wind around their feet as they approached the edge of unknown.

"Is this the end of the river?" asked Rachel.

"I didn't get a good view while I was down there because I was flapping for my life, but it was definitely not the end of the river. It's a cliff."

Rachel leaned out to get a better look down, causing Charley to grasp her arm and pull her back.

"Be careful," Charley warned.

Instead, Rachel got down on her belly and reached into the mist. She scooped up a handful of nothing. She looked up at Charley with a confused expression.

"It's just fog."

She waved her hand to sweep the mist away, revealing nothing but more gray. Standing, she threw up her hands.

Charley became more annoyed and angrier rather than frightened or worried. She shouted a wordless curse out into the blankness to the unseen powers-that-be who were responsible for this predicament.

"What do we do now?"

Rachel sat with legs crossed at the fog's edge and calmly pulled some jerky out of her backpack. Charley kicked at the ground in a mini-tantrum. Rachel chewed patiently, enjoying her performance.

"Charley, why don't you sit and relax. We need to think, not scream at the wind."

Charley plopped down and stated flatly. "We're out of stones. We're stuck here."

She stood inches away from the mist and looked out thoughtfully. Rachel scooted close to join her. Charley crossed her arms and gripped her chin with a filthy hand. They thought for quite a few seconds before footsteps behind them broke the silence.

The girls turned to see a tall, pretty, young woman walk up to them and stop at the fog's edge. She was dressed in a white silk shirt with tailored charcoal slacks. She wore expensive and high-heeled shoes that were wildly inappropriate for traversing down the river, but she appeared to be suffering no discomfort. Her long hair was pinned up in a casual yet elegant style, and her eyes were smiling. She tilted her head in a relaxed manner and looked down at the two girls who stared back dumbly.

Charley craned her neck to look up at the woman.

"Hello," she blurted.

"Hello, yourself," replied the woman. She surveyed her surroundings with an air of authority. She dipped a shoe into the mist and pulled it back.

"My name is Caroline. And you are?"

Neither girl could muster enough wits to provide an answer.

"Do you have something to tell me? Are you supposed to be some kind of spirit guide?"

Both girls shrugged their shoulders and held out their hands palm-skyward in ignorance.

"Are you just going to sit there and stare? Because I'm in kind of a hurry." She looked at them expectantly.

Charley was still too surprised to think clearly. She pointed back the way they had come. "Did you...? What about...?"

The woman cocked her head and gave Charley a quizzical look.

Charley pointed at the sea of mist. She sputtered, "The fog... Can't... We... Cliff... Caroline..."

The woman gave up.

"Alright then. Thank you. You've been so very helpful, but as I said, I'm in a hurry."

She saluted them and took one step into the mist, feeling her way. Satisfied with her footing she continued carefully. The friends watched as she strode confidently into the mist. She appeared to walk down a gradual slope, her head eventually disappearing, without looking back.

The girls waited in shock, expecting to hear her screaming as she plummeted to certain death far below. When nothing of the kind happened, they looked at each other and decided in silent agreement to follow her. They shouldered their belongings and tentatively walked into the vapor up to their ankles. Their feet were no longer visible, but so far, so good. They advanced to their knees and then cautiously to their waists.

Charley held up her arms as if she was walking into an ice-cold mountain lake. They stopped and turned to face each other.

"It feels weird," said Charley.

Rachel nodded in agreement. Charley remained on her tip toes in the second position, waiting for Rachel to do something. She gasped as Rachel dunked her body beneath the surface. She spun around, whimpering with a panicked expression, looking for Rachel. Rachel popped up in front of her, causing her to shriek.

"Don't do that!" she shouted, pushing Rachel backward.

"Just keep walking, Charley. We'll be alright." She grabbed her friend's free hand. Charley lifted her chin to breathe precious air for as long as she could as she was pulled forward into and ultimately below the surface.

Charley held her breath for the whole ordeal as they walked quickly down through the thick wetness. A few seconds of walking took them down out of the befuddling cloud and onto a moderately steep slope which evened out, eventually sloping into the serene scenic river valley to which they were accustomed. They looked up to find the sea of fog was now a gray, cloudy sky. At their back, nothing seemed unusual, just valley. To their left and right, the hedges stood resolutely. One face made a fleeting appearance and disappeared downstream on a breeze. Of the beautiful woman, there was no sign.

Charley held out her arms and spun around, "Come on! Where's Caroline? We were right behind her!" She pumped her fists in fury. "Rachel, we were right behind her. I am sick and tired of mysteries."

Rachel had no explanation. Charley paused to take a deep breath resulting in a short coughing fit.

"Charley, are you okay?"

"I was hoping when you fixed me that you fixed everything." More coughing ensued. "I guess not."

"I'm sorry. We'll think of something. Here. Have some water."

She offered her canteen to Charley who accepted it with shaking hands and drank deeply.

"There's nothing you can do about it."

"Come on. We can't just sit here. I need to get home."

The riverbanks were wider here, covered with cool, springy turf. If not for their sour moods and the coming night, they might have enjoyed themselves. Charley muttered under her breath and cursed cottonwood seeds for floating on the breeze. Rachel hummed a tune as she scampered up one slope and back down, leaping over the rocks in the middle to climb the opposite slope and down again. Charley sneered at her as she passed, puttering along slowly, stumbling in the stream bed.

A loud roaring blast from upstream startled them both. They looked at each other in panic. Rachel grabbed Charley by the wrist and dragged her away. They felt the ground shake, and another roar shook the leaves on the trees and caused birds to take flight. Charley let out a terrified scream and froze in place. "He's back!" Rachel lifted a finger to shush her and pulled her to a tree on their right. She helped Charley up. "Climb as high and as fast as you can."

Rachel followed her, climbing rapidly to be hidden by the leaves. They felt the vibrations from the giant's enormous feet pounding the earth and coming their way. Rachel grabbed hold of Charley's ankle to stop her and held a finger to her lips to silence her. Charley's eyes were as wide as fried eggs, but she suppressed the urge to scream again.

The girls waited as the pounding and bounding grew louder.

They wrapped their arms around the nearest sturdy branch to avoid being shaken loose like ripe pears to be squashed by the approaching monster. He came into view through the foliage and slowed to a stop. His drooling, snotty-nosed head was at their level. From their hiding place, they got their first good look at his large head in profile. His bulging bloodshot eye panned and searched the ground below. He snorted and raised his long bulbous drippy nose to sniff the air. The monster took in a deep breath and let out another eardrum-splitting roar.

"CHICKENFINGERS!"

He leapt straight up and came down with a heavy earth-quaking thud which almost shook the girls loose from their perch. Then there was silence. His head turned from side to side watching for any movement.

On the opposite bank, the hedge rippled, and the semblance of two green girls appeared. From their perch in the tree, the real live girls were amazed to see the imposters draw the monster's attention to themselves. The monster spotted them and scrambled up the slope toward the illusions. The figures appeared to run downstream, and the monster gave chase, disappearing but leaving his stench behind.

The girls waited for a few minutes, barely breathing for that very reason. Rachel gave Charley the signal to climb down. When they reached the ground, Charley hugged Rachel. "He won't give up," she said.

Rachel agreed, "He's like a dog with a bone."

"We're lucky the hedge helped us for a change," observed Charley. "I wonder why he stopped here. Do you think he could smell us?"

"I doubt he can smell anything besides himself." She waved her hand in front of her face. "This smell needs its own species."

"What do we do now? If we follow him, we'll get caught."

"Well, we can't go back. That's obvious." She looked around and up at the tree that had been their hiding place. "We're in trouble."

"Perhaps, I could help," said a voice.

Charley instinctively put Rachel between herself and the voice. She looked around Rachel to see Stefano standing on the top of the right bank, leaning against a pine tree. He now wore a buckskin vest over a white ruffled shirt tucked into buckskin pants. He had a raccoon hat on his head with the tail hanging over his right ear.

"I'm so glad that we meet again. Our last meeting was too short." He walked down the slope with a cocky swagger, smiling and waving as if he was walking onto a stage in front of an adoring crowd. Charley stared at him as Rachel looked around to find the crowd who was cheering his arrival. Charley stepped around Rachel and approached him without concern. In a monotone voice she said, "Yes, we could use your help again. You found us just in time. We had given up hope."

"Of course, I can help. One of my homes is close by."

The boy reached Charley and took her hand. "You're that charming young lady I found on Death's door. If I hadn't come along, you would be a charming young ghost right now."

He stroked her palm with his finger, examining it for any lingering swelling or tenderness. Charley giggled as if it tickled.

"Allow me to re-introduce myself. I am Stefano, and you will be my guest. Do you have any bags, any belongings? Could I help carry something for you?"

Rachel gripped the straps of her backpack tightly and said, "We don't need any help."

Charley sneered at her. "Don't mind Rachel. She was scared silly by that monster."

The boy looked at Charley with incredulity and an arched eyebrow.

"Of course, I wasn't frightened at all. He's probably harmless," said Charley.

"Oh no, he's a killing machine. He would have torn you limb from limb," said Stefano casually, shocking the smile from Charley's face.

"It's rare to see Stink hunting during the day. He must be on a mission. Wait a minute. Is he hunting you? Did you hurt his feelings? He can be quite sensitive."

Charley tried to be vague as she looked back and forth between Rachel and Stefano. "I may have done something that might be the reason he is looking for us."

Rachel gave her a dirty look.

"Looking for me, I mean," admitted Charley.

Rachel shook her head slightly and gave her a look that meant, 'Don't say anything else.'

Stefano appeared to be satisfied with her answer. He maintained his hold on Charley's hand.

"Well, the day is nearing its end. Shall we go?"

Rachel motioned for Charley to huddle and discuss their options. Their recent affirmation of sisterhood was apparently forgotten, as Charley had no interest in hearing what Rachel had to say. Stefano offered her his arm and Charley could not suppress another small giggle. She slid her hand over his arm, and they began to walk downstream again. She looked back at Rachel following with a gleeful, excited expression as if she had been chosen to be Princess by Prince Charming.

CHAPTER TWENTY-SEVEN

They strolled, too slowly for Rachel. A gap in the hedge led to another dry riverbed leading back and away at a sharp angle. Charley, holding hands with her new best friend, entered the gap and moseyed along, chatting away as if ravenous monsters didn't exist and night was not about to fall. Charley paid no attention to the strangeness surrounding them.

Rachel called to her friend. "Charley, it's getting dark. Shouldn't we be hurrying?"

Charley looked up at Stefano, not bothering to turn in Rachel's direction.

"We are close to your home, aren't we?" she asked.

"Don't worry. You're perfectly safe with me," he said as he patted her hand.

Rachel was not convinced, so she trotted to scout ahead. The river bent slightly, and she hesitated, not wanting to be out of sight of the happy young couple. The hedges in this area were taller. Leafy trees also lined both sides of the riverbed, further blocking the waning sunlight. The air was still, and the usual constant music of birds or insects was gone. The only sound was the crunch of her footsteps on cool, wet leaves.

She waited.

Charley and her boyfriend had picked up their pace. Charley was still beaming and chattering on while Stefano's face betrayed a hint of fear and possible annoyance. Charley disengaged from Stefano's arm and ran ahead to speak with Rachel. Stefano ignored them both and trotted past.

She breathlessly recounted their short time alone. "We're having the best time, Rachel. Stefano was telling the coolest stories. Did you know he once killed a giant spider with a baseball bat?"

Rachel dragged Charley forward by the hand. "Oh yeah, I read all about it in the newspaper."

"There's a newspaper here?"

"No, Charley," said Rachel with a sigh of exhaustion. Charley ignored her tone and kept prattling along.

"Then he took silk from the spider and twisted it into a rope. He said it's magic. He's going to show it to me."

"Great, if we live that long. Come on."

They hurried to catch up with him as night fell. Blazing torches lined the riverbed leading the way toward a cheery gingerbread-style house surrounded by a ring of sturdy oak trees. Stefano stood between two torches many yards away with a forced smile. He beckoned them forward with his hat in his hand. Charley pulled free and skipped ahead to join him.

While Charley caught up to Stefano and inserted her hand into his, Rachel hesitated at the limit of the lighted path, frozen in suspicion. She looked at the couple and her vision blurred. The smoky torchlight stung her eyes forcing her to look away.

When her eyes adjusted, she found herself flanked by gnarled and lifeless and leafless black trees. The healthy and sturdy green hedge was gone. She gagged at the moldy sickly odor swirling visibly around her head. She held up her hand to block torchlight and peered in Charley's direction to see the path was now a gloomy tunnel ending in a greenish vortex of mist. As she focused her attention on the mist, the mist's attention became focused on her. The vapor solidified and advanced toward her through the tunnel. The air pulsed with pres-sure, wreaking havoc with her heartbeat, and assaulting her eardrums.

Her first primal reaction was to back away. As she blindly retreated, her foot landed on a large, squishy mushroom causing her to slip and fall awkwardly and land on her side. The odor of moldy leaves and decay made her retch. She hurriedly pushed her upper half up off the ground to find fresh air, steadying herself on her right hand. A long slimy centipede slinked onto her middle finger and attempted to climb her arm. With a flick of her hand and a short involuntary squeak, she saved the centipede hundreds of thousands of steps by flinging it far away. She scrambled to her feet.

"Charley! Where are you?"

Charley's voice grounded her. "Come on, Rachel! Stop fooling around!"

Charley was less than twenty steps away. The surrounding area was suddenly filled with sounds of the forest again. What was once a throbbing attack of dread was now a symphony of trilling, buzzing, chirping, and croaking. The light from the torches gleamed and flickered, reflecting off the moist trunks of tall, healthy trees. All seemed normal.

Rachel stirred to join her friend. Charley and their host turned to leave her behind. Before she could take a step, the torches to her right and left guttered and died, plunging her into blackness. The musty smell of dying leaves returned to her nostrils. Directly behind her, the rumbling sound of something large taking in an enormous gulp of air was followed quickly by a blast of hot, fetid breath on the nape of her neck. It propelled her forward like the crack of a starter's pistol.

With the presence of a gigantic marauding beast at her back as motivation, she sprinted along the path to catch up to Charley. As she sped, the torches blinked out behind her. Something slithering with a malevolent purpose was scant yards behind her. She didn't dare slow down or turn. Ahead, Charley and Stefano had reached the front door of the house. Charley turned in time to see Rachel, her eyes wide in terror, crash into her arms. They both fell in a heap at Stefano's feet.

He reached down to help Charley to her feet while Rachel remained seated and scrambled to put her back to the solid door of his home. Stefano steadied Charley by holding her arms with his hands. He gave her a concerned look and reached up to brush the hair from her face.

"Are you alright?"

Charley was still frozen in surprised silence from Rachel's violent arrival and, as a result, all she could do was nod.

"You must be starving. Let's get inside and see what's for dinner, shall we?"

He pushed the door open, and Rachel fell inside. She crawled away into the house as Charley allowed herself to be ushered in by their host. When the door closed, they both remained motionless while Stefano tossed his hat onto a rack and called out, "Gustav, I'm home!" He continued down a hallway and disappeared around a corner.

Charley scowled down at Rachel and whispered harshly, "What is wrong with you? You're acting like a maniac."

"There's something out there," said Rachel with a shaking voice.

Charley dismissed her fears. "And we don't have to worry about it because Stefano is going to protect us. Honestly, you're acting like a two-year-old."

Rachel stood and tried to pull herself together. "I don't trust him," she stated with certainty and conviction.

"Don't be silly. We'd be out there in the dark right now if it weren't for him. Now, get a grip."

Charley took a moment to look in a mirror on the wall and straighten her hair.

She frowned. "Oh my god, I look awful. He's going to think I'm a wild animal."

Rachel continued to warn Charley. "There's something wrong about him... and this place." She looked around at a faded and dismally dated foyer.

Charley rounded on Rachel and pointed to the door. "Then leave. Go outside and see if Stink will keep you safe and feed you."

"Something's not right, Charley. I'm not letting you out of my sight."

Charley was about to respond when Stefano poked his head around the corner. "What are you doing out there? Come on in."

He waved to the girls and disappeared again.

Following his lead, they turned the corner and walked down a thin hallway with white plaster walls riddled with spidery cracks. The wooden floor creaked despite the light tread of two young girls. Charley led confidently with Rachel close behind.

They found themselves outside a cluttered living area with a low ceiling, brightly lit by dozens of small candles on a wide railing circling the room. Stefano was inside, lighting the last of the candles. Overlapping rugs of different colors and styles covered the floor, and plump cushions were strewn about for seating. The candles tried their best to give the room a fuzzy, comfortable glow, but their efforts failed to soften or warm a wide stone fireplace gaping cold and dark on one wall. The light bounced off a barrier of icy air. The girls backed away from the entrance, almost spilling into another room behind them.

"Come in. Have a seat. I'll see if Gustav has something cool for us to drink. I'll be right back."

He left them again. The girls entered the room and Rachel stooped to pick up a cushion, never taking her eyes off the fireplace. She placed it next to the cushion at Charley's feet, and they both sat down, comfortable, but not at ease.

Stefano returned quickly, carrying a silver tray holding a pitcher of a dark liquid and two glasses. Placing the tray on the table, he filled the glasses and carried them over to the girls.

"This is a cider Gustav makes from apples and pomegranates. It's quite good warmed, for cold winter nights, but I like it better cold. It's very refreshing."

He handed one glass to Charley and clinked it with his own. Tipping it back, he drained the glass. Charley paused for a moment and took a sip out of politeness.

"Aaahh, so good. Now, to see about dinner."

He walked to the table, placed the glass down on the tray, and left the room, bowing to them on his way out. Charley tipped back her own glass and made pretend-gulping sounds.

Rachel leaned over and whispered, "He could have poured me a glass. Now, can you see he's not Mr. Wonderful? And you can stop with the glug-glug-glug. You're not fooling anybody."

Charley looked down to hide her guilty expression. Rachel walked to the table and picked up the pitcher. She sniffed it and looked at Charley.

"Do you feel dizzy? Is it drugged?"

"Of course not. If you were nicer to him, he would probably be friendlier to you. You have been kind of mean to him."

"Can't you see this place is creepy? We don't know anything about him."

"He told me all about himself and his family while you were being rude."

"Rude?" She closed her eyes and waved Charley's accusation away. "So, what did he tell you?"

"I don't remember," said Charley, looking puzzled. "That's weird."

"You probably don't remember because it was you who was doing all the talking."

Charley took a long gulp from her glass. Rachel took another sniff and then a swig directly from the pitcher. She cocked her head, stuck out her lower lip and said, "Hmmm, not bad." She carried the pitcher to Charley and poured more cider into her glass.

"I still think there's something wrong about this place and your boyfriend."

Charley turned red from embarrassment. "He's not my boyfriend, Rachel. Why would you say that?"

"Oh, please. You're practically drooling. Well, anyway I don't trust him, and I'm the one who's going to protect you from him."

She looked toward the fireplace and pointed adamantly, "That. That is bad, Charley. Evil bad."

Charley nodded in agreement. "I don't like it either. I feel like it's watching us."

Rachel took Charley's hand and pulled her to her feet. "Let's get out of here."

Charley refused to budge. "No, Rachel, we can't."

"I mean this room. We're trapped in this house tonight, but we don't have to stay here in this room."

Charley placed her glass on the tray, and together they peered outside the room. Hand in hand, they took cautious steps across the entrance hall. The room opposite was unlit, but the light from the living room illuminated the edge of a gray tarpaulin covering a large mound which almost filled the room. It was taller than the girls. Rachel took a step inside and squatted down to lift the tarpaulin. Her fingertips stuck to the tacky cloth, causing her to recoil and shake her hand free. She pulled away and looked back to consult with Charley to find her staring blankly and chewing her hair.

Rachel reached for the tarp again. With thumb and forefinger, she lifted a corner a few inches off the floor. This slight action triggered a shudder to ripple through the mound beneath, accompanied by a pitiful and despondent sigh. She flicked her fingers to release the cloth and Charley grabbed her by the collar, yanking her backward to the uncertain safety of the hallway.

Rachel sat heavily on her backside. She gurgled and pawed at her neck until Charley let go of her collar. Neither of the girls could take her eyes off the mound.

"I don't want to see what's under there, Rachel."

Rachel gasped. "Couldn't you have just said so instead of strangling me?" She got to her feet and straightened her shirt.

"Now, you're getting the picture. We're in danger here."

Charley attempted to put on a brave face. "No. No. Come on, Rachel. That's not why I don't want to see. This is none of our business, that's all. Let's go. Stefano must be this way."

She spun to her left and left the undulating mound behind. Rachel caught up, and they linked arms to walk side by side down the cramped hall lit weakly by smoky candles. The first room they passed had a large dining table and chairs with virtually every inch of wall covered by paintings of men in hunting clothes. They continued past a series of unlit rooms on both the right and the left. Charley frowned. Her forehead wrinkled in concern and her nose wrinkled in disgust at the noisome sickness emanating from the rooms. Their eyes burned and watered from the oily smoke.

Charley whispered, "I don't think anyone has ever lived in

these rooms."

"It's probably more accurate to say nothing living has ever been in these rooms."

Charley pulled her close and held her arm. "Stop it. You're scaring me."

Rachel nodded once and wagged a pointing finger under Charley's nose.

"Good, now you might use some sense. As long as we stick together, we'll be fine."

They moved forward together, steps synchronized, and arms linked. Voices emanated from a room not far ahead and light spilled into the hallway. When the girls reached what turned out to be the kitchen, they found Stefano staring at them with a grim and menacing look on his face. His stern gaze turned angry, flickered for a second to raging, and then softened back to stern again. The girls huddle close together. Despite his stature, the teenage boy wore the look of a disapproving, even dangerous, adult. A tense moment passed while they waited for him to announce the appropriate punishment for exploring the house without permission. Instead, Stefano smiled. They relaxed slightly as his cruel and savage gaze softened.

"I was about to come and tell you dinner will be served momentarily."

He took Charley's hand and gave it a delicate kiss. "I hope you'll be pleased."

He then turned his back to return to the preparations. Rachel mouthed a string of words proper ladies don't use, directly into Charley's face. Charley responded silently with glaring eyes and a shushy mouth. Rachel relented and shoved Charley into the warm kitchen where Stefano dipped a large spoon into a pot.

The pot sat on an old black stove along with an enormous, cooked turkey in a pan and three other pots a-simmer, each with its own mouth-watering aroma. Thick slices of bread were arranged, still steaming, in a wicker basket on a butcher block table in the middle of the room. An icebox stood in a corner, and a cart with plates and silverware was tucked inside the doorway. They waited nervously for some direction as Stefano sipped from the spoon and smacked his lips.

A tall, lanky man carrying a carving knife melted into the kitchen from a pantry, eliciting a pair of brief shrieks from the girls. Long locks of straight jet-black hair ran down his forehead like drips down the sides of a paint can. The streaks stretched to meet a pale, expressionless, and totally hairless face. He wore a black shirt, black tie, and pressed black slacks. He wore no shoes. An apron covered with flour and dark red stains protected his dress clothes. He stopped for a moment to look at the girls and disregarded them instantly.

"This is Gustav. He's been with the family for years. He's a talented chef, and he's been working hard all day. I asked him to prepare something extravagant for this special occasion. Say hello, Gustav."

Gustav reluctantly tilted his head to the absolute minimum angle, and for the absolute minimum length of time necessary to be considered a nod. Stefano appeared satisfied and attempted to get the girls excited about the impending dinner.

"There's turkey, potatoes, stuffing, collard greens, turnip, and those pearl onions everyone loves. And there's pie for dessert if Gustav didn't eat it all himself. Are you starving? You must be starving."

Rachel tilted her head from side to side, "I could eat."

Charley waved her hand in Rachel's face and turned to Stefano saying, "I'm starving. It's nice of you to go to so much trouble just for us."

Something made a clucking sound at the stove.

"It is nothing. It is the custom in my family to fill guests with food until they can't fit out the door, but with someone as tiny as you, that would take years of meals."

Charley blushed. "I doubt I could ever get that big. My mother says I eat like a bird."

"Your mother sounds delightful."

Gustav cleared his throat to get Stefano's attention. The boy was in the way, leaning against the stove. Stefano moved away, allowing Gustav to pull down the oven door. He reached in with bare hands to pull out a baking dish holding a deep golden-brown pie with a dark red liquid bubbling and oozing out of the top. He appeared not to notice the dish was as hot as lava. The girls looked at each other, amazed.

Rachel whispered, "How could Gustav be working all day on this meal, when we only ran into Stefano a little while ago?"

Charley chewed her lip and thought for a second with a furrowed brow. She toyed with a lock of her hair, unable to answer the question.

Before she could use her enhanced intelligence to guess at the riddle, Stefano spun and put his arm around her, leading her out of the kitchen. He distracted her with more flattery and compliments while Gustav loaded up the cart with dinner under Rachel's watchful eye. It did look delicious, and she was starving. She looked up from the feast before her to find Gustav standing to one side, sharpening a carving knife with a stone as he glared at her.

Finished honing his weapon, he reached for the cart. Rachel had to jump out of his way to avoid being run over. She followed him to find Stefano holding Charley's hand and reading her palm. Charley was enthralled. Rachel tapped her on the shoulder to distract her and pointed down the hall where Gustav was still pushing the cart.

"Our dinner is getting away."

Stefano bowed to Charley, retaining his hold on her hand. "Shall we dine?" he asked, placing Charley's hand on his right arm. He covered it with his own and led her away with Rachel close behind.

Rachel listened to the cart ahead as it rattled down the dingy hallway. The happy couple followed, Charley prattling on as if she were enjoying a sunshine stroll along the riverbank. Rachel thought back to the expression on Stefano's face and the counterfeit smile he bestowed on his young admirer. Everything about him seemed false. She chewed a dirty finger, wondering how to break the spell he had cast on Charley. Candles flickered as she passed by. She told herself it was due to the movement of the whole group, but the hair on the nape of her neck tickled as if, once again, something in the darkness followed close on her heels.

Faint sounds leaked out from the side rooms as they passed. Rachel quickened her pace and daringly jumped around Charley and Stefano as they walked down the center of the hallway. She darted ahead in order to avoid presenting herself as a target to any hand, claw, or tentacle that might be interested in dragging her to her doom. Light bulged out of the dining room, repelling the darkness of the hall away from the entrance. Like finding shelter from the rain, she stepped into the light and shivered to shake off the darkness.

Turning around, she realized she had left Charley far behind while fearing for her own safety. In the hallway, the pair walked stiffly toward her. Charley had stopped talking. Her eyes were wide and unfocused. Her mouth hung open, fixed with a slack-jawed smile. She continued to march without wavering. Stefano could have been taking a terrier for a walk. Charley was oblivious.

Stefano looked annoyed and determined, anxious to get to his nefarious plans. He shook Charley's hand off his arm and grabbed it to pull her along. He stopped in front of Rachel, outside the dining room, and Charley staggered to a halt, waiting for direction. He ducked inside, leaving them alone. Rachel faced Charley and grasped her hands.

"Charley! Charley! Are you in there? You have to come back!"

Charley stood silent and still, without meeting Rachel's eyes. She smiled, but it was the smile of one who might be daydreaming about the time they had won a giant stuffed monkey at the carnival. Rachel took Charley's face in her hands and squished her smile away, only to see it return when she let go. She shook Charley by the shoulders, and the only reaction was a tiny giggle.

Stefano popped out of the dining room, but before Rachel could scream at him, he snapped his fingers and took Charley's hand, pulling her away from Rachel.

"Come along. We mustn't let the food get cold, Charlotte."

As she passed, the old Charley gave Rachel an excited smile.

Aloud to Stefano, she said, "No, we mustn't." To Rachel she

mouthed the words, "Isn't he amazing?"

They disappeared into the room leaving Rachel fuming outside. She looked at the ceiling, trying to compose herself. Movement far back up the hallway drew her attention. Black whispering shapes, like jets of ink from octopi, began to billow out of the rooms to darken the smoky gray dimness. They swallowed whatever light could be absorbed from the remaining weak, defenseless candles. More shadows joined them, crowding into the corridor and gusting toward Rachel. The blackness thickened and a chorus of whispers grew in volume and despair. She stared at the approaching storm as it gained speed and shadows. A wave of howling hunger and sadness preceded it, pushing her backward, battering her mentally and physically. There was only one escape, into the dining room where an even more powerful peril waited. Rachel ducked inside before being swept up into the black tsunami of souls.

CHAPTER TWENTY-EIGHT

"**R**achel, look. It's a feast."

Rachel tore her eyes from the empty, black doorway to see Gustav at work, lighting long tapers in the centerpiece of a long table covered with a stained and shabby tablecloth. Rising despair took hold, and her mind reeled with questions. Platters and bowls wheeled out of the kitchen moments ago overflowed with steaming food. An oily wall of onyx guarded the doorway against escape. She shivered with a feeling of complete and utter hopelessness. The only thing keeping her from lying down on the floor terrified and curled into a ball was seeing Charley, oblivious and carefree again.

Their host sat at the head of the table with Charley to his right. His eyes were fixed on Charley with a look of malevolent avarice. His plate empty; napkin and silverware untouched. Charley wasted no time and loaded up her plate. A place was set to Stefano's left. He motioned for Rachel to join them. His gaze focused on her, and Rachel quailed. Her legs wobbled beneath her as she staggered to her chair. She clutched the high back and collapsed onto the seat.

His deep voice slapped her.

"I understand you have been Charlotte's guide. She has told me you have been... How did she put it? Kind of okay."

Rachel stared at her empty plate, avoiding his gaze.

Charley half-heartedly corrected him, her mouth full of food, "Rachel's my best friend, Stefano. She's been mostly very nice. It's just that sometimes she's kind of a killjoy."

Rachel flinched as her heart sank even further. Tears welled in her eyes as Charley picked up a turkey leg and took a bite. Stefano smiled at her dismay.

"You should eat."

"Yeah, Rachel, everything's delicious," said Charley without the slightest awareness of Rachel's mental state.

For appearance's sake, Rachel made an effort to lift her arm and reach for a serving spoon in a bowl. She scooped out mashed sweet potato and deposited it on her plate. She reached for a fork and stabbed at her dish only to plunge the fork into a slimy patty of moldy, worm-filled filth. She gasped and threw the fork to the floor. Stefano laughed at her, relishing her fright.

Charley could not be bothered to lift her head from her plate to notice. Noodles hung from her mouth as she chewed and slurped and lapped up food with super-human speed. Dribbles of gravy dangled off her bobbing chin. Her concentration was solely focused on feeding. She gave up all pretense of paying attention to the confrontation in front of her. Her fists rested on either side of the dish. Her fork, no longer being employed, stuck up out of her right hand. She ate like a hog, her nose almost buried in the slop and her hair forming a curtain around the plate. Rachel's stomach turned as she watched and listened to her friend's gulping and sucking and smacking.

The nauseating sounds stopped, and Charley slowly lifted her head an inch. Eyes opened dully in a face that looked like it had been hit with a turkey pot pie. Rachel gasped and covered her mouth with her hand, mortified to see the gluttonous display.

Stefano broke the silence. "Gustav, Charlotte appears to have finished her plate. Could you prepare another for her?"

Gustav, who had been standing motionless in the corner with his hands clasped in front of him, sprang into action, taking and quickly filling Charley's plate. He used a handful of Charley's hair to lift her head and slid the plate beneath it. Her face stared blankly at nothing until he tilted her head back down to an inch above the food. Charley immediately resumed feeding; her hair now rested in the mash of vegetables and potatoes and gravy.

Rachel rose angrily, and her chair flew back to smack the wall with a crack and tip over, landing with a thud on the rug. Charley didn't stop eating to take note.

"Why are you doing this to her? You're a fiendish monster!"

Stefano remained seated. He calmly spread his hands on the table in front of him. "Fiendish monster? Is that not a matter of opinion and degree? You may be right in your mind, but I, myself, do not feel the need to judge myself. It only leads to jealousy and bitterness. I am what I am. You are what you are."

"This seems like an opportune time to ask." He paused and looked at her with real puzzlement. "What are you?"

Rachel stumbled for an answer. "I'm her friend," she said finally.

"That is what you are to her. Surely, it is not all that defines you," said Stefano with ghoulish calm.

"It's the only thing that matters as far as you're concerned. We are leaving," she said with stiffening defiance.

Rachel circled the table and stood behind Charley. She pulled the young girl's shoulders back to lift her head from the plate. Charley's head snapped up and around to growl at her with teeth bared. Rachel started at her friend's frightening visage. Having been released, Charley returned to her feeding.

"You are feisty," Stefano said as he calmly and gracefully rose from his chair. Rachel's eyes widened as he changed. He was now over six feet tall, and his face sported a thin mustache. He wore a burgundy smoking jacket over a cream-colored shirt tucked into silken black pants. The shirt was unbuttoned to expose a large circular scar on his chest. Symbols and words in an arcane language were tattooed in and around the circle. He slid the chair under the table and watched Charley with cruel gleeful interest as she licked the plate clean. Rachel stood between Stefano and her friend. He leaned casually, his elbow resting casually on his chair back, his expression a bemused frown. Rachel stood defiantly, her arms crossed and feet spread apart. They faced off for a long moment.

"That's enough," he said at last. "Gustav, take care of all this and then prepare the den." He turned his back on Rachel and walked to a sideboard to pour himself a drink from a decanter.

Gustav approached Charley's side of the table. Rachel positioned herself between the servant and her friend. He ignored her. Bending down, he placed his hands under the table and, without a sound or any indication of effort, flung the table up and over to crash against the wall. Rachel rushed to put her arms around Charley, who sat, open-mouthed and motionless. Gustav gave them a sneering look and spun on his bare feet to head for the doorway. He strode out of the room without hesitation to be absorbed into the void of blackness.

The sound of glass clinking caused Rachel to spin her head around once again. Stefano, his back still turned, was pouring himself another glass. After drinking, he threw the glass toward the over-turned table, shattering it and causing Rachel to shriek.

He turned toward the girls and addressed them calmly. "You asked why I am doing this to her. The answer is, I am preparing her."

He waited for her to respond. Rachel waited for him.

"I am surprised you are not curious."

"It doesn't matter. I'm not going to let anything happen to her," said Rachel in defiance.

"You are powerless to stop me."

He stared at her for a moment as if trying to recall where they might have met before.

"Whatever you may be, you are unusual. I rarely have the chance to hold forth to an audience. So much of my work is done in private. I will explain."

He began to pace. "Are you sure you do not have any questions to ask about my work?"

Rachel remained silent, standing with her arms still tightly wrapped around Charley and her chair.

"So, you won't interrupt me once I start?"

"Get on with it, weirdo!" shouted Rachel.

"You see, young Charlotte is being prepared for my master. The monster's master, if you will. You might say my master feeds on life, on youth, on beauty and innocence, on what you would call good-ness. Though, it is more accurate to say he grows stronger when the force of goodness weakens."

Rachel had recovered some of her courage. "Charley won't be a very satisfying meal for your master then. She's sick."

"You promised not to interrupt."

He waved his hand, unconcerned. "I am aware of her flaws, but her malady is inconsequential. I have strengthened her sufficiently. There is kindness, compassion, and virtue within; useless traits though they are."

Rachel interrupted again, while Charley's eyes drooped closed. "And then when you're done with her, she'll turn into one of those things in the hall; those shadows?"

Stefano looked toward the door. "Are you referring to my pets? No, they were never living beings. They simply enjoy my company. Wherever I travel, they follow along. Lesser monsters, as it were."

"You're evil," stated Rachel plainly.

Stefano continued his stroll around the room. "You speak as if there is such a concept in absolute. Good and evil; they are weights on a scale. Evil or good, I do what I do. I make no choices, nor do I seek reward, nor do I feel the need to question. I serve a higher power. I am my master's tool. That is what I am."

"Take me instead," offered Rachel.

"I am still unsure of what you are. No, my master will be sufficiently pleased by Charlotte's gift. Tomorrow, another will pass through, and I will present him or her as well. I cull the herd, you see. Enough." He snapped his fingers again, releasing Charley.

Charley stirred. Rachel dropped to her knees to search the sickening mask on her face for signs of intelligent life.

"Charley! Charley! Are you alright?"

Charley shook her head. "I feel funny, but okay. Did I fall asleep?"

Rachel looked up to see Stefano standing behind Charley, a teenager again.

He spoke. "You were sleepy, Charlotte, after such a big meal. We let you nap."

Charlotte brightened, "Oh good. You two are friends now."

Rachel shook her head, "Not even close."

Charley scowled and leaned close to whisper in Rachel's ear.

"You are being rude, Rachel. You don't have the right to tell me who I can and can't be friends with."

Rachel stood and didn't bother to whisper. "Your pal Stefano is a monster. He is going to kill you and feed you to his master!"

Charlotte jumped up and turned around, her mouth opening wide in horror. For many seconds no one spoke. Stefano waited patiently, unconcerned.

"Rachel! Oh my god! You are terrible."

Charley lifted her hands to her face and felt the mess covering it like a beard. She scraped away the food as she circled Rachel. "Tell me that was a joke. That was a joke, right?"

She turned to Stefano and asked him, "She's kidding, right?"

"I will put it this way. She is wrong," said Stefano.

She spun to face Rachel again. "And he's going to drink my blood too, right? Very funny, Rachel."

Seeing neither of them smiling, Charley grew nervous. She shrieked when Gustav's head and shoulder popped into the room from out of the wall of shadow pets.

Stefano kept his eyes on the girls and asked Gustav, "Is everything in order?"

"Yes," replied Gustav in a voice like boots on gravel.

"Marvelous," said Stefano. With a wave of his hand, Charley returned to terrier state.

Rachel screamed, "Noooo!" and attempted to hug Charley. When Stefano approached, she screamed, "No! No! No!" and lashed out at him with her fists. The blows did not do the damage intended, however. Her fists punched through his body, striking nothing. In fact, they had no effect on Stefano at all. He looked as surprised as Rachel to see her left arm buried up to the elbow in his chest.

"How curious."

Rachel snatched her hand out of the nothingness that was Stefano.

"You are something unfamiliar to me, Rachel, definitely worthy of consideration," he said, eyeing her like a torturer examining his victim for weaknesses. "Perhaps later we will talk. I have work to do."

He took Charley by the hand and led her toward the door. Rachel grasped her friend's free hand and pulled. Her futile efforts resulted only in her being towed along. First Stefano, then Charley, disappeared into the bulging, writhing mass at the door. Afraid of being left behind, she held on to Charley's hand for dear life. She closed her eyes, held her breath, and allowed herself to be pulled into the black death.

CHAPTER TWENTY-NINE

Rachel emerged, tripping face first into the living room. Her ears were assailed by a piercing scream of terror which ended abruptly once she realized the source of the scream was her own throat. Her head pounded and although she had spent mere seconds passing through a dark limbo filled by echoes of tormented whispers, the emotional attack continued to pound inside her skull.

From her hands and knees, she searched the room for Charley and found her sitting calmly on a stool in the middle of the room facing the foreboding fireplace. Stefano's adult persona strode around the room kicking rugs and pillows aside to reveal a hard-packed dirt floor. Gustav stood by, waiting patiently, with a coil of gray rope. Rachel rose to her feet and rounded to face Charley, staring blankly ahead with her hands in her lap. She dragged Charley off the stool to collapse limply to the ground.

"Charley, wake up! You have to wake up."

Rachel tried slapping and shaking and pinching, but Charley did not react at all. She grabbed Charley by the armpits and dragged her away from the chair, but there was nowhere to go. The wall of blackness stood guard. Rachel collapsed down to the earthen floor with Charley.

Stefano's long legs stepped into her circle of vision. His hand reached down to place a finger under her chin, and Charley lifted her head, her expression an oblivious, adoring stupor. She took Stefano's hand and rose. They walked to the center of the room, and she resumed her place on the stool.

As Rachel wearily returned to her feet, she noticed for the first time, patterns in the earthen floor surrounding the stool. Curved iron bars like the heating elements of an electric stove surface formed concentric circles around Charley's seat. Black wrought iron strips connected the circles. The stool sat on a disk of a dull, silvery metal with long spars extending out like sun rays into the fireplace.

Stefano stepped up, snapped his fingers, and passed his hand in front of Charley's face. She shook her head, regaining consciousness. She blinked several times and her gaze settled on him, the vacuous smile remaining on her face as she turned her face to survey her surroundings. She spotted Rachel in a corner, her shoulders slumped, and head bowed.

"Rachel, you look awful. You should take a nap. Stefano and I will be talking for hours, I'm sure," said Charley, blithely unaware of any danger.

Rachel lifted her head to connect with Charley, but Stefano stepped between them.

"Yes. Charlotte. Do you recall the story I told you about the spider and the rope I fashioned from its silk?"

Charley clapped her hands. "Yes. You hit it with a baseball bat until its head split."

Stefano's face betrayed his annoyance. "To be precise, in the story I told you, I used the femur from a former prisoner's skeleton which was lying in a cage nearby. Regardless, neither story is true."

Charley looked confused. Stefano beckoned Gustav forward.

"In any case, would you like to see the rope now?"

"Sure." She twisted to follow Stefano's gaze.

Gustav approached her and handed her one end of the rope.

She handled it carefully. "It's sticky. Well, that makes sense, I guess."

Gustav continued to walk, circling Charley, and playing out the rope as he followed the path of the iron in the floor. Stefano stood in front of Charley and smiled, drawing her entire rapt attention in return. Charley was being bound, but loosely. The trap was drawing closed.

Rachel ignored the pain in her head and sprang at Gustav to block him from his task, but she moved through him just as she had when attacking Stefano. Failing to stop him, she stood between Gustav and Charley. She tried grabbing the rope to lift it over Charley, but Gustav yanked it taut, binding the girls together, back-to-back. Rachel was able to wriggle enough to twist and face in Charley's direction, with one arm free to wrap around Charley's shoulders. That was that. They were caught together now.

Charley's breath was taken momentarily when the rope tightened further, and her arms were pinned to her sides. The pain from the binding sharpened her wits.

"Hey, that hurts. Stefano, he's hurting me. Rachel, what's going on?"

Rachel whispered in her ear, "I'm here, Charley. We're going to be alright."

"You let us go right now. Nonnie is going to be really angry."

Stefano snorted and smiled at the threat. He disappeared out of their view as Gustav continued to wind the rope around the pair. Rachel closed her eyes and sighed, the pain in her head finally subsiding to a dull roar. Charley's head swung wildly as she looked around for Stefano.

"This is not funny. You let us go, right now. Do you hear me? I'm warning you!" She began to shriek, bringing the return of the stabbing pain to assault Rachel's brain.

Rachel begged, "Charley, stop! You're killing me." She bent her head forward and bit Charley's shoulder, hard.

"Owww! Rachel, what are you doing?" Charley's voice had turned into a terrified sob.

Rachel shouted in her ear now. "Stop screaming and think, Charley."

The voice of Stefano boomed. "Enough, children!"

He chanted in a guttural, ugly language neither girl understood. A humming coursed rhythmically in the air around them. The unearthly ethereal beings massed outside the room started a keening which quickly rose in volume and pitch. The throbbing in the air beat on their eardrums and battered all hope of escape out of them.

A sickly green orb surrounded by swirling clouds of gray and silver appeared in the center of the fireplace, drawing their attention. The vortex Rachel had seen outside was now in the fireplace watching them, ravenous and lusting for their souls. Tall and menacing, Stefano continued his chant as he walked into view. He faced the fireplace and bowed. As his voice rose in intensity, the iron in the floor began to glow. The gray was burned away from the network of metal. Lines of molten orange formed a circular prison around the disk where they awaited their fate. The only path leading away was a thin lane of bubbling lava between the spars, leading directly toward the vortex. Heat shimmered from the floor, and acrid smoke rose to fill the room, making the girls cough.

Stefano stopped his chant and bowed to the fireplace. He then spun to face them. Charley gasped, seeing this Stefano for the first time. His eyes glittered as he leered and bared sharp rotted teeth. She twisted to avoid his gaze. Rachel whispered in her ear. "Charley. Charley. I'm here. Snap out of it. I'm here."

Charley thrashed with her legs, but the stool was fixed to the silvery plate, and her efforts were futile. Rachel continued to try and calm her. She hugged her closer.

"Think, Charley. Has Stefano said anything that could help?"

Charley was hysterical. "That isn't Stefano! That's a beast! I want to go home, Rachel. I want to see my mother and father again. I wish I had never come here!"

Stefano floated toward them, stopping inches away. A halo of green framed his grinning face as the red glow of the iron cast his features in demonic radiance. His voice was mocking and cold.

"It is time, children. Allow me to introduce you to my master."

He floated to the side, and the terrified girls were compelled by the monstrosity in the fireplace. As if sensing them, a palpable, amorphous form began to take shape in the whirlpool of sickness and decay, like a being of evil searching for prey. It had no face or body, only a baleful, diabolic shadow that hungered and pulsated. The being's focus sharpened to form a greedy, hungry maw casting about for a target. It settled on the girls, trembling in terror.

The reality of the room faltered. The ceiling and walls creaked and groaned as if the room was being rocked and twisted. The girls struggled desperately against their bonds. Candles flickered, and the hair on their heads stood on end. Gustav handed the remaining rope to Stefano.

Charley was beyond reason with fear. "Rachel! Help!"

"Charley, anything? Did he say anything?"

Charley tore her eyes away from the fireplace. "What about stones? I might have one left."

Rachel squirmed and contorted unsuccessfully, trying to reach into Charley's bag. Stefano watched with an amused expression and shook his head.

"I am more powerful than your foolish fairy godmother, and I am not subject to the whims of your pitiful stones. I am a servant of the Null. You are powerless in my presence."

"Let me out!" screamed Charley.

The candles sputtered and died. The crimson glow of the iron gave way to an emerald sickness spreading from the fireplace across the walls and ceiling. A single shadow from the doorway streaked overhead to be swallowed up in the vortex. Rachel turned her head to see more separate from the doorway and disappear into the gulf of the fireplace.

Stefano bowed toward his master and turned to the girls. "It is time."

He tossed the remaining length of twisted web into the fireplace. The power within pulled the rope taut, causing the girls to lurch and recoil. Rachel dug in her heels and braced herself to match evil's pull with all her strength.

Seated and unable to help, Charley could only plead desperately. "Hold on, Rachel!"

Rachel began to lose the battle, inch by inch. A stream of shadows, along with pillows and carpets hurtled past them, caught in the vacuum created by the master's relentless hunger. The frame of the house groaned, and still Rachel resisted. Stefano watched casually, unaffected by the forces at play.

Gustav came into view wearing a cadaverous smile, enjoying

210

the maelstrom. He neared the fireplace, and whatever stuff he was made of collapsed and was swallowed by the vortex.

In the chaos, Stefano had to raise his voice to be heard above the din.

"You are strong, whatever you are! My master has never before been challenged to such a degree! You are quite a puzzle!"

Rachel was past the point of fear now. "Together we're stronger than you and your master! I won't let her go!"

"Foolish girl. You have no power here. You will go together."

He stepped forward and kicked the stool out from under Charley, causing Rachel to lose her balance. She stumbled forward and would have fallen if not for Charley gaining her feet and adding her strength to the effort.

The howling of the vortex increased. The two girls leaned back to fight the pull of the rope. Their combined efforts brought them a few feet of distance from their enemy.

Rachel shouted above the din. "Charley! I can't keep this up much longer!"

A tinkling near Charley's ear caused her to turn and she caught a glimpse of Rachel's butterfly pendant hovering, wings beating furiously, above her shoulder.

"Wait! Can you reach Butter?" asked Charley with a shout of renewed hope.

Rachel desperately tried to bend her wrist and free hand inside their binding to get a grip on the knife hidden in Charley's sweatshirt. She was able to get two fingers on it, but her loss of concentration caused them to slip closer to the fireplace. Charley yelped, and they renewed their efforts, re-gaining a step. Rachel made another attempt for the knife, and this time her fingers wrapped around the hilt. She flicked away the scabbard and clumsily applied as much as pressure as she could to the rope near her bound arm. She ignored the pain as it drew blood. It sliced through the rope like a shark fin through water. The slight unraveling of the rope allowed Charley to wriggle an arm free.

Stefano approached them from the side, intending to hurl them into his master's embrace. He sidled between them and the fireplace, his face twisted in unconcealed anger. Charley took the split-second opportunity to grab the knife from Rachel and viciously saw the rope that stretched into the glowing green void.

The blade severed the rope and the free end flicked wildly, attaching itself to the nearest object and wrapping itself around Stefano's shoulders, pulling him off his feet. Charley and Rachel scrambled backwards , landing outside the circle of hot iron as the deafening destruction of the house continued around them. Charley sawed away at the rope, allowing them to break free. She flattened herself on the ground, and Rachel crawled over to cover her. Stefano lay flat, his belly on the ground, desperately clinging to red-hot iron with his fingertips. A misty cloud billowed to envelop him.

He managed to scream, "This cannot be! I am elemental! I am a force of nature! Master, no, this world is mine!"

His wail died suddenly. Whatever malevolent essence sustained Stefano's form detached from his body and sailed into the fireplace. His body remained behind, lifeless. The girls continued to lay as flat as possible to avoid the cyclonic winds pulling the room down around them.

As the maelstrom of force dissipated, Rachel rose unsteadily and assessed the situation. Charley stood as well. They found themselves back in the dying grove where Rachel had first encountered the vortex. In the direction of the infernal fireplace, the green mist swirled between nearby trees, apparently satiated for now. A cold wind blew, sending dead leaves between and around their feet to bury the iron circles in decay. A timid dawn greeted them quietly.

As their eyes adjusted to the dim light, they surveyed the scene around them. The entire house was missing, and in its place, two rows of steaming mounds stretched far into the woods beyond. Rachel dragged herself toward what was left of Stefano. Above the collar of a moldy jacket, blackened and decomposing skin stretched taut over a skull, face down in the dirt. Decayed hands stretched from the sleeves like claws hooked into the ground. She backed away without examining the corpse further.

Charley asked from a respectable distance, "Is he dead?"

"I'm hoping, yes. Though I don't know for sure if he was ever alive."

Charley's voice was hopeful. "So, it's over? We're safe?"

Rachel nodded. "Unless you want to hang around here for another night."

She pointed to the nearest mound. "I think we were supposed to end up in one of those after that horror in the fireplace drained the life out of us."

Charley let out a whoop. "We did it! Well, you did it! No, we did it!"

Her voice echoed strangely in this forest. The trees had become accustomed to screams and wails, so Charley's joyful spirit rang unfamiliar to them.

"You did it, Charley. If you hadn't thought of Butter, we might have been Stefano's newest bat groupies. But we're not out of these woods yet."

"It was my present. I knew that butterfly was magical. Does this mean I'm a wizard, or a witch, or whatever?"

"It's a good question, Charley. But can we discuss it later?"

She turned Charley toward the mist. "See that? We have to get out of here. Evil never gives up. We're still not safe."

Her voice trailed off, and she swayed as she stood. Charley seemed not to care. She was back to being her obliviously carefree self for now.

"I'm safe as long as I'm traveling with you. And I feel great, too."

Rachel tilted her head and smiled briefly. "Aww. How sweet. Let's go."

Charley returned Butter to the scabbard in the kangaroo pocket of her sweatshirt. They took their first steps upstream, their legs wobbly from their exertions. Rachel faltered and nearly fell. Charley

ducked under her arm to support her. Together, they shambled out of
the foul hollow, leaving the misty vortex behind. Rachel was almost
dead on her feet.

Charley tried to lighten the mood. "Stink better watch out too.
We're coming for him next. Right, Rachel?"

"Charley, you're too much. Now you know why I dance with
butterflies. Fighting monsters is dangerous. And exhausting."

They trudged out of Stefano's valley, as quickly as possible.
Upon arriving at the spot of their last encounter with Stink, both girls
looked around with dread. The exhilaration of escaping from the fiend
in the forest was fading away. Rachel was barely able to put one foot
in front of the other. She suggested they stop to rest.

"Here?" complained Charley.

"I'm sorry, but I'm wiped out. We can find a place under the
pine trees up there. It should be fairly comfortable," said Rachel,
pointing a hundred yards downstream.

Charley thought about it for the length of a yawn.

"Maybe a quick power nap."

With Rachel leaning heavily on her friend, they hiked down
and then up the slope on the opposite side. They found a comfortable
grassy spot in the shade and Charley let Rachel slide down to the
ground. She intended to keep watch over her friend, but soon joined
her in slumber.

CHAPTER THIRTY

The sun beat down on the two girls. Charley woke up refreshed from her nap with a good drool from a few uninterrupted hours of deep slumber. She stretched languorously and purred with contentment. She rolled over to find Rachel curled into fetal position, panting weakly.

She started bolt upright. "Rachel, wake up! Wake up!"

Rachel did not respond. Charley shook her by the shoulder, resulting in a slight unwinding of Rachel's curved spine. Charley knelt to intensify her efforts to revive her. She eventually uncoiled and opened her eyes for a brief flicker of recognition before staring off blankly.

Charley dared to slap her face lightly as she begged Rachel to snap out of her spell.

"Rachel, it's Charley. Come back. Wake up!"

Her voice grew steadily more desperate.

"You have to get up! What's wrong with you? I wish I had a wish."

She rose to her feet and searched the grass nearby for a stone. Casting an ever-widening net, she hunted for a wish that could bring Rachel back to her senses.

She strayed farther and farther away from her friend, calling out in an attempt to rouse Rachel from a distance.

"Did Stefano cast some kind of spell over you? Rachel! Wake up."

Downstream, around a bend, she spied a stone glowing amongst the ordinary river stones. She looked back and realized that to reach the stone, she would lose sight of the prone form of Rachel. She wavered at the bend, leaning left and right.

"Rachel! Can you crawl a little closer? There's a stone here, but I don't want to let you out of my sight. Rachel!"

Her angry tone did nothing to rouse her friend. She huffed and puffed, agonizing over which direction to take her next step. She threw up her hands and chose upstream. Before her foot fell, a faraway voice called from upriver.

A chilling cry of "CHICKENFINGERS!" rolled down the valley.

Charley didn't hesitate. She raced back to Rachel to find her in worse condition. Her breathing was very shallow and her lips blue. Charley considered her options for an instant until that voice scrambled her thoughts. Stink was closing in on them.

"CHICKENFINGERS! SMELL YOU!"

Charley knelt at her friend's side and placed her hand on Rachel's cheek.

"I could go face him, but I can't leave you here. He'd step on me, and you'd die here alone. If I wait here with you, he'll squash both of us. I guess I'll have to carry you and see how far we get."

She grabbed Rachel's backpack and settled the straps on her shoulders. She bent down and dug her hands under Rachel's limp body and preemptively grunted under the strain of her weight. As she attempted to rise, her expression changed from a teeth-gritting grimace to surprised relief. She stood straight and tall, easily cradling Rachel in her arms.

"Ha, you're as light as a feather, Rachel."

She stood, marveling at her own strength, until the ground began to shake under her feet.

"Gotta go!"

She started walking with urgency downstream. When she discovered her burden wouldn't be a problem, she sped up, into a trot.

"STINK SMELL CHICKENFINGERS!"

"He's coming, Charley," murmured Rachel.

Charley almost dropped her in surprise. Instead, she picked up the pace. She passed the glowing stone and surveyed the countryside ahead, searching for the smoothest path. The ground vibrated with the weight of the crazed giant's strides. A hundred yards downstream, they passed an opening in the hedge on the left where a separate branch of the river led away. Charley spun around quickly and retraced her steps to take the alternate path.

She continued until the new course bent sharply. Rounding the bend, she veered up the bank. As she knelt to gently lay Rachel at the foot of the hedge, a face appeared to look on her with a prideful smile. She ignored the face and listened for signs of pursuit. Stink's presence was no longer felt or smelled. She held Rachel's hand tightly.

Rachel stirred and managed to raise herself up to rest on her right elbow. Her eyelids grudgingly allowed her to see Charley looking down at her with a smirk.

"What happened to Stink?" asked Rachel.

"He must have missed that fork. I think we're safe for now."

To the hedge, she barked, "Stop staring at me, goofball."

She swung her arm through the branches to swish the face away.

"What's up with you? You had me scared to death. I thought you were dying."

"All of a sudden, I couldn't think or catch my breath. Maybe I caught something in that house. I'm a little dizzy, but I'll be alright."

"I'm glad you're feeling better. I picked you up and carried you here. You know; like a superhero."

"You're a true friend, Charley. Thank you for saving me."

Charley offered her hand to Rachel and helped her to her feet. The older girl encircled Charley with her arms and gave her a long, crushing hug and a kiss on the cheek.

They broke off the embrace to find a dozen faces in the hedges watching them with knowing expressions. Charley wriggled out of the backpack and handed it to Rachel who seemed to be back to normal, physically.

"I don't think I'll ever understand this place, Rachel. Where do all of these river branches come from?"

"We've passed plenty of places where streams merge. What's the big mystery?"

"It's just that I didn't see this when I was up there flying," said Charley, jabbing a thumb skyward. "I didn't see any other branches. There was one river and nothing else but forest, forever."

Rachel shrugged her shoulders. "I don't know what to tell you, Charley. It is confusing. I can't explain it."

Charley fumed. "I'm not confused. I'm mad!"

She stomped around in a circle shaking her fists, searching for a victim until her eyes lit on Rachel.

Rachel raised her hands to protect herself from a possible death blow.

"Take it easy, Charley. You don't want to take it out on me. I'm warning you."

Charley unclenched her fists, but her scowl remained. The faces dispersed as she let out an explosive breath toward the sky which would have been, had she been a dragon, a gout of flame.

Rachel patted her on the back, and they set off once again.

CHAPTER THIRTY-ONE

Charley's temper cooled over time, and she turned her attention to her surroundings. After a short and pleasant stroll, she held Rachel up with something new that was bothering her.

"Does the hedge look shorter to you?" she asked.

"You know, you're right. What do you think it means?"

"I hope it means I can finally get out of here."

Charley jogged toward the hedge and a female face appeared to stare at her with a questioning glare.

"What's your problem, needle nose?"

She looked back at Rachel with a smile on her own face, looking for kudos for such a clever insult. Rachel grudgingly nodded.

"Good one, Charley."

When she turned back to give the hedge more attitude, the face was not pleased. Charley grabbed its ears and shook the branches violently, erasing it. She clapped her hands to clean them of shrub.

Charley glared left and right to address the whole river-long length of tormenting greenery. "I'm going to tell my Dad to chop you down when I get home! This is getting annoying. Do you think it would burn if I wished for a fire?"

"I doubt it. And I wouldn't test it if I were you. Remember how your wish for water turned out."

Charley regarded her friend with a sour expression. "I'm much smarter now, remember?"

"Still, why don't we just ignore the hedge and be on our way?"

"Might as well. There's nothing to do here anyway."

"That's the spirit."

Charley had no trouble catching her sarcastic tone. She affected an excited little girl voice and clasped her hands in front of her chest.

"I'll bet there's a friendly herd of unicorns grazing in a field of lollipops and candy corn around the bend. Wouldn't that be delightful?"

Rachel nodded in appreciation of such an acerbic and well-executed dramatic retort.

"You have a real future in the theater. You've got the looks, the loud voice, and the narcissism."

"What's narcissism?"

"It means you're confident. Can we go now?"

As they rounded the next bend in the river, the first impression of what lay before them was delivered in the form of a putrid assault on the olfactory sense. They slowed and began to wave in front of their faces to break through a cloud of stench. Charley grabbed Rachel's sleeve and pulled her back away from the smell. When they had back-pedaled far enough to breathe clean air again, they stopped and gasped, greedily inhaling the welcome scents of grass, dirt, and even their own considerable body odor.

"That was gross," cried Charley.

"I'm not sure but I think there's a dead whale ahead," suggested Rachel.

Charley looked defeated. "What do we do now? I thought I could handle anything but now I'm not so narcissist. I didn't think anything could smell worse than Stink, but I was wrong."

"We have to go through it, Charley."

"What if it is Stink? We'd be walking right into his arms." An involuntary shudder shook her whole body.

"It didn't smell like Stink to me. He's got superhuman b.o. but that was different," replied Rachel.

"So, what? We just hold our breath and stroll on through?" scoffed Charley.

"We could tie something around our face to breathe through," suggested Rachel.

Charley's expression of open-mouthed overbite, rolled eyes, and furrowed brow reduced Rachel to an embarrassed, teary-eyed child for having the nerve to suggest such an idiotic idea. At least, that was her intention. Instead, Rachel took one stomp toward her with fists clenched and Charley flinched reflexively.

"Give me a stone, Charlotte".

Charley complied without hesitation. Rachel took the stone and muttered a few words. A folded cloth appeared in her free hand. She scowled at Charley as she dropped the stone and tore the cloth in two. She handed one piece to Charley and proceeded to tie the remaining piece over face, covering her nose as well as her mouth. Charley was standing still, biting her lower lip, as she watched Rachel. The scowl was hidden, but the anger in the older girl's eyes still focused on Charley.

She would normally bristle when someone used her formal given name, but something told her that a measure of sass or a slightly dirty look might be dangerous and painful. She copied Rachel in securing the cloth on her face. Her own eyes were looking everywhere but at Rachel.

"Are you ready, Charley? Sometimes, to get where you want to go, you'll have to deal with unpleasant things. A little smell is nothing compared to what some people live with."

Charley's mouth moved under her makeshift mask as she nodded, but she was careful not to make a sound. Rachel noticed the muscles twitching in her face, but she ignored Charley's silent rebellion.

Rachel grabbed Charley's hand and with only a slight drag, they made their way back toward the wall of odor. Pointlessly, they both reached out with a hand to feel their way slowly, the other hand held the cloth close to the neck to prevent unfiltered air from stabbing them in the nose. They moved forward one step at a time groping the air as if they were blinded by the masks.

Before long they were in it. The masks were partially effective, making the air breathable, but they didn't protect their eyes which stung and watered. Rachel tugged Charley harder, and they began to walk faster with jerking steps that lengthened into running strides.

The area that they had entered was wide and flat, bounded by a stone wall on both sides with the hedge sitting atop giving a two layer effect. The center of the riverbed was its usual stone course, but narrower than usual. To either side, the ground was ashen, broken, and uneven with wisps of smoke or vapor escaping to add more putrefaction to the mantle of rot that pressed down on the ground and against the cloths around their faces. The only plant specimens were sporadic tufts of black crabgrass.

The whole area was also littered with hundreds of glowing stones, some as close as a few footsteps away. They glittered enticingly in the darkness of the waning daylight and the gray oppressive atmosphere. Charley veered very slightly to the right, but Rachel's grip on her hand prevented her from leaving the path.

She swung around to clutch Charley's shoulders and hold her in place. They stared at each other over their masks and Charley got Rachel's message.

"Don't worry. I'm not going out there. I don't need a stone that bad," she said, assuring Rachel.

"Good, let's get going. Don't fall behind," warned Rachel.

The girls were forced to march in single file to avoid stepping off onto the noisome plain of crusty slag. They picked their way as carefully and quickly as possible. Rachel, leading the way, repeated, 'Almost there. Almost there. Almost there.' Charley answered her with a simple staccato, 'Go. Go. Go. Go. Go'. They hurried for a time without incident, dealing with the oppressive atmosphere and its constant assault on their senses. As time dragged on, their energy flagged, slowing their pace to a trudge.

When Rachel stopped short, Charley didn't crash into her so much as dock herself onto Rachel's back and bury her face next to the backpack. She shouted with a raspy cracking voice, "What is it, Rachel? Are we almost out of this place?"

Rachel said nothing for a moment. She called over her back to Charley. "Don't freak out, Charley, but there's a skeleton on the ground in front of me."

To Rachel's surprise, Charley did not freak out. Instead, she carefully and slowly detached herself enough to peek around from Rachel's back to look down. The skeleton of a tall male stretched across the path on his back. He was dressed in jeans and a leather coat, and he appeared to have just laid down to rest and never rose again. Rachel stepped toward the body and Charley shuffled after her. When Rachel stepped over the skeleton, Charley let out a small whimper.

"He's not going to grab your ankle, Charley. Come on," said Rachel. Her voice was insistent with a hint of panic. Charley whimpered with genuine panic before steeling herself and leaping over the body to smash into Rachel's arms.

"You're fine," Rachel comforted.

Charley tried to pull herself together. "I preferred the ghosts."

She decided to take the lead and they resumed their trek with renewed speed spurred by the possibility that the skeleton's nap was over, and he was stalking them now. Moments later, they came upon another skeleton. This one was a young woman curled into a fetal position. Her clothes were well-made, and her shoes were entirely inappropriate for walking on the stones of a riverbed. Her arms were crossed as if she had been shivering as she lie on her side. Charley stared at her for quite some time before turning to Rachel.

"Why did she just lie down here, in this dead place?" asked Charley.

"I do not know. The only one who possibly can answer that is her and she might not have known why. We can wonder about it later when we're out of here." Rachel's worried tone spurred Charley back into action.

They passed or stepped over other bone-dry skeletons and some less decomposed corpses, each one adding a measure of dread to their already ragged state. Rachel was back in the lead trying to shelter Charley from some of the more gruesome sights. She hoped that Charley hadn't noticed the forms of other bodies lying on the ground out among the gleaming stones. But Charley had noticed, and she was closing in on hysteria. The powerful sulfuric smell was no longer foremost in her mind. She clutched the back of Rachel's shirt, effectively being towed downstream.

The path was still not wide enough for two, so Rachel couldn't comfort Charley in the manner that she wanted to. She could only reach back with her arms to form bumpers that kept Charley from staggering or stumbling off the path. They made their way slowly through a landscape that looked like a cemetery with bodies strewn about as if they had been displaced by an earthquake.

Charley was now chanting her mantra loudly, trying to block out the input from any other senses. Rachel didn't mind since it meant she could tell that her friend was still with her and not wandering away to lie down herself. They continued forward at a snail's pace. The air around them was crushing them, robbing them of the will to continue.

Just when Rachel was sure that they couldn't move a step further, she distinguished another voice a few yards away to their right. The two girls had almost passed a familiar figure standing casually, softly humming and swaying. Chilly stood in a trance, showing no awareness of their presence. He reached up to roughly rub his own face, massaging his temples. He rolled his head, stretching his neck, and then began to collapse slowly to first one knee and then the other. He rocked side to side as he knelt and his chest expanded, drawing in deep lungfuls of the corrupting air.

Rachel lowered her arms for a second and Charley scampered off the path toward him. Rachel squawked in alarm. "Charley, come back!"
Charley reached Chilly before he could stretch out for the last time. She tried shaking him, but it had no effect. She dug her arms under his right shoulder and tried to pull him to the center of the stream. She called out to Rachel. "Help me, please! It's not too late."

Rachel had no choice but to follow in Charley's footsteps. She assisted by pulling Charley by the hips and together they dragged him back to the path. Charley shook and slapped him for a few minutes, and, although he was breathing, he did not come to. She even tried lifting her mask and kissing him on the lips as if she was Princess Charming. She looked up at Rachel for suggestions only to see her looking away downstream.

She turned back to Charley. "I don't know. You've been beating him pretty severely for a long time and he hasn't woken up. I'm not surprised kissing him didn't work either."

"Do you have anything constructive to say? We have to get him out of here," she cried. "He's too heavy to carry."

"We only need to drag him a little farther," said Rachel.

"What are you talking about? We're trapped in this poisonous wasteland. This is life or death here! How can you be so relaxed?"

"Look."

Rachel moved aside so Charley could see the direction she had been looking. No more than a few strides downstream, the familiar riverscape beckoned. Charley looked around to find them on the edge of the nightmare badlands. Bodies were no longer visible and the lights from the stones were dim specks.

"Don't just stand there, Rachel. Help me drag him all the way out of here."

Their combined strength and energy was enough to pull him onto a grassy riverbank where they both collapsed next to him. A few moments of rest later, Rachel fished a canteen out of her backpack, tore her mask off, and took a hearty swallow. She handed the canteen to Charley who greedily gulped her own share. She then poured some water on Chilly's face. She continued to pour until Rachel reached for the canteen to stop her.

"That's enough. It's considered torture at this point."

"But why doesn't he wake up?" asked Charley.

"Maybe I should kiss him," suggested Rachel.

"Funny," Charley retorted. "I'll try CPR."

Charley applied a few pumps to Chilly's chest, and he roused to cough out the poison in his lungs. He raised one hand to his rub his forehead and groaned, long and loud. They watched him rock side to side attempting to roll over. He was finally able to reach escape velocity and defy gravity enough to roll and rise to his hands and knees. He looked around squinting and eventually his gaze settled on Charley.

"Charley, I don't believe it. Where did you come from? How did I get here?"

Charley's eyes sparkled. Tears welled in her eyes and she launched into his arms. She buried her face in his shoulder and whispered, "We saved you."

CHAPTER THIRTY-TWO

Still on his knees, Chilly held Charley at arm's length. A wide toothy grin split his face.

"Girl, this place is crazy. I've been looking for you for weeks, asking everybody I meet. No one's seen the most beautiful little girl in the world."

Charley tried to ignore the 'little girl' part of the compliment. "That was like two days ago, Chilly."

"That's impossible. I've been kicking around, going up and downstream, sleeping in cabins, and tree houses, and caves. It's been at least two weeks."

He released his grip on her shoulders and rose unsteadily. Charley looked to Rachel for an explanation.

"Maybe time moves differently for everybody."

Charley threw up her hands. "Sure, why not? Nothing about this place needs to make sense."

Chilly coughed up some more toxic air. He wriggled his shoulders to remove a backpack. Kneeling, he rooted around until he found a canteen and brought it to his lips for a drink.

"Where did you get that?" asked Charley.

"I used a stone to wish for it, of course. I'm already handsome."

Charley gave him a sneering smile, acknowledging his dig.

"Well, you were half-dead in a poisonous landfill a couple of minutes ago and now you're walking and talking, thanks to me. If you've recovered from your near-death experience, maybe we can get going. While we walk you can tell me about all the people you met who didn't save your life."

Rachel nodded approvingly.

"Sorry, that is bad manners. Last thing I remember before you resurrected me was walking into this field full of stones and the sun set like someone flipped a switch. I just kept taking steps in one direction, hoping nothing cut me down. Then I woke up with you pounding on my chest. If you found me in there, how come you weren't affected the same way?"

"We stayed on the path," said Rachel.

Charley adopted a haughty tone. "You weren't on the path. It was almost unbearable, but I guess it was worse out in the field."

Chilly rose and shouldered his backpack. "Hmm, a path. Lucky for you."

He looked around at their surroundings, stalling while he searched for words. The girls also prepared to move on.

"Charley, thanks for what you did. I'm still alive and there's still hope we can get back home. Let's call it even and hope neither of us has to save anyone's life ever again."

"Deal."

They all stood awkwardly in place, shuffling their feet. Rachel was the first to initiate some movement. She opened her arms to take her friends into a group hug. Charley followed suit, wrapping her arms around Chilly's chest. Chilly closed his eyes and smiled as he hugged them both. They stood, rocking like a young tree in a strong wind, for a long time until they broke the embrace. With a few sniffles, they silently agreed to set out once more. They walked downstream, three abreast, with renewed energy and hope for a happy ending to their journey just around the next bend.

CHAPTER THIRTY-THREE

A soft, tangy breeze blew in their faces as they walked. Seagulls mewed loudly overhead. Charley stopped suddenly and sniffed the air. She looked at Rachel with wide eyes and a wide-open mouth.

"Do you smell that? Is that the ocean?"

"That is the sea, girl. I'd know that smell anywhere," Chilly confirmed.

Chilly and Charley laughed and took the opportunity to start an impromptu dance party. Rachel stood to the side, smiling with a wistful expression as she watched the pair dance with joyful abandon.

Suddenly, their celebration was interrupted by the familiar thumping sound of a persistent behemoth's foot stomps. Charley wasted no time in shifting into panicked racing mode.

"Run!"

She sprinted toward the shore with Rachel and Chilly right behind her.

There were no trees to climb or tall grass in which to hide as they ran. Even the hedge was gone. They kept on running to find the ground at their feet was now packed sand. The soft green grass they were used to from the river banks had been replaced by beach grass. Charley stopped, searching desperately for a place to hide. The others kept on going a few more paces.

Stink appeared, thunder in his stride. Rachel called to Charley, "Don't stop now. We have to keep going."

Charley stopped dead in her tracks.

"This is the end, Rachel. I have to face him. You keep going. It's me he wants."

Rachel returned and grabbed her hand. "We're a team, Charley. Come on."

Chilly didn't bother to try to convince her. He bent and picked her up, throwing her over a shoulder.

Charley let herself be carried forward. From her bouncing

vantage point, she saw the bloodshot eye of the debt collector focus on them. Less than ten steps later, Chilly jumped to a halt in the sand. Charley looked in both directions to see the backs of dozens of people traveling in the same direction. They milled about on the white sand of a wide beach. Chilly set Charley down and the three friends darted into the throng shouting, "Look out! Run for your lives! It's a giant!"

They startled some of the young people who looked at them like they were crazy. Some pointed and laughed. A few shook their heads and sneered. However, the people around them, as a whole, appeared to be rather uninterested in the news regarding a possible assault by a Titan.

A loud blast of frustrated rage shook the sand.

"CHICKENFINGERS!"

The girls clung to each other for comfort, hoping that seeking refuge among a crowd of other humans would confuse Stink.

"CHICKENFINGERS! COME OUT!" he trumpeted.

Chilly and the girls crept out toward the edge of the protective swarm. They peered from between the bodies to see Stink, standing at the edge of the beach. He searched the strand, scratching his under-arm and drooling.

A few of the people towards the back of the crowd glanced his way disinterestedly for a moment, only to return to facing the shore and craning their necks for a glimpse of the water. Charley and Rachel were stunned at their indifference. They looked back at Stink.

He was staring down at the sand, hesitating. He hopped back and forth from foot to foot and shook his fists, menacing but impo-tent. Charley approached to stand just outside the boundary of his odor. Chilly and Rachel flanked her as backup.

"Here I am, Stink. You're just going to have to go home and tell your brother I got away. No squishing for you today."

A defeated expression crossed the bully's ugly face.

"You're lucky, Charley. You got away with it," said Rachel, at her back.

Charley turned around with a satisfied smile on her face. She shrugged.

"I didn't do anything wrong, anyway."

"Nothing?" asked Rachel, one eyebrow raised.

Charley's face turned sour. Her eyes rolled, and her lip curled into a sneer. Instead of responding, she turned back to Stink.

"Run along, now. Go home and take a bath."

Stink raised a foot and gauged the distance from his quarry. Finding her outside of stomping range, he accepted failure. He blasted out one more cry of "CHICKENFINGERS!" and stalked away whence he came.

The friends stood together in awkward silence. Some in the crowd around them looked up as if they had heard something, but most continued to stare seaward, oblivious. From time to time, the whole mass of people shuffled forward a few steps and then settled back into nervous anticipation mode. This left them on the periphery, anxious and hopeful the worst was behind them.

As the feeling of being hunted disappeared, they were able to relax and better survey their surroundings. Looking up and down the beach, they saw other river outlets. Figures trickled out on foot from some to join the crowd on the beach. From others, boats crowded with people sailed right on through and presumably out to sea. Charley pointed them out.

"Hey, that's not fair! They're cheating!"

She stomped her foot, but the sand deadened the effect she was hoping for. Her voice softened into a grumbling curse.

"Why did we have to walk all the way when those people get a ride?"

Rachel squinted in the direction of the lucky passengers.

Chilly answered, "Some people have to fight and scrap and claw to get through life, and some people get to sail on through. That's just how it is."

Charley's face grimaced with sorrow at the unfairness of it all. She kicked at the sand, taking out her anger on the beach.

More latecomers hurried out from their own familiar riverbed to join the beach party. None seemed to be affected by an angry giant recently passing through their midst. It appeared he really had given up the chase.

One passerby took notice of Charley's angry fit and stopped to express concern. A tall, tanned young lady with long shiny brown hair and a winning smile knelt on one knee and looked Charley in the eye.

"Aren't you adorable. You don't have to worry. We're all in this together."

She chucked Charley under the chin and bobbed her face in front of Charley, attempting to get the younger girl to look her in the eye.

"My name is Mia. What's yours?

Charley shook her head to clear away her unhappiness and extended her hand.

"I'm Charley. Very glad to meet you."

Rachel and Chilly's jaws dropped simultaneously. The young lady reached out and pulled Charley's head close, so their foreheads touched.

"Well, Charley, you are a beautiful, intelligent, and special girl. Don't let life get you down. Bad times are like sand in your shoes. You just pull them off, pour it out, and away you go."

"Thank you," said Charley.

Mia rose and patted Charley on the cheek. Her smile widened even further somehow. She beamed at Chilly and Rachel as well and turned to go. The friends allowed more youngsters to pass them by and even climbed higher up the beach to get a better look. The crowd before them consisted entirely of young people in their late teens or early twenties. They came in all shapes, colors, and sizes, dress, and physical condition, moving slowly with various degrees of eagerness, to the water's edge.

Rachel tapped Charley on the shoulder.

"You were very pleasant just now. Are you feeling alright?" asked Rachel.

"She was just being nice. I've never seen a kinder smile."

Rachel and Chilly began trying out different smiles, attempting to charm Charley in the same a stranger had just warmed her heart. Charley pursed her lips as her friends mugged and grinned until she could not hold back the laughter anymore.

"Okay, okay. Knock it off."

The dread from being hunted had disappeared and the flow of travelers emerging from their riverbed had stopped. The trio began trudging across the sand toward the sea, bringing up the rear of the crowd. Lifeguard towers faintly lit by lanterns were regularly spaced along the beach in both directions, visible above the heads of the travelers. Though the crashing waves were hidden from view, the sound of the surf was audible, and the breeze carried a salty sea tang.

Charley turned to Rachel and asked with a sigh of relief, "Are we finally here? Can we go home now?"

"Looks like it," said Chilly.

"Has it been so horrible, traveling with me?" asked Rachel.

Charley began to protest and disagree, but the look on Rachel's face was one of wistful introspection rather than an accusation. There was also a sadness Charley did not understand.

"It's been scary and awful and dangerous... and fun," she admitted. "I've never had an adventure before; unless you count emergency rooms and hospitals."

Charley squatted to pick up a handful of sand. She looked up at Rachel and asked, "Wouldn't it be cool if each grain of sand was a wishing stone?"

Chilly chuckled. "Life is hard work, Charley."

Rachel sighed. "Haven't you learned by now? You don't get what you just because you want it. You don't become what you're meant to be by wishing for it. It's not that easy."

"It's easy for some people. All they have to do is ask for something, and they get every single thing they want," said Charley.

Her older friends continued to show patience and calm.

"You have a lot to learn, girl," said Chilly.

"Every single thing," Rachel said, stressing the word 'thing'.

"Things aren't important. Your family is important. Your friends are important. Creating something that is uniquely yours is important. Inspiring others is important. Doing something positive that makes a difference for other people is important."

Charley was genuinely touched. "How come I've never had friends like you before?"

Chilly rested his arm on Charley's shoulders and led her toward the beach, walking on her left side.

"Let's go, girl. I think it's time to get outta here."

Rachel caught up to them and took her right hand. Together they moved to join the crowd on their march to the sea. People moved forward steadily, but slowly. Everyone was now waddling slightly, in the manner of penguins, constantly swaying to look past the person ahead of them. As they neared the water, the chatter became more subdued. The sun had set behind them, and the moon's light provided scant illumination.

CHAPTER THIRTY-FOUR

Chilly and the girls were in the back of the pack. They strode casually and separately, in silence now. Charley sneaked a quick glance behind them in case a rogue flesh-eating beast was prowling the sand for an easy meal.

As they waddled, one of the lifeguard towers came into view, directly in their path. They could see a figure atop, scanning and speaking in an animated manner to the people shuffling past below. As they got closer, they saw her flashing gestures while keeping up a flow of steady commentary to the travelers. Sometimes she used words of encouragement and other times she shouted instructions or advice. It seemed she was fluent in many languages as she slipped rapidly in and out of dialects and tongues to communicate. There was even the occasional heated curse for the odd, unruly individual, but through it all, the current of wanderers kept flowing.

Charley's excitement built as the inexorable beating of waves beckoned them forward. She took advantage of the sand and stood en pointe, peeking through bodies, impatient for their turn to pass through and reach their destination.

Up and down the beach, the crowd passed by the lifeguards. Bringing up the rear, the three friends were the last to reach their rickety wooden tower. The sea was still not visible, but the waves crashed loudly. The lifeguard above them was a gangly, crisply tanned spider of a woman with long, white hair poking up out of an orange visor. She had keen eyes, the whites starkly contrasting with her tanned skin, and a long, sagging nose covered in zinc oxide. She wore a bright orange vest that clashed nauseatingly with her brown shorts. She sat erect in her seat, looking them up and down with a frown on her face.

Chilly led the way, passing the lifeguard's post and receiving a respectful salute. Charley looked up at the woman perched above, gave her a friendly wave, and tried to walk past. The guard loudly and violently cleared her throat causing Charley to halt her confident stride and cringe with anxiety.

"Where do you think you're going?" barked the lifeguard.

Charley's cringe deepened. Her teeth clenched. Her shoulders rose high enough to hide her ears. Her two small tight fists were held knuckle-to-knuckle in front of her chest. She mustered a meek smile and slowly turned. Pointing toward the water with both index fingers, she cleared her throat and batted her eyes as she looked up at the lifeguard.

"That way?"

A second later, she flinched as the lifeguard spastically extricated herself from her seat and leapt to land on the sand in front of her. Charley stumbled backward into Rachel's arms. Chilly tried to come to her defense, but one long arachnoid arm snapped as rigid as a spear and stopped him in his tracks. A single bony finger hovered an inch from the bridge of Chilly's nose.

Keeping her eyes fixed firmly on Charley, the lifeguard told Chilly sternly, "You may go."

"But, why can't...?"

"They are waiting for you. Go," the lifeguard said dismissively.

Chilly spoke to Charley around the lifeguard. "What's going on, Charley? What did you do?"

Rachel helped Charley to straighten up. She brushed herself off and faced the lifeguard with a look of righteous anger and indignation. Her expression combined with the clenched fists resting on her hips in a challenging stance would scare almost any small child. The lifeguard simply cocked her head and directed a single muscle in her cheek to pull off an artificial half-smile. Her eyes blazed eagerly as if she was daring the little girl to pounce at her. Her condescending, imperious attitude set Charley's nitroglycerine-filled kettle boiling. She pulled out her most threatening voice.

"Oh, I am going that way, and no walking Slim Jim is going to stop me."

The lifeguard's tiny half-smile blossomed into a three-quarter-smile.

"You are not ready, child," she told her in a stern voice.

"Who are you to tell me I'm not ready?" Her face clouded with anger and confusion. "Ready for what?"

"Ready to go on. You are not even meant to be here," she told her.

"I know I'm not supposed to be here," she spat. "I'm supposed to be at home sleeping with my cat. Now, get out of our way!"

"You are a special case. We are looking into how you came to be here." She eyed Charley with suspicion and wonder. "Very curious, indeed. Achilles may go. A boat is waiting for him. It is his time."

"What makes him better than me?" whined Charley.

Charley looked at Chilly for some explanation, but he looked nearly as mystified as she did. The lifeguard relaxed her arm and Chilly came to kneel at Charley's feet and took her hands.

"It's not like I'm better than you, Charley. I'm just older. I think she's sayin' I can go on because I'm not a kid anymore. It's time for me to make my own way in the big wide world."

Charley fought back tears. "I'm not a kid. I don't want you to go away again. I don't have enough friends. I can't lose any."

He pulled her close and hugged her with fierce strength. When she sniffled, he pulled back and held her shoulders.

"You're a gangster princess warrior, Charley. You're gonna be fine. I got a feeling about you. You just need some seasoning to build up some armor. You're a tough, smart kid, but you're still a kid."

A few days ago, Charley would have fought anyone calling her that with bared claws, but she was tired, and beaten. She didn't have the energy to pretend to be miserable in return for pity. Her tears were genuine, and her head hung in unaffected sadness.

"It's just not fair," she said with all the outrage she could muster as she sank to her knees.

Rachel walked up and put her hand on her shoulder.

"Charley, we should be happy for Chilly. Who wants to grow up anyway, right?"

Chilly tried to cheer her up as well. "Hey, Princess. We'll see each other again. We make a good team."

Charley sniffled and regained enough energy to stand with Rachel's assistance backing her up. She brushed sand off her knees.

"Don't make promises you won't keep. People lie to me all the time, you know. I'm pretty good at telling when people are lying to me. "

He held out his hand for her to shake. "I promise we'll meet again, Charley. When you're a famous singer-slash-actress, I'll give you a call. Make sure you answer, though. Don't go all big-time on me."

"I'll tell my agent to put you through," she responded with a small smile.

"That's cool. Well, I better be going before the boat leaves without me. Take it easy, girl."

He gave Charley's hand, and consequently her whole frail body, a vigorous shake and then knelt down to pull her in for another hug.

Charley pushed him away playfully. He tumbled backwards with exaggerated force to lay flat on the sand. The recently concluded arrangements for the future had gone a long way toward brightening Charley's gloomy mood. She turned to Rachel with a beaming smile.

"We'll have a reunion every year. It'll be like Christmas," she said with every confidence it would happen. Rachel gave Charley a reassuring nod.

Rachel waved goodbye. "Take care, Chilly. Thank you for helping us."

Chilly got to his feet and shook a sand pail full of beach out of his clothes. "It's been a trip. I'm still amazed you made it through on your own."

"It's good to have a friend by your side, and wishing stones help too. Now, get outta here."

He flashed them a peace sign and turned to jog away.

Rachel called out "Bon voyage," to their hastily departing friend.

Charley watched until he disappeared from sight as night collapsed around them.

CHAPTER THIRTY-FIVE

The smile vanished from her face immediately as the realization hit her that they were alone again and without shelter. She looked about for Rachel and found her standing next to the lifeguard, leaning cross-armed against his tower. The lantern glowed weakly, barely illuminating the small area around them. A mist crept in from the sea and swirled around them.

Rachel stared at the sand with a strange distant expression. The lifeguard pushed herself off the tower and approached Charley. She answered the girl's question before she asked it.

"There are no beasts, monsters, or fiends allowed on the beach, child. You need not fear."

With no zombies or spiders or wolves to fear, Charley's apprehension turned to anger. "So Chilly can go, but Rachel and I have to stay here forever? So, what, we turn into a freak like you and get a job torturing teenagers?"

The lifeguard could have been sympathetic to Charley's circumstances. She could have understood she was lashing out at her out of fear and helplessness. Perhaps she actually was sympathetic, and she actually did understand. Her job required her to deal with all sorts of young people with their own personalities, anxieties, and shortcomings. She had learned many different tactics over the years to deal with the many different situations presented by travelers as they passed beneath her little tower. In Charley's case, she chose to bend down and look directly into her eyes with a calm and steady gaze. She paused for a long moment and then proceeded to yell directly into her face at a volume comparable to one of Stink's bellows.

"YOU ARE A CHILD!"

Charley backed up awkwardly and landed abruptly on her butt in the sand. She sat still with her eyes blinking and her mouth moving, incapable of producing words at this time.

The lifeguard sat beside her, cross-legged and resumed speaking at normal volume.

"You presume to speak as if you are wise in the ways of the world when, in reality, you know next to nothing."

Rachel sat cross-legged across from them and for a time they stared at each other in silence. The darkness closed in, encasing them in a misty, rapidly chilling, dome of light. Rachel traced in the sand with a reed while Charley sought to regain her composure and dignity.

"I'm sorry I called you a freak."

"I take no offense, Charlotte. You are a child throwing a tantrum," she said matter-of-factly.

"Rachel, are you going to let her talk to me this way?" Rachel shrugged her shoulders.

"Are you going to say anything? You've barely spoken since we got here. Don't you think we deserve an explanation?" demanded Charley, regaining some of her feistiness.

"Just listen to her, Charley."

"No, I have some questions first." She rose to her knees, turned toward the lifeguard, and sat on her heels.

She nodded. "Proceed. Do not test my patience, though, little one. If I have an answer to your question, I will provide one. If I do not, will you burst into tears?"

This adult's low opinion of her level of maturity was not lost on Charley. She bit her tongue, not wanting to offend her now that she had agreed to the spillage of some beans. She took a deep breath.

She started with, "Where do the boats go?"

"My job is to watch out for passengers who are not ready for their voyage. I provide encouragement and sometimes discipline to the rest. When they appear at my chair, they are on the shore of their own destiny. Where they land once they set sail from here, I do not know."

Charley let off some steam audibly with her lips. "But not me somehow. Let's try this. How do you know our names? We never told you."

"Ah, it is one of my powers. I am able to pull it from you. Reading your mind, if you will."

"Can you tell what I'm thinking now?" asked Charley with mischief in her eyes.

She waved dismissively, without a hint of a sense of humor. "Next question."

Charley contemplated. She had many questions, but considering the lifeguard's demeanor, she assumed answers were in short supply. This called for artifice and guile. She continued on her current innocuous tack.

"What is your name?"

She drew in a deep breath and puffed himself up as if she were going to give a speech of great import. "I have been called many names. My story goes back in time to a distant land forgotten by..."

Charley cleared her throat ferociously and without a hint of subtlety. "What should I call you?"

The lifeguard's eyes narrowed, and her lip curled into a sneer. "My mother named me Ariana. In my native tongue, it means 'short-tempered'.

Charley got her message. Hoping to catch her off-guard, she affected a casual air and asked her most important question. "Why can't I go on?"

She sighed. "I believe I already told you. You are a child."

Charley's jaws clenched and her eyes widened, pupils dilating. Unsatisfied, she hissed her frustration with a barely civil tone. "Says who?"

The lifeguard considered her and eventually explained.

"Travelers take the voyage when they reach a level of maturity and a threshold of competence. Some are gifted and eager. Some are capable and apprehensive. Still others are ill-equipped and terrified. However, when the time comes, they must leave immaturity and dependence behind. Your time has not come."

"But, what about everything we've gone through? What I've gone through? We were almost killed about ten times!"

She seemed unimpressed with Charley's declaration. "Every

traveler on the river encounters some measure of danger.”

Charley wouldn’t accept her dismissive attitude. She pointed toward the ocean. “I seriously doubt every one of those kids had to deal with what we did.” She actually felt rather proud of herself for surviving the last few days.

“Such as?” asked the irritatingly calm lifeguard.

“Such as being hunted by a giant! Such as almost getting sucked into a demonic fireplace! Such as almost drowning in a flood!”

“And how did those admittedly dangerous situations come about?”

“Well, we… I let my friend Cecil out of a cage. And I trusted this boy who turned out to be some kind of devil, I guess.” Her voice trailed off, and she chewed her lower lip. “The other time I wished for water. Help me out here, Rachel.”

She turned to Rachel for help, but she was deep in thought. “What? I’m sorry, Charley. What were you saying?”

“What’s wrong with you? Tell her how we should be able to go on. How we survived all sorts of dangers to get here.”

“We did get in a lot of trouble. But…we… some of it was kind of avoidable,” she said, dodging Charley’s glare.

Charley hexed her with a look of accusation and turned her attention back to the lifeguard.

“So, it was all my fault. I got us into some trouble. Big deal. The point is we survived.”

“The point is your decisions led to your troubles. You had to be protected and guided along the way or else you would have been lost.”

“Protected? You mean Rachel?” Charley scoffed.

“Yes, Rachel, and others. Did you think your ancestors in the hedge were watching a play? You are not succeeding in making your case.”

“Even if some of it was my fault, we’re still here. Doesn’t that count for something?”

Her head bobbled as she considered her question. “I wondered why the Giggleton boy was sniffing around. And I heard about the flood. You caused that?"

"It was an honest mistake," squeaked Charley.

"It seems you also narrowly escaped another, more terrible fate. There are beings coming and going on the river who are utterly evil. This boy or demon sounds like one of those chaotic, malevolent forces that take travelers from time to time before they can reach us here. How did you escape?"

Charley looked sideways at Rachel. "Rachel cut me loose, and then I was able to cut the rope and set us free."

"You have an extraordinarily special protector, child."

Rachel relaxed, sitting down with only a hint of a satisfied smile.

"I guess so," admitted Charley.

"I tell you this before you go," she began.

"Before we go where?" Charley interjected.

"Do not interrupt me again."

Charley raised her hands in submission.

"You came here with faults and weaknesses, like everyone else. Perhaps you have been plagued by more than the normal share of difficulties, but you prevailed together."

"Thank you," responded Charley with exaggerated sarcasm.

She ignored it. "That is to your credit. There are many dangers on the river. Some are natural and random. Some exist due to the cruelty and vices of brutish human predators. Then there are the ones you described-- the ones you create yourselves."

Charley sighed. "Enough. The past is the past."

She continued, disregarding Charley's hurt feelings. "Charlotte, you are not the first to unleash ills upon the world as a result of carelessness. You aren't the first to make an enemy in the course of doing what you think is right. You are also not the first to misjudge another at your peril."

"Please get to the point," Charley whined.

The lifeguard maintained her patience despite Charley's thick-headedness. "My point is..."

"You aren't ready yet, Charley," said Rachel. "You're a funny, smart, and typically mixed-up kid. Why can't you just be happy with that?"

Charley couldn't disguise the petulance in her voice. "I hate being treated like a child. You don't understand."

Rachel explained, "I understand. All those people we saw on the beach understand. Everybody feels that way when they're your age."

Charley pressed on, not yet able to escape the confines of her own small, self-absorbed bubble. "Why does my life have to be so hard?"

"Do not presume to compare your life to others," snapped the lifeguard. Her tone shook Charley from her misery like a slap on the cheek.

"You have carried a heavy burden in your short life. It is true. Nevertheless, there are others struggling in this world with no hope and no help against forces over which they have no control. Some unfortunates spin round and round on a carousel macabre until tragedy or disease or inhumanity put an end to their misery."

Silence meshed with the darkness, draping the group with melancholy.

"Well, that's cheerful," said Charley. "I feel so much better."

A smile broke free on Rachel's face. The lifeguard frowned more severely.

Charley gave in. "I guess we can't change your mind. We can't set sail. We can't wish ourselves home. So, what do we do now?"

The lifeguard rose and climbed her tower. Rachel approached Charley and enveloped the smaller girl in her arms. "It's time to go home."

The lifeguard climbed back down with the lantern and handed it to Charley.

Gesturing up-river, she said, "The way is open now. Rachel will guide you home. I wish you well, Charlotte. Your friend Achilles was right. You have the heart and strength of the heroes of old. You have other gifts as well. Don't waste them."

"Thanks, Ariana. Good talk."

Charley fished her only stone from her pocket.

"Here. Could you make sure this gets to Mr. Giggleton? It's all I have left."

She tossed it to Ariana, bouncing it off her chest. She slowly looked down at the stone and then panned back up to look Charley in the eyes, her expression blank. Charley inhaled audibly through gritted teeth.

"That... Umm... Sorry. So, let's hit the river again, Rachel."

She took measured steps hesitantly, peering forward through gloom resistant to the feeble light from the lantern.

"We have a magic lantern now that keeps the monsters away, hopefully."

Rachel hung back and made a point to shake the lifeguard's hand, surprising the woman. "Thank you for being patient. I know she can be difficult to deal with."

The lifeguard returned the handshake and even bowed to her. "You are an impressive individual yourself. Your assistance has been heroic, and we have noticed."

An incongruous smile appeared on her otherwise despondent face. "Thank you, Ariana. I'd better go, or she'll fall down a well or something."

She placed a hand on her shoulder. "Vade in pace, Rachel."

She nodded and turned away to chase after her friend.

"Until we meet again, Charlotte!" called the lifeguard.

CHAPTER THIRTY-SIX

Charley stopped and turned to say goodbye once more, but she found the woman and her tower had disappeared. The lantern was now blazing with intensity. She placed it on the ground and stood alone for a moment until Rachel stepped into the circle of light. Somehow, in the space of a few steps, they were back to the spot where they had met. The sea mist was gone, and the familiar scents of the riverbed returned. The silence was abruptly broken with a vengeance by the sound of crickets and other insects conducting multiple chirpy conversations. The stoic shrubbery walls penned them in again, with a crescent moon above to cast a silver tinge on the stones at their feet. The girls faced each other, trapped in an awkward pause.

Rachel was the first to speak. "So here we are. Alone again."

Charley was truly repentant. "I'm sorry if I hurt your feelings, Rachel. It felt like you and the old lady were ganging up on me."

"I wasn't attacking you. I was trying to get you to listen to her. She's pretty wise."

"For an alien."

Rachel smiled. "Maybe she is. Who knows?"

They faced each other, awkwardly kicking small stones. They inhaled deeply, pent-up air puffing out their cheeks. In unison, with flapping of lips, they exhaled audibly. They both burst into laughter, and their loud carrying-on echoed in the valley. Realizing there was no shelter nearby and it was the middle of the night, Rachel tried to shush Charley. Their laughter tapered to quiet girlish giggling despite the possibility of a monster attack.

"It's time, Charley," said Rachel finally.

Charley frowned, realizing for the first time that going home meant going their separate ways. "Oh, Rachel. This is hard. I am so tired."

Rachel nodded and gripped her friend's hands. "I know."

"Why don't you come home with me? Our house is huge, and

you could have your own room and help around the farm."

Rachel shook her head. "I can't Charley. I don't belong there."

Charley persisted. "You said you couldn't live with your Mom and Dad. You're old enough to live wherever you want, aren't you?"

Rachel shook her head. "Well, yes...no. It's complicated. I just can't live with you, Charley."

"I don't get it. You wanted to be best friends, and now you're ditching me," said Charley with genuine pain in her voice.

Rachel was distressed and at a loss for a reasonable explanation. "I don't know, Charley. I have a lot to do."

"You're my *only* friend. When am I gonna see you again?" said Charley, on the verge of tears.

Rachel bit her lower lip, guilty over the anguish clouding her friend's dirty, pathetic, and authentically and abjectly heartbroken face. Charley's expression brightened for a second as her mind hatched a plan. She tried one more suggestion.

"How about this? You come home with me tonight, sleep over, and then you can go home tomorrow?"

Rachel resisted the idea at first, but after some consideration, she gave in. "Alright, Charley. One night," she said with a forced smile.

Charley clapped and danced around her older friend. She performed an awkward semblance of a cartwheel, giving Rachel a chance to question what gifts the lifeguard was referring to.

Charley picked up the lantern and walked toward the hedge on her right. "Follow me, Rachel," she said with unwarranted confidence.

She stopped walking half-way up the bank and scanned the hedge for a door or gap. She turned around. "Wait a minute. Is this right? Rachel, is there supposed to be a door or something?"

Rachel remained at the bottom of the valley. "First of all, your farm is on the other side of that hedge," she said, pointing at the opposite riverbank.

Although embarrassed, Charley curiously didn't feel the need to lash out in anger. She simply said, "Hmm," and skipped downhill to join her friend.

Together, they looked up at the hedge.

Charley said, "I feel different, Rachel."

"That's not surprising. You've got a best friend now. That's got to be a good feeling."

"That might be why," Charley agreed.

Charley gasped when a face appeared above them in the branches. "I forgot how creepy they are. They don't look familiar to me at all.

"They aren't creepy, Charley," chided Rachel. "You should show respect."

Charley scratched her itchy scalp. "I think my family tree is a Creeping Willow."

Rachel suppressed a laugh. When they looked up again, the face had been joined by three others.

"Alright, I will," relented Charley

She bowed and said with only a thin layer of impertinence, "Oh, Faces of the Hedge, Ariana, Lifeguard from the Planet of the Leather Spider People has granted our wish to leave this place. Please let us pass so we may return to my home and take a long hot bath."

A bustle in the hedgerow slowly twisted and bent into a crease between the faces. Charley gasped, "That worked?"

Rachel laughed at her reaction. "Yes, see what being polite gets you?"

"Maybe Ariana is a magic word.

Maybe I really am a wizard," she said with a giant smile.

The faces disappeared as the branches in the crease shook and rolled apart, leaving an opening wide enough for an exhausted, hungry, homesick little girl to squeeze through. She raced up the bank, the lantern swinging wildly. Rachel followed at a more leisurely pace.

At the gap, Charley tentatively reached out, half-expecting the path to either be a mirage or snap close on her arm. It was real enough, and she turned to Rachel with genuine excitement despite her condition. Rachel smiled and nodded. "Lead the way, Charley."

Charley held the lantern high with one hand and grasped Rachel's hand with the other. Together they squirmed through an uncomfortably tight path. Again, the branches poked and prodded and held, causing Charley to mutter a string of gibberish, sprinkled with minor curses and growls.

Rachel followed Charley closely until the confines of the path pressed Charley into violent flailing. She released Rachel's hand to beat at the shrub's many scratching green arms. The branches pulled the strap of her satchel from her shoulder. She left it behind and maintained her grip on the lantern, trying to keep up a brave front.

"Why the heck is this so bleeping difficult?" she shouted at their virtual prison of evergreen foliage. Her salty language stirred up the memory of her father and her determination was renewed. She pushed forward again, but her reserve of energy was gone. The light from the lantern was dimming by degree, in synergy with Charley's weakening state. She felt the familiar dizziness which used to accompany her spells.

"Rachel, we're almost there! It won't be long now."

The light from the lantern sputtered and gave out. Charley swayed and fought, finally reaching the outer wall of the hedge. She was able to see the tops of cornstalks pointing up at the night sky like an army of spearmen. She dropped the heavy lantern. With a final push, using the last of her remaining strength, she stepped out into nothingness and slipped down, down, sliding and rolling to a stop by the side of the rutted dirt road bounding her family's corn field.

CHAPTER THIRTY-SEVEN

The pickup truck rumbled slowly, its shocks failing miserably to absorb the jolts from the uneven dirt road. The headlights bobbed, searching the darkness ahead while flashlights shining from the windows of the cab threw diffuse sprays of illumination at the roadside vegetation. To the left, the corn field allowed a few feet of penetration for one questing flashlight. On the right, the hedge defiantly snubbed the other's weak and paltry glare.

"CHARLEY!" called her mother from the truck. Her voice was raw and strangled by emotion. Charley's father's voice called out for his daughter from the driver's side. His worried and urgent shout of 'CHARLOTTE ROSE!' rustled the stalks as they passed.

Minutes slipped away while they called into the night for their daughter. They had been searching since nightfall when Charley did not turn up for dinner. Their meal was long cold, still on the table, and they were desperate.

Cecilia Stanton faced out the window, not wanting to take her eyes off the side of the road. Thomas Stanton stepped on the brakes and stopped the truck. He reached for his wife's shoulder and pulled her close to face him.

"We'll find her, CeCe. Everyone is out looking. It's only a matter of time."

Her eyes were wild and red from crying. "I can't lose her, Tom. I can't lose another."

He reached for her hand. His voice cracked as he tried to calm her, thanks to the gigantic lump in his throat.

"She's so tough. You know that."

She squeezed his hand and tried to respond, but no words came out. She could not hold back more tears. He slid closer on the seat, and they huddled together for mutual support. Charley's father wept silently while his wife's tears fell with frightened gasps. He held her tighter and kissed her forehead. His lips muttered words of hope for her comfort, pleas for Charley to hear, and angry threats for whichever person or deity was responsible for Charley's disappearance.

She broke off their embrace and motioned for her husband to start driving again. She slid back to point the flashlight out the window. He reached for the shift when a crackle from their walkie-talkie alarmed them. Before either could grab it from the seat between them, another squawk of static followed by a garbled voice caused them to hold their breath.

Tom Stanton grabbed the radio with a death grip and shouted into it.

"Again, what was that? Please repeat!"

The seconds ticked by while they waited for an answer.

"I say, come again! This is Tom," he shouted, the walkie-talkie shaking in his hand.

A lifetime later, a crackle shocked them again. "Tom, this is Carlos. We've found her!"

Tom dropped the radio in his wife's lap and shifted into drive. She picked it up and spoke carefully into it like it was Charley's own ear.

"Carlos, is she alright? Is she alright? God, she has to be alright."

The truck was bouncing along, rarely with all four tires touching the ground.

"Mrs. Stanton, this is Carlos. It looks like she's sleeping."

CeCe gasped and bit her lip.

"Should I wake her? Mrs. Stanton?"

"Where are you, Carlos? Where is Charley?"

The next transmission was garbled. Tom Stanton cursed.

"Carlos, where is she?" shouted CeCe.

"Field 5, southeast corner," came the reply.

CeCe looked at her husband. He managed to growl, "Three minutes," before he re-clenched his jaw to fight the violent rocking of the truck as it shot through the night. CeCe was unable to hold the walkie-talkie to her mouth to respond.

"Should we wake her?" asked Carlos. "Mrs. Stanton! What should we do?"

CeCe held one hand anxiously over her mouth and, the other braced against the dashboard.

"Two minutes, Carlos! We'll be there in two minutes!"

Tom Stanton drove his truck to a skidding halt, sending a cloud of dust into the torch-lit night sky. Dozens of their farmhands held torches and flashlights, illuminating the side of the road. They both jumped out of the cab and ran to their daughter, CeCe clutching a medical kit. The expressions of the farmhands were apprehensive and scared.

Carlos rose from Charley's side and tried to set their mind at ease as they approached. "I don't see any injuries, Tom. I covered her with my coat. I hope that's okay."

CeCe knelt at Charley's side and lifted the coat to examine her daughter.

"It's fine, Carlos. Thank you," said Tom.

Carlos tried to explain, "It's the damnedest thing, you know. We looked here before. We looked everywhere before. She wasn't here, and the next time we came by, she was."

Tom nodded as his wife looked Charley over. "I know what you mean. I drove by here earlier myself."

CeCe felt Charley's face with both hands. She looked up at her husband and said, "She feels normal. She's breathing normal. What should we do?"

Her husband knelt beside her and bent down to kiss Charley on the cheek. To his surprise, her eyes opened once and then fluttered when she realized whose face was in front of her. Charley threw up her arms to hug her father. CeCe gasped, and the crowd gathered round threw up a cheer.

Charley let her father go and reached for her mother. They embraced and held each other for a long, long time. Carlos placed his hand on his boss' shoulder and squeezed.

"She's good?" he asked.

"It seems so." His shoulders sagged in relief as he placed his arms around his family.

CeCe wouldn't let Charley go. From her mother's bear hug, Charley managed to squeak out, "I'm sorry."

CeCe held Charley at arm's length and stared hard at her daughter. "You really are," she said in surprise.

Charley sat up quickly and looked around. "Where's Rachel?"

Her father gulped, and her mother's breath caught at the name. They stared at each other; eyes unable to decide what type of tears to form.

Charley scanned the area around her and up the small rise. A dozen flashlights pointed simultaneously in the direction of her gaze. At the top of the rise, the beams of light illuminated a face in the hedge; the face of a teenage girl. Charley gasped and covered her mouth with a grubby hand. Disbelief and wonder fought for room on the faces of her parents. The search party began to mutter, some making the sign of the cross. The face disappeared before their eyes.

"Rachel!" cried Charley. "Don't go." She blinked back tears. Her friend had not followed her home.

CeCe pulled Charley close again, squeezing hard. Charley felt her sadness drain away as if her mother was drawing it out of her. Her father, smelling of liniment and nature, wrapped his strong arms around them both. Although Charley was effectively bound in her parents' embrace, she didn't mind. After a time, she was barely able to squeak out, "Mom."

CeCe relaxed and drew her sleeve across her face, drying her tears. She looked down at her daughter. "Yes, Charley?"

Charley's normal expression of exasperation and disrespect was nowhere to be found on her face. Instead, her face was relaxed and even innocent.

"I've been doing a lot of thinking over the past few days." She chattered on, oblivious to her mother's confusion. "Mom, I'm going to start being nicer to you."

CeCe didn't know what to say.

"And Dad too."

Tom was at a loss for words as well, "Charley..."

"I want to be like you, Mom. Because you're smart and tough and just amazing."

CeCe eyes started to water again. "I... I don't know what brought this on. Let's all start over, Charley. You've been through so much already. Whatever life has in store for us in the future, we'll get through it together."

"I know we will. I have you and Dad, and I'm getting better. I'm sorry I was gone so long. I didn't mean to scare you."

"Charley, it doesn't matter now. What's important is you're safe now," she said with a smile. "And filthy. Very, very filthy."

Charley laughed. "But am I smarter?"

"You're brilliant, Charley."

"Am I more beautiful?"

"We'll see after a bath. Let's get you home."

"Can you teach me how to make pancakes?"

CeCe laughed in relief and surprise.

"And I'll tell you all about my new friend Rachel."

Tom Stanton shared a questioning glance with his wife. He lifted Charley from her mother's arms and carried her to the pickup. He walked to the driver's side and placed her on the bench seat inside. CeCe slid in next to her daughter and wrapped an arm around her. Tom slid into the driver's seat and gave his wife a puzzled look. She shrugged her shoulders and mimed the words, 'I don't know'. As they pulled away, passing through smiling farmhands waving and pounding the truck, CeCe's confused tears flowed freely and without restraint.

"Charley," said her mother.

"Yes?"

"We have to have a talk."

"I know. I've been awful."

They rode without speaking for a ways. The only sound in the night was the squeaking of the truck's springs and the rumbling cough of its engine.

Tom and CeCe looked intently at each other. When Tom nodded, CeCe said, "No, darling. It's just that there's something we haven't told you."

Charley looked up into her mother's eyes.
CeCe's voice shook. "You see, before you were born... we had another child. It's time we told you about your sister."

ACKNOWLEDGMENTS

If you're lucky you'll find someone who not only recognizes and accepts you despite your long list of flaws, they're also willing to expose their own flaws to you. I've been married to such a forgiving soul for over 32 years and without her support and understanding this book would never have been written. Thank you, Debbie, for our family, our health, and our partnership. You share equally in all my successes.

To my boys, thank you. I'm immensely proud of you all, but please don't follow my lead and wait until you start breaking down to aspire to great things. Regret adds up. To quote Al Czervik, "Let's go. While we're young!"

To Mom, Dad, and my siblings. I have you to thank for fine tuning my cognitive ability and creative process during my formative years. In return for this recognition, I ask only that you never reveal my secrets to anyone.

To Kate, Melissa, and Otherwords Press, thank you for believing in my story and for all your hard work, wisdom, and expertise.

To my readers, thank you for your input and your suggestions. You improved my story, and I will always be grateful.

To Mike Scott, thank you for composing the current that inspired me and carried my idea to reality.

That was the river. This is the sea.

www.ingramcontent.com/pod-product-compliance
Lightning Source LLC
Chambersburg PA
CBHW070453300726
48975CB00007B/2157